LOOK FOR THESE TITLES FROM A. C. FOX

Now Available

The Warriors of Love & Magic Series

The General's Hostage (Book One)
The Captive Prince (Book Two)
The Dragon Hunter (Book Three)
The Warrior's Mage (Book Four)
The Gladiator's Slave (Book Five)
Marked (Book Six)

Other Titles

Chains
Hold the Sky

THE DRAGON HUNTER

The Warriors of Love & Magic Book Three

A. C. FOX

etopia
press

Etopia Press
1643 Warwick Ave., #124
Warwick, RI 02889
http://www.etopia-press.net

THE DRAGON HUNTER

Print ISBN: 978-1-947135-05-5
Digital ISBN: 978-1-944138-86-8

First Etopia Press electronic publication: March 2017

First Etopia Press print publication: May 2017

~ DEDICATION ~

For JKJ and his dog.

CHAPTER ONE

Rycard Serod's dog moved closer, nearly pressing against his legs as Rycard led his horse down the muddy, churned-up road winding into town. The smoke and ash in the air probably made the dog nervous. Rycard reached down and stroked Charza's head, trying to reassure him. The dog whined and lapped nervously at his hand.

A battle of some kind had raged around Shademere, and not very long ago. Dark smoke billowed from the remains of a large stone structure near the center of the settlement. Some sort of stronghold, most like. The fire was almost out. The smoke cloud was dissipating, but the air still stank of char. Large sections of the hewn logs forming the town's palisade wall had been smashed or burned. The gates were shattered into scorched splinters. Arrows protruded from the mud of the surrounding fields as if they'd been fired desperately into the air by the hundreds, only to fall back to the earth without finding their target. Boa Visk guards in dark, spiked armor patrolled the charred gaps in the wall, most of them bearing polearms or bows.

Gansen trotted over on his destrier and reined up beside Rycard, the horse's hooves spattering mud on Rycard's legs. Rycard, who had dismounted to rest his horse and now walked at the pace of their three wagons, ignored it. A little more mud certainly didn't matter now.

"Dragons," Gansen said in a deep grumble and spat into the mud. "Of course it was dragons. Fire's always caused by dragons. It's never something as simple as a lightning strike or a drunken fool with a lamp." Gansen was a bear of a man with a heavy brow and aggressively bushy beard. He wore odd bits of chainmail and leather armor and carried a two-handed ax nearly as tall as Rycard. "We should never have come here."

"We go where the money is," Rycard said placidly.

Gansen settled his hand around the thick haft of his war ax as if he wanted to strangle something. "Do you really think to collect a bounty on a dragon? There's no bloody dragons anymore. All I smell is some cowardly garrison commander who got his fortress burned down by rebels. Instead of admitting defeat, he cries dragon."

"It's the biggest bounty we've ever been offered."

"And that alone should tell you something."

Rycard remained silent. Best to let Gansen complain and get it over with. If it wasn't the dragon, it was the mud, the food, the blood flies, or how often his horse farted.

Gansen shaded his eyes as he stared at the distant town. "Besides, it's hard to stomach working for those Boa Visk bastards."

"We've done it before."

Gansen spat again into the mud. "Aye, we've done it before. But there's always a last time. And this might as well be it."

Rycard didn't bother to reply. He hated the Boa Visk as much as Gansen. Few humans in the land did not. When the Boa Visk had poured across the Drahahn Mountains in an endless tide, none of the human nations had been left standing. The magic of the Boa Visk was strange and powerful, their beasts of war terrifying and difficult to kill. The Boa Visk armies invaded and enslaved, plundering without mercy, until most of the human kingdoms were crushed under their boot heels. Their home, Shomogar, was one of those nations.

Gansen urged his horse forward to continue patrolling

around their wagons. His horse's hooves splattered more mud with every step. Rycard let him go. He didn't want to talk about the bounty. Gansen was right. The size of the bounty should have set alarm bells ringing in his head. But they needed the money. And Rycard needed one last payoff—a big one—and then he could retire from this dirty, wet, thankless work and maybe buy a little cabin on a plot of land by the river somewhere that he could farm until he died from the plague or the boot rot or starvation like everyone else.

The town of Shademere was situated on a rise, far enough above the banks of a narrow river to avoid the spring floods when the snow melted in the mountains. Reeds and cattails dotted the riverbanks, and masses of birds flocked from one side of the river to the other, as if they were as agitated as his dog. The distant mountains made a craggy, purple-and-gray wall to the north, with snow dusting the highest slopes and the river winding its way to the flatlands. Fields of wheat, barley, and oats spread out from around the palisade wall as far as the eye could see.

Rycard scanned the fields outside the town. No sign of fire damage. That struck him as odd. If a dragon truly were involved, surely it would have blackened the ground for leagues around. The mill on the river had also escaped the flames.

He trudged onward toward the smoldering fortress, the mud squelching around his boots as the wagons creaked and groaned beside him. He wanted to ride again but was giving his horse, Redmane, a rest. Earlier, they'd had to use both his and Yero's horses to help drag one of the wagons out of yet another muddy trench. It had rained most of the way here, compounding everyone's misery. Their three wagons were loaded with provisions and weapons, making the wheels sink up to the axles in mud at seemingly every turn. The entire journey had been an exhausting, filthy struggle. But they were finally here.

Only to find part of the town burned to cinders.

They drew up to the shattered town gates beside the burned-out remains of a guard tower. The half dozen Boa Visk sentries at the gate spread out and made their way toward Rycard and his convoy. Beneath their spiked helms, their yellow-green scales looked sinister and snakelike, their orange-and-black eyes watched Rycard and his hunters like predators. They wore brown and black armor, ornamented with spikes and black braided cords that revealed their ranks and battle history. Each carried a carska spear, a weapon with a long haft and three black blades on the end like a W with an elongated center blade.

It was probably poisoned. The Boa Visk liked to poison their blades. They also liked to bite their adversaries with their sharp yellow teeth, poisoning with their saliva. They made his skin crawl, especially when they stared at him with those reptilian eyes, as if he were prey to toy with.

"What have we here?" one of the Boa Visk growled, narrowing his eyes as he looked them over. He glanced up at the flag that flew from one of their wagons. A red chain and white arrow against a black background. Then he turned to his comrades and grinned, showing his pointed yellow teeth. "Muddy little humans pretending to be warriors? Now that tickles me."

Gansen spurred his horse closer. Timval, one of their mage adepts and their newest and youngest member, dropped his hand to the knife sheathed at his side.

Gods be damned, the little fool. Rycard stepped forward and shot him a look heavy with warning. The sandy-haired young man scowled but removed his hand from his knife and sat easy in the saddle again. Rycard wasn't about to allow a hothead to provoke a fight before they even entered the town.

He turned back to the guards and withdrew the parchment with the bounty offer from his saddlebag. He held it up before anything else could go wrong. "I'm Rycard Serod of the Splitchain Hunters." He gestured toward his companions, the seven hunters and the three wagon drivers who doubled as cooks, tinkers, hedge smiths, and guards.

"We've been summoned to solve your monster problem."

The gate guard's expression turned nasty. "You're vultures, you mean. You come here, sniffing around corpses, searching for gold. Well, you're too late. We already killed the dragon."

Cold dismay washed through him. If they'd traveled all this way for nothing…

They needed that gold. Rycard had staked his leadership of the Splitchain Hunters on this rainy-season journey. Horses had to be fed, supplies purchased, hunters paid, armor repaired—the list was endless. They'd spent much of their profit from the last few bounties fleeing the plague back in Landilar. After the capital had been sealed off, escaping the city had been a nightmare. Bribes had been needed…and food had cost a fortune. Two of his hunters, Dormier and Casten, had died of the bleeding lung.

Winter was coming on. They'd have to hole up until spring, and that meant money for three months' worth of provisions for his men and the animals. This was the last job they'd be able to take before the ice storms hit. As it was, so late in the season, they'd be lucky to get back to their winter camp without freezing to death on the road.

If the dragon was dead, there would be no bounty. No monster to hunt, no gold to collect. They might as well have stayed in the plague-ridden Landilar. They'd be just as dead.

Rycard met the Boa Visk's stare. "So the dragon attacked Shademere, and the garrison brought it down?" He kept his tone carefully neutral. Not weak, but not overtly challenging, either.

The Boa Visk guard planted his carska spear and leaned on it. "Are you a fool? I said as much, didn't I? We killed the dragon, protecting this pisshole town. Riddled it with arrows and bolts and seared it with kovohl magic. So run along."

"Strange. I don't see a dead dragon anywhere," Dezarie quipped, peering around theatrically from horseback, her short, dark braid sliding over the shoulders of her light armor as she turned her head. Like the rest of them, mud-spatter dotted her legs and her horse's flanks. The woman was the other of their two mage adepts. Both she and Timval specialized in trap spells, tracking, and control magic, but Timval relied more on his magic and Dezarie more on her sword. "I'd like to at least see the fantastical beast since we came all this way."

The guard slitted his orange eyes as he nudged one of his comrades. "Bad enough the males act as if they can fight. Now they hide behind the skirts of their females."

"I'd be nice to her if I were you," Gansen warned with a cheery note to his voice. "Unless you want her to hex your head down to the size of an apple."

Rycard held up a hand for peace as the Boa Visk guards edged closer, their expressions darkening. The Boa Visk were always dangerously volatile, and his hunters weren't exactly helping matters. He'd had about all he could stomach of these guards, but his small band couldn't survive a fight with the entire garrison.

"I have a commission to hunt a dragon from Gardzar Malak Telk," Rycard said. "I will speak with him in person. If you've already killed the dragon, the gardzar will terminate our commission. If not…well, I'm certain the gardzar would not be pleased to learn a mere sentry turned away the hunters he sent for."

The guard gave him one last lingering stare of contempt before spitting again and waving them through. "Go on then, vermin. The gardzar is in his pavilion near what's left of the fort. But he won't have any more use for you than I do. No doubt that dragon is as good as bled out by now."

"No doubt," Rycard agreed, mounting Redmane again and urging her forward. Charza stayed close on his right. He whistled to the wagon drivers and signaled for them to move out. With a clatter of hooves and wagon wheels over the rutted road, their little band started through what remained of the palisade wall as the Boa Visk stood aside and eyed them with clear dislike.

Once inside the fortress walls, they headed for the town square. Townsfolk and merchants, all human, watched them pass with frightened, sullen eyes. They did not wave or speak. Many of them fled inside when the hunters approached. A beaten people. Rycard had seen it all over the lands of Shomogar and in Tyrdenva, where the Boa Visk ruled commoners and nobility alike with an iron fist.

The stink and haze of smoke still lingered in the streets as they made their way toward Shademere's town center. The smoldering ruins were indeed some kind of stronghold. The stone was charred and scorched, and in places, the stones looked as if they'd been melted. Entire sections of the fort had collapsed into smoking rubble.

Yero was staring at the fort uneasily, his small, dark eyes slit-like beneath his heavy dark brows. "That stone's *melted*. Imagine the heat it took to do that."

"Don't worry, Yero," Timval said, grinning as if this were a game. "Just keep back and you won't get singed. You only need one adept to take down the big, scary lizard."

Rycard sighed but held his tongue. The kid was going to give him a bleeding stomach lesion.

Not far ahead, Rycard finally spotted what he thought must be the gardzar's temporary pavilion, his quarters now that the stronghold had apparently been melted by dragonfire. "I'm going to go see about the bounty," he said, glancing around at his company. "Stay here. Behave yourselves."

"While you're in there, demand a raise," Brockon said nervously as he eyed the damage around them. It was hard to tell if the lean archer with the hawkish-face was jesting or not. Rycard had seen Brockon's spelled recurve bow send arrows through the armored plates on monsters as easily as daggers through bread. So if Brockon was uneasy, it meant they had cause to be.

Rycard swung down from his saddle and handed his reins to Brockon. Whistling for Charza to follow, he made his way to the pavilion, where two Boa Visk guards in crimson armor raised curved swords to stop him. Their expressions were cold, their orange-and black serpent eyes hostile.

Rycard pulled out the bounty letter. "Rycard Serod, here to eliminate your dragon problem."

The Boa Visk made a noise halfway between a grunt and a snarl. "Go find somewhere else to wait, dragon snack. You'll be summoned at the gardzar's leisure. And no mammal pets permitted. Unless they're meant to be eaten."

Rycard knew the game. These two would keep him waiting endlessly, looking for bribes for quicker access to the gardzar. Rycard didn't have time for games.

"We'll see him now," he said and backhanded the guard across the face. He grabbed the dagger from the Boa

Visk's belt and pressed the blade against his scaled throat. "And I know you aren't insulting the strength and power of the great Malak Telk, the honored gardzar of Shademere, by insinuating he has anything to fear from a *mammal pet*."

The guard froze, his nostrils flaring and his orange-and-black eyes wide as Rycard pressed the edge of the blade harder against his scales on his neck. The other guard moved far enough back to draw his sword, though he did not pull the blade from its sheath.

"I would never stain the honor of Gardzar Telk," the Boa Visk said, still careful not to move. No doubt the blade Rycard held was poisoned. "If you have a summons, go inside."

Rycard nodded and shoved the guard away from him. Then he stepped forward and sheathed the poisoned knife back in the guard's belt as if the whole thing had been nothing more than a passing whim.

"I thought he said behave?" Gansen groused behind him.

Dezarie laughed. "When did he ever listen to his own advice?"

Rycard glanced back at them and glared at them to quiet down, showing more bravado than he actually felt.

His hunters had gathered around the wagons parked on the road. They looked tired and uneasy and filthy with mud. His heart tightened in his chest, the ache there deepening. They were his people; they were counting on him. Nine men and one woman. His responsibility. He'd led them here chasing the biggest bounty he'd ever seen...and now he was about to learn if he had doomed them all with his gamble.

Steeling himself, he brushed past the guards without another glance, as if they didn't present the slightest threat to him. Charza padded along at his side, his mouth open and tongue out. Almost as if his *mammal pet* were laughing.

He stepped inside the dark pavilion, not certain if he was ready to face the venomous gardzar who ruled this sorry, borderland town, this Boa Visk called Malak Telk, who had offered such an outlandish sum for the death of a creature no one had laid eyes upon in generations.

He probably should have taken his chances with the plague in Landilar.

* * *

Something woke Vorgon Graydalon from his healing

trance before he was ready. He sniffed the air around him and took note of the icy stream that babbled around his blue and white scales. The fire in his core had burned low, depleted by the attack, by the pain and loss of blood that sapped his stamina. He'd intended to retreat to his home in the labyrinthine tunnels of his cave in Blackgap Canyon, but the wounds he'd ignored in the heat of battle had finally grounded him. By the time he'd found a safe place to hide, he'd become dangerously weak. He'd circled down toward a gully between the mountains but landed badly, sliding down a slope of skree and into a stream of runoff from the snow in the mountains.

For a while, all he could do was lie there. He knew he'd left a trail of blood across the fields after the battle. They would come for him, come to kill him. He didn't dare change to human form, though it would've been easier to hide that way. His dragon-self was far more closely linked to his magic and to the power from the Ygatar, the ancestor gods of all dragonkin. He needed his power to heal.

He raised his head, curving his long neck around to see what had roused him, but he saw nothing. He heard a sound in the distance, an animal of some sort, bleating in pain or fear. Pain throbbed and pulsed through him with every beat of his heart as he took account of the damage he'd suffered. A meter-long scorpion bolt had pierced his scales near his hindquarters—that one was the worst. Of the half dozen or so arrows that had hit him, only a few had pierced completely through the armor of his scales. His left side was badly scarred and burned. Not by fire, which could not singe his scales, but by some kind of acid mist one of the Boa Visk sorcerers had cast at him. Right before Vorgon had chomped him in two.

He'd lost time as he'd slipped into the near-comatose state, yielding himself completely to the healing as he burned through his body's stores of energy to aid in the repairs to his flesh. Lying in an icy stream wasn't helping. But he didn't have enough stamina yet to rise.

And now something had woken him from the healing trance early.

He laid his head back down on the rocks of the streambed. That's when he saw it. A human. A male child. He couldn't tell the child's exact age. He found it difficult to differentiate age in a species that lived such a short time. But he was certain it was only a child.

A shepherd. The boy wore woolens, leather boots suitable for hiking the rocky crags around the foothills, and a wide-brimmed hat. He carried both a sling and a long staff. His skin was browned by the sun. His dark eyes were wide with fascination and more than a little fear.

Vorgon didn't smile at the boy. When he smiled in

dragon form, humans fled in terror. He had a lot of very sharp teeth.

"What is it, little one?" he called, his deep voice rumbling and echoing in the rocky gorge between the slopes of the foothills.

The boy flinched and jumped back. Then he caught his courage and bowed. "Dragon. You're hurt."

"I am aware of that, thank you." The scorpion bolt was still lodged in his flesh, although it had nearly been pushed free as his muscle and scales had begun to heal imperfectly around it, forcing it out. A glance showed him the other wounds were still visible as jagged scars and splits in his coat of scales, the ones above the waterline painted nearly black with dried blood.

He never thought he'd come out of the attack on the Boa Visk unscathed, but neither had he been fully prepared for the ferocity of their defense. Before this year, it had been a long time since he'd warred with any two-legged species. Magic was always a threat, but the power of their bows had increased as well, and the siege weapons they'd turned on him might've killed him, had he not been so maneuverable in the sky. Maneuverable or not, that scorpion bolt had nearly brought him down for good.

"Great dragon," the boy said, seeming to build up his nerve again. He pointed at two sheep farther up the slope, hitched around a scraggly tree. Vorgon could hear their fearful bleating. "I bring you a meal from the shepherd tribes. Please don't eat me."

Vorgon raised one ridged brow at the boy. "Are you sure you don't wish to be eaten? I hear boys your age are quite tender."

The child immediately paled and stumbled backward. He tripped over a rock and fell on his rear. Then he scrambled backward up the slope of skree, his eyes wide.

"Peace. Peace, child," Vorgon said quickly, regretting teasing the boy. He should've known better. His thoughts were still fuzzy from exhaustion, and the fires in his core had not yet returned to full strength. "I was only jesting. I don't eat humans."

The smell of the sheep gave him the stamina he needed to rise. He pulled his wings tight against his body as he put his weight on his legs, balancing himself with his long tail. The movement rewarded him with several points of throbbing pain and deep aches, especially around the scorpion bolt. He craned his neck until he could grip the metal and wood bolt in his mouth. It was difficult work biting down without shattering it. A surge of pain seared his flank as he pulled the bolt free. The wound still ached, but it felt cleaner without the filthy bolt stuck in his flesh. He crunched the scorpion bolt to splinters, which seemed to impress the boy.

The wound started to seep blood so dark it was nearly purple. The boy stared at the blood and wandered closer. "You're hurt again."

"It's nothing." He glanced at the sheep. After expending so much energy, first in the attack and then healing himself, he was famished. He felt a wave of gratitude for the humans in the valley, especially the shepherds, who had provided him with meal from their own flocks.

So it had always been between the humans and Vorgon—they'd given sheep and goats in return for protection from the monsters that wandered down from the mountains or across the wilds. But after the Boa Visk conquered Shomogar and slew the human king, things had rapidly changed. It wasn't long before the Boa Visk arrived at this isolated place and tried to slay him.

Instead, he'd slain the Boa Visk. Burned and scattered them. In revenge, they'd murdered many of the shepherds who camped with their flocks in the fields and foothills, trying to lure Vorgon out. Yesterday had only been the latest skirmish.

He turned his gaze to the boy again. "The town... Were any humans hurt?"

The boy appeared uneasy. "Some. The fires spread. The Boa Visk made the townsfolk fight the fire at the stronghold."

Vorgon had feared as much. He had done his best not to set fire to any of the townsfolk's homes or fields, but fire, especially dragonfire, spread quickly. That humans had been hurt weighed heavy on his heart. "Do they hate me?"

The boy shrugged, stepping closer. "Some do. Some always do. But not most. Not the shepherds. Most know you were fighting the Boa Visk. The mayor has promised to rebuild the homes that were burned. If the Boa Visk let us."

Vorgon grunted. Knowing the Boa Visk, they would conscript most of the town into rebuilding their stronghold first. He'd intended to wipe out the Boa Visk garrison completely, but the wounds he'd taken in the battle had driven him off before he could.

"I'm not finished with the Boa Visk," Vorgon assured him. "What is your name, boy?"

The boy looked at him, still not quite sure of his intentions. "I'm called Donnel."

"Well met, Donnel. I am Vorgon Graydalon." He tilted his head, eyeing the boy. "How did you find me?"

"Eren and Old Shem saw you go down here when they were grazing the flocks. We've all been watching out for you, in case the Boa Visk came. I just followed the blood."

The blood. He must have left quite a lot of it behind. "No one from the town followed you?"

Donnel shook his head. "No one pays attention to shepherds. Or children."

He laughed softly. "You're very brave. Thank you for coming, Donnel. I will gladly accept the gift from your people. Give them my deepest thanks."

The boy took another tentative step closer. His expression remained wary. "There's more. Hunters have arrived in town. Everyone thinks they're here for you."

Hunters? He did not fear hunters. Perhaps the boy was mistaken. "Boa Visk? Sorcerers or assassins?"

Donnel shook his head. "Human hunters. A band of them. We first saw their wagons a day ago. We were watching them in case they were rebels. But the elder says they hunt monsters."

Monsters. He'd been called that before. After one had lived hundreds of years, petty insults held no power. Neither did human hunters.

"I appreciate the warning," Vorgon told the boy. He only needed a few more hours of rest to finish healing, and a meal of fresh mutton, then he would fly back to Blackgap Canyon. Now that most of the bleeding had stopped, these hunters wouldn't be able to track him to his lair and kill him. Soon enough they would tire of the hunt and go back to wherever they'd come from, and Vorgon wouldn't have to kill them, either.

The boy edged closer and put out a trembling hand as if to touch him. But then he shied away. "Can you fly?"

"I must finish healing first. Your gift will do much to aid me. But if you wish to earn even higher favor, ask the shepherds to keep an eye out for these hunters or for any Boa Visk who come searching for me."

The boy nodded. "We will."

Vorgon smiled. The boy's eyes widened a little at his rows of teeth. "Don't worry," he said gently. "Have you ever touched a dragon before?"

The boy whipped his head back and forth in an emphatic no.

"Go ahead."

The boy stepped into the rocky shallows and reached one small hand out to Vorgon's side. In dragon form, with the heavy protection of his scales, he could barely feel the touch in the physical realm, but there was far more to it than that.

Vorgon was a creature of flesh and bone, energy and magic. His control over wind magic allowed his wings to lift his solid bulk and keep him aloft for hours. The fires inside him were fed by magic, keeping his need for physical food far lower than that of a purely physical being of his size. And magic fueled his mind, enabling him to link to the minds of others when they made physical contact. It was one of the reasons dragons often preferred the company of their own kind, since the dragonriders were exiled long ago. And it was one of the reasons he didn't kill humans unless they forced him to. The sensation of knowing the fear and pain of sentient prey was not something he enjoyed.

Allowing the boy to touch him was an honor the child would not fully understand, but Vorgon wanted to show his gratitude. He gave the boy a memory—a glimpse of dragon flight. The wind roaring against his body. The trees and homes so very tiny below him. The incredible sense of joy and freedom as he turned and climbed and dove and rode the currents in the air.

In turn, he caught a simple memory from the boy, not consciously communicated, just there. In the memory, Donnel was sitting at a campfire, listening to one of the shepherds tell a tale of the gods. The tale of Vraxis, the sun god of Quinylan myth, and Efon, the moon god. The two gods had been lovers and shared the sky, but had fought over the birth of humans in the world and drifted apart in strife. Now they forever chased each other through the sky, never together, except for the rarest of times when the moon and sun touched again. It was a melancholy tale. But in the memory, the boy had been fascinated, both by the tale and by the wide expanse of thousands of stars overhead. The boy's feeling of pride at being able to stay up late to listen to the stories, his awe at the stars, his delight in the warmth from the fire, all blended into a feeling of contentment and joy. His mind was so achingly young and curious that it lifted Vorgon's heart and made him smile.

The boy finally drew back his hand. "Was that what it's like to fly?"

Vorgon nodded. "When you touch a dragon, we can share thoughts, memories, feelings."

Donnel was quiet for a moment, biting at his lip. "You felt hot."

"That is good. The magic is like a furnace at my core. I need it to survive. To heal."

The boy seemed to consider this before nodding and then scurrying up the far slope of the gully toward the sheep. "My father says I'm not allowed to watch you eat. You won't tell him, will you?"

He chuckled, enjoying the boy's spirit. "You should mind your father. A dragon's meal will give you nightmares."

Donnel turned around and glared. "It will not! I'm no baby."

He grinned at the boy. "Of course you aren't. You have touched a dragon, and flown. But now you must go. I would eat alone. And then I must sleep, and heal."

The boy turned and headed up the scree, turning back

to glance at him once more before disappearing around a bend.

Vorgon would eat this gift of mutton and then he'd slip back into his healing trance. With the shepherds watching out for him, he would be safe enough until he finally made it back home. And after he had recovered, he could begin plotting to drive the Boa Visk from Shademere and the valley once and for all.

CHAPTER TWO

It was dark and close inside the pavilion when Rycard entered. The smells of charcoal, smoke, and seared meat filled the air. It took a moment for his eyes to adjust to the gloom, broken only by a single lamp and the red glow from a brazier. A small shrine with an onyx statue of the six-tailed snake god sat in the corner.

A Boa Visk dressed in dark armor with two blades at his side and elaborate rank braids hanging from his shoulders glanced up when Rycard entered. He sat at a crude wooden desk, writing by the light of the lamp. His cold, orange eyes narrowed as he looked Rycard over from head to toe, then eyed Charza with a frown. Slowly, he set down his quill.

"So you are here to end my dragon problem," Malak Telk said. "I overheard the little fracas outside my tent. You are bold, I'll give you that."

"I'm Rycard Serod of the Splitchain Hunters." Once again he pulled out the letter he'd received offering the contract. "We were summoned."

The Boa Visk smirked, eyeing the creased parchment. "Summoned, were you? I sent out half a hundred of those bounty letters."

"And how many hunters answered the call?"

For a moment, Malak's expression hardened. Then he showed his yellow teeth in what Rycard took to be a grin. "Only you. I suppose that leaves me little choice in the matter." He stood from the writing desk and walked to the sideboard where he poured himself a drink. He offered none to Rycard.

"I am Malak Telk, Gardzar of Shademere." He stepped directly in front of Rycard and took a sip from his cup. "Your mercenary company has an odd name."

"We are monster hunters, not mercenaries."

As for their name, Rycard didn't bother to explain it. The history behind the Splitchain Hunters wouldn't matter to this creature. Worse, it might even count against them. Their founder, Mordecan of Averal, was an escaped slave from Guqesh, capital city of the Boa Visk's Undlev Empire. He'd split the chains off the other slaves around him with a maul and led them south to the Shomogar swamplands. Those few who survived the escape banded together and lived on monster bounties as their reputation grew. Or so the story went. It had happened over sixty years before Rycard was born, nearly a hundred years ago from where Rycard stood now.

"Whatever you are," Malak said, "you will not be paid until you bring the dragon back to me. Alive."

That caught him by surprise. On occasion they'd been hired to trap monsters, instead of kill them, smaller ones to put on display as curiosities. But a dragon?

"How do you intend to imprison a dragon?"

"I don't. I intend to kill him slowly for the destruction he has caused. This creature will suffer exquisitely for as long as I can keep him alive. Until I sever his head from his body and drain his blood as a gift for the kovohl mages."

Rycard's dislike deepened, something he hadn't believed was possible. Taking down a deadly monster in a hunt was one thing. Torturing it was another thing entirely. The dragon's attacks had cost Malak his stronghold and his men, but such was war. Rycard suspected what enraged the leader the most was his loss of face. That meant he had to be very careful dealing with Malak. No more dangerously skirting the line as he'd done moments ago, antagonizing the sentry. Antagonizing Malak might prove extremely dangerous.

As was trying to take a dragon alive.

Not dangerous. Impossible.

Dread settled in the pit of his stomach. Gansen had been right. This was turning out to be an unqualified disaster.

As was life as they knew it without this bounty. Without it, the Splitchain Hunters were finished. Especially if they couldn't escape Shomogar before the plague spread across the countryside.

But if he could pull this off, get his people back out again safely and flush with gold, then he could be done with this life forever. Find that river. Settle down. Just him, Charza, and Redmane and a whole lot of time.

"Taking a dragon alive might prove difficult," he said.

Malak Telk, Gardzar of Shademere, flashed a smile and licked the poisonous saliva off his yellow teeth. "You have come to collect the bounty. Collect it you shall. If you fail, you will be flogged until you cannot stand, then your pitiful company will crawl out of this town without weapons, horses, or wagons until the vultures pick the flesh from your bones." He cut a glance toward the entrance to the pavilion. "Now go. Consider yourself fortunate that I do not have you executed for drawing steel on my sentry. You have amused me. But now I grow weary of you."

Rycard headed for the door. "The guards at the gate were certain the dragon is dead, or dying," he said carefully.

Malak waved a hand dismissively. "They are fools. Dragons have magic at their core. This makes them strong, difficult to kill, and...valuable. It took a bolt from one of our scorpions and a few arrows. I believe one of our kovohl mages struck home with a burning spell before being killed." He made a hissing, sighing sound and tapped his chin. "This isn't the first time we've clashed with this dragon. There have been attacks against garrison patrols and foragers after we culled a little of the surrounding human population. But this is the first time he has dared attack the town. This escalation...this provocation...will not be tolerated."

The talk of culling chilled him to the bone, though it didn't surprise him. Still, Rycard found it strange how the surrounding fields hadn't been burned. The mill was untouched. It was almost as if the dragon had specific targets in mind. Specific Boa Visk targets. "He destroyed the garrison stronghold."

"Yesterday morning. It took us most of a day to put the fires out completely. The support timbers in the fortress walls continue to smolder. The garrison is down to under fifty percent effectiveness." He took his drink to a chair and sat, leaning back into the cushions and crossing his ankles in front of him. "It is an outrage."

"Why did you put out the call for hunters?" Admitting he needed help must have rankled the gardzar—especially help from lowly human bounty chasers. "Before the dragon attacked Shademere, I mean. The amount of gold offered is considerable. Why not bring in your own reinforcements?" The Boa Visk armies had plenty of archers, ballistae and kovohl—mage adepts using the dark, strange magic of the Boa Visk. Unless most of them were all off in Tyrdenva trying to squash the rebellion there... He'd heard rumors the human armies had taken Illunvia and Redfall and reclaimed almost half the kingdom.

Malak's lips tightened. "At first I believed this to be...vermin control at best. A force of my best soldiers was dispatched to hunt the dragon down. They were unsuccessful in finding his lair." He sipped his drink, which Rycard could smell from where he stood, a stink like putrefying flesh.

"And then?"

"My soldiers killed some sheep and shepherds to lure the dragon out. He did not take the bait. Then, on their way back to this filthy hovel of a town, the dragon attacked my soldiers. I lost my second in command and half the garrison. The better half."

Dragons were said to be both powerful and highly

intelligent. Not monsters, the way other lesser creatures were monsters, but more like the gods. Rycard kept his tone noncommittal. "Did they not underestimate him, perhaps?"

Malak bristled. "The Boa Visk know plenty about dragons. We've forgotten more than humankind ever knew. Dragons are nothing more than cowards. Flying about where they cannot be reached, burning brave warriors from the safety of the sky, and then fleeing." He turned and spat through his yellow teeth. The wad of his saliva ran down the canvas side of the pavilion, sizzling as it dripped.

"It will be difficult to track something that flies. And taking something so dangerous alive?" Wary of provoking Malak, Rycard decided to play it safe. "If half a garrison of the best Boa Visk couldn't take this dragon, how to do you expect a troop of mere humans to do so?"

Malak watched him through half-lidded eyes. "Your whining disgusts me. I hope I did not hire toothless monster hunters."

Rycard kept a hand on Charza's head, calming the dog. He could feel the tension in Charza, although he also felt pride in how still his dog remained at his side. "We have teeth enough."

"I suppose we shall see. I care little for how you take him. I want results. I want the dragon alive. Hurt him if you must, but he must be *alive* when you deliver him to me."

Malak took another sip of his foul drink. "Dragons can shift into the shape of a human using their magic. It is their greatest weakness, and why the Boa Visk saved the world by driving them from Anzin."

Apparently they missed one. But Rycard wasn't going to point that out.

Malak continued. "Being able to shift into human form is no doubt why this dragon shows an inordinate amount of care for the safety of the human vermin infesting this land. Yet this is also the dragon's greatest vulnerability. I'll give you a suggestion on where to start. Take hostages and kill them until he surrenders."

"You tried that already. It only made him mad."

"But *you* are humans," Malak snarled, eyeing him as if he were an utter fool. "He will not want to kill you. You can strike while he wrestles with his honor, or whatever passes for honor in a dragon." Then Malak shrugged and grinned. "Or I'm wrong and he will eat you all. It hardly matters to me. You don't see any gold until you bring me the dragon alive. Take him when he's human. That is how I want him before me. Weak and debased and weeping, begging for his life."

"You wish to torment this creature so badly?" The thought sickened him. The possibility that he'd have to participate in something so dishonorable, so foul, made him sicker. The sudden urge to pull his blade and drive it through this Boa Visk's eye flashed inside him. Then they could try fighting their way out of town. Maybe the dragon would fly in and help them escape.

And maybes were for fools.

"Torment him?" Malak repeated, his voice turning eager. "You cannot even comprehend what I have planned. He has humiliated me and openly challenged the divine right of the Boa Visk to rule these lands. He will be made an example of. One that will never be forgotten. Now take your flea-ridden mammal and get out. Meet the demands of the bounty or die. I care not which. Either will bring me a certain pleasure."

This was a nightmare. What the hell had he gotten them into?

He pushed through the tent flap and left the pavilion. Charza growled at the two guards until Rycard put a calming hand on his head. Together they made their way to the wagons.

Brockon was leaning against one of the wagons, his hand on his bow. He grinned as Rycard headed his way, but the look in his eyes held no humor. "For a while there, I was half convinced we'd trudged all the way to the ass-end of the world, through plagues and mud and more mud, to fight for our lives against a garrison of Boa Visk over an insult to your dog."

"What changed your mind?" Rycard quipped as he headed around the wagon to where Redmane was tethered.

Brockon threw back his head and groaned with frustration.

The rest of the hunters and wagon drivers came over to him, ready for orders. He knew they were exhausted and filthy after the long journey. There was no way they could set out after the dragon tonight, even if it meant the trail growing colder than it already was. He had to balance the bounty against their safety. Tangling with a dragon who had burned half a Boa Visk garrison to ashes was a death sentence to begin with. They needed rest and food, and Rycard needed a plan.

He motioned the hunters in closer. "Tonight we rest. On our way in, we passed an inn that looked big enough to take us, if we double up."

Yero nodded. "Better than sleeping in the mud."

"Is it true about this dragon?" Gansen demanded. "This wasn't the work of rebels? It was an actual flying lizard that pisses fire?"

"No rebels. This was a dragon."

They were all silent, watching him. He could feel their unease settling deeper, getting its teeth in them. He had to head this off fast or he might be out there hunting this thing alone.

"This is no different than any other hunt. We track it. We trap it."

"No different?" Urson said. The wagon driver was bald and meaty, with sideburns that came down to his chin. "This isn't some dumb sand squid or graskin fang. Dragons were the steeds of the gods. You don't mess with the steeds of the *gods*."

Rycard eyed him. "Well, until some god shows up and tells us not to mess with his steed, we're going to fulfill this contract."

"You said 'trap it,'" Dezarie said, frowning at him. "Clearly, you meant 'kill it.'"

"I said trap it; I meant trap it. We kill it, we don't get paid."

"We *don't* kill it, we don't get paid, either," Dezarie replied. "Because we'll get *eaten*."

"That's disturbing," Brockon said.

Gansen nodded as he tugged at the frizzy mass of hair he called a beard. "We have the tools to kill it…most like. But how are we going to trap it without getting fried?"

"We force it into human form," Rycard answered.

"How?"

Rycard gathered up Redmane's reins and mounted. "I'm working on that."

"I can do it," Timval said, his expression brightening. He touched one of the square leather pouches slung at his side. "I know form-bindings. I have exactly the thing. Only I have to be close."

"Then we'll get you close," Rycard said. "But right now I have another use for your magic. The Boa Visk claim they wounded the dragon. Find its blood, mark it, track it. Let me know where it went. Yero, go with him. Watch his back."

"He'll only get in the way and slow me down," Timval said quickly. "This will be delicate tracking."

"And you have the delicacy of a charging boar," Yero complained. "The boy and I will find where it's holed up."

"I'm no boy, you goat-faced troll. And I don't need your stink giving us away."

"Enough," Rycard snapped. "You're worse than a bunch of children. You're giving me a headache." He turned to Timval and held the young man's gaze.

Blood had power. Timval could use a spell that would enable them to follow the path of the dragon's blood. It was one of their trade secrets and saved them weeks of beating the bush, trying to flush out the monsters they hunted.

"Do this just like we always do. Follow the blood. Find where it's hiding. Then come right back."

"Of course. I know what I'm doing."

"Do not get close to it," Rycard continued. "And don't let it know we're hunting it. Right now, we only need to find its lair. After that, we can decide how to flush it out and bring it down."

Timval nodded, a pleased smile spreading across his youthful face. Rycard had a sudden flash of misgiving. Of all the people he would have picked for this job, Timval was the last. Still, the boy's magic was better at tracking than Dezarie's, and he didn't want to humiliate Timval by insisting Yero go with him. The kid was young, but they'd all been young once. What the kid needed most was experience.

Telling himself that didn't make Rycard feel any better.

When the young adept took a step toward the town the gates, Rycard nudged Redmane forward and put a restraining hand on the boy's shoulder. "Remember what I said. Be careful. I don't want to be writing a letter to your mother explaining how her son was eaten by a dragon."

Timval snorted. "Good thing I'm an orphan then."

Rycard gave him a stern look.

The grin never left Timval's face. "Relax. This is easy magic. Barely worth my time. But as long as there's a bonus in it, I'm all in. I'll be doing most of the work after all."

Rycard frowned. "Do the job right and we'll discuss bonuses. But it'll take all of us to bring this dragon back alive."

Timval gave him a considering look. "Actually, I have some ideas on that—"

"And I'll be happy to hear them out later tonight. For now, get tracking that dragon before the trail turns to ice. And remember what I said."

Timval rolled his eyes and headed for the town gates. Rycard watched him for a moment, increasingly worried he'd made a mistake sending the kid. But he couldn't baby the young man forever. He knew the risks when he signed on. None of them had the luxury of guarantees in this life.

Finally he turned to run his gaze over the remaining hunters. "Listen well. We hunt tomorrow. I want you all well rested and ready to move out at dawn. Now let's get our gear stowed and get something to eat."

From their reactions, that was the most popular thing he'd said in days.

* * *

Donnel woke him again. The boy was pushing at his

side with all his might, though he couldn't budge Vorgon's mass. His voice was sharp and panicky. "Wake up! Dragon, wake up!"

Vorgon lifted his head and blinked at the boy, then peered around him. Dusk had fallen. Purple shadows lined the rocks around him in the darkening gorge. He saw nothing. He drew in a breath, searching for a scent on the air. He smelled nothing other than the boy. The stream bubbled and gurgled over the rocks, but he heard nothing else.

"What is it?" he demanded, getting to his feet and bringing his tail around to shield them from whatever it was that the boy feared. He allowed the skin of his second eyelid to descend, letting him see the varying levels of heat in the landscape around him, searching for living things that could be a threat. Still he saw nothing except the boy.

"A hunter," Donnel said quickly. "He's following you like I did. With your blood. He's almost here. I came as fast as I could, but he has a horse."

Vorgon didn't feel fear, only the tightly focused attention that came to him before a battle. The fires in his core flared. He felt better, thought he might be healed enough to fly away and leave the hunter far behind. He inspected his wounds. They were sealed, no longer seeping blood. They would leave no trail for the hunter to track.

But there was the boy to think of. He didn't know who

this hunter was, or whether he'd harm the boy. The Boa Visk had killed enough humans, and he wouldn't risk the boy's life.

It came to him then in the gathering darkness. The sharp sweet tang of magic, brushing against his mind like a breeze.

"Run," he told the boy.

The boy held his ground, fumbling a sling from his belt. A moment later, a man on a horse rode into view at the mouth of the gorge. Magic, faint at this distance, but distinct, teased Vorgon's senses.

So they'd sent not only a hunter, but an adept. That made him far more dangerous.

The aura of the man's magic swirled around him, rippling in Vorgon's vision like the heat shimmer off the rocks of the canyon in high summer. He rode cautiously up the gorge toward them, dressed in gray ringmail and leather—a hunter's garb—with a deep purple hooded cloak.

The boy stepped in front of Vorgon as if to shield him. Another time and another place, he would've found it touching. But not now. Vorgon bumped Donnel with his head, nudging him to step aside, and roared at him in a tone that brooked no argument. "This is not the hour for foolish bravery, Donnel. *Run.* I will deal with this."

The boy took one last look at him and threw his arms

onto Vorgon's side as if to hug his wide body. Then he sprinted away, splashing over the rocky stream and disappearing into the crags above.

Vorgon grunted his approval. The hunter would have a harder time tracking the boy through the streambed. If he were interested in the boy at all.

Vorgon turned to face the hunter riding toward him—the hunter adept—drawing himself up to his full height. The sun was sinking below the jagged horizon to the west, painting long cold shadows over the gorge, and a ghost moon floated in the south, just above the mountain peaks. A random thought flashed through his mind—the boy's memory of the tale of the sun and moon gods and the humans who'd killed their love. Vorgon watched the human hunter ride steadily toward him, energy swirling around him like a vortex.

When the hunter drew within a hundred meters of him, the horse caught Vorgon's scent and shied. The hunter had a hard time controlling his mount as it paced around in a circle, fighting at the bit. Foolish human. Did he think his horse would willingly ignore the scent of a predator, especially one such as him?

The horse finally put his head down and bucked. The hunter barely had time to clear the saddle before the horse leaped back and bucked again, leaving the hunter on his backside on the rocky ground. Then the horse darted off the way he'd come.

The hunter scrambled to his feet with his purple cloak tangling about his legs, staring after his horse so sadly that Vorgon felt a moment's pity for him. But the flight of his horse didn't distract the hunter long. He turned back and approached Vorgon on foot. Slowly.

He wore a sword and dirk at his side, but he did not draw his weapons. The human was grown but still young. Brave. Or foolish. But that did not mean the young adept wasn't dangerous.

Vorgon watched him come, waiting. Every moment he waited gave the shepherd boy who dreamed of suns and moons more time to escape.

When the young human hunter came within a dozen meters of him, he stopped. "Beast," he shouted up to him. His voice echoed up and down the gorge and from the slopes around them. "Do you speak the common tongue?"

Vorgon lazily tilted his head and looked him over. So much noise from such a small creature. "Go away," Vorgon finally said, his voice a deep rumble like a rockslide. The warning would've been enough to frighten off most humans. Even a madman, as this one must be.

"Monster! You attacked a helpless town and burned it to the ground."

Vorgon took a step forward and moved his massive wings, as if threatening to unfurl them. "I burned the stronghold of the Boa Visk, not the human town. I bear the people of Shademere no enmity. Now go. If the Boa Visk are paying you, then return their money and leave this place. Their friends are my enemies."

Uncowed, the hunter adept took a step forward. "You are a liar. The town's gate is smashed. Its walls are destroyed, its buildings burned, and its people terrified. You are the cause of great suffering."

"You should flee," Vorgon warned again, letting smoke seep from between his teeth, each longer than a human's hand. "If you truly wish to face me, find yourself heavier armor and a very large shield. And bring some comrades. To mourn you."

The foolish human held his ground. "I need none of those things to bring you down. You will face justice for your crimes."

Vorgon looked down at him. "All alone? Your people sent a single boy by himself to bring down a dragon? Either you're all fools, or all mad."

"I'm all they need," the boy hunter said. "As you shall see. I am Timval Deyswift."

Brave or mad, the small human was certainly tenacious. "How much are they paying you to kill me?"

Vorgon let a casual breath of fire hiss out toward a cluster of rocks not far from the hunter's feet, leaving them scorched and glowing, the scent of burnt earth lingering in the air. "No amount of gold is worth your life."

"Oh, I don't intend to kill you. I only intend to collar you and drag you back to the gardzar."

"The Boa Visk," Vorgon snarled. "You think to be a hero, child? No one will praise you for selling out your kind to those murderous creatures. They enslave and murder any who speak against them. That is what their gold buys you. The murder of your own kind."

The hunter edged a step closer. They faced each other at a distance of ten meters in the shadow of the defile as the sun slowly dipped behind the mountains. The air had turned colder. Even mostly healed, Vorgon's wounds still ached, and the acid burn on his side still throbbed with dull pain. Why would this human choose Boa Visk gold over the lives of his own kind?

Vorgon grew weary of the sadness of it all. "The entire garrison tried to kill me and failed. What makes you think a pup like you can succeed where they did not?"

"Don't call me that, beast!"

"You grow tiresome, pup. I will show you mercy because you are young and lack the wisdom of years to recognize your own folly." Vorgon leaned in closer, narrowing his eyes, letting a few drops of burning slaver drip from between his teeth and scorch the ground. "Leave now, before you strain my patience to the breaking point."

With that, he spread his wings to take flight.

As he did so, Timval ran toward him, chanting words of power as he dug into one of his pouches. The very recklessness of his actions caught Vorgon off guard. In all his long years, he never thought a living creature could be so rashly insane.

Vorgon wheeled back to face Timval and drew deep upon his inner core of fire. Before he could release a breath, the hunter pulled a bright blue stone the size of a plum from his pouch and threw it at him. Vorgon recognized the stone instantly for what it was, for the magic that had been bound to its surface and swirled around it like a halo. For what that magic could do to him.

From this distance, it could not miss.

When it struck Vorgon on the side, the stone's magic burst into twisted lightning chains that encircled him from all directions. The energy burned across his skin, searing him, filling him with agony.

Binding his magic.

He roared in pain, then drew in breath to spit fire as the bluish energy crackled around him. His concentration fragmented as the stone's magic worked against him, feeding upon Vorgon's power like a parasite.

The stone's magic did not stop at binding Vorgon's power. He screamed as the stone's magic reached its full power, forcing him to change forms, to shift into his human body. He was helpless to stop it. He screamed again as the change consumed him and ripped through his body in a blaze of blue heat and power and pain.

The world shifted wildly, spinning and whirling in a disorienting blur. His vision changed from dragon sight to human. Naked, he sank to one weak, human knee in the tufts of grass that poked up between the rocks. He gasped for breath, his human body shuddering. Usually he changed forms smoothly and painlessly. But the change forced by the magic was harsh and primitive, as if he were being torn apart and sewn back together in an instant that seemed to last an eternity.

A moment later, Timval stood over him with a dagger at Vorgon's vulnerable, human throat. "So arrogant," Timval said. "And now look at you."

A stone struck Timval's head, sending him staggering with a cry of pain. He raised his free hand to clutch the place where the stone had split his skin. Blood ran through his fingers.

Donnel, standing on a rocky outcrop not far away, lowered his sling.

Vorgon gathered all the strength he had left and launched himself for Timval, grabbing his knife hand. He turned Timval's wrist to point the blade toward the hunter's chest and shoved, hard. The knife blade stabbed into the hunter, sliding past his ribs to pierce his heart. Dark heart's blood began to seep from the wound, flowing around the blade.

"I'm sorry," Vorgon whispered, startled momentarily by the softness of his human voice. The young hunter clutched at him, gazing at him desperately with wide eyes, gasping as he tried to conjure another spell. But he could not. He went still, mouth moving slightly as he sighed out a long, rattling breath.

The magic from the binding stone died with him and wafted away like a scent on the breeze.

Vorgon lowered him gently to the ground. Timval's eyes still gazed off into the distance, wide and sightless. Vorgon closed those staring eyes with deep sorrow in his heart. Why hadn't the foolish boy listened?

He hadn't meant for it to come to this. Yet it was his fault. He'd baited the reckless young man. He'd meant to cow him, but he should've seen that the hunter adept was too prideful, too committed to taking Vorgon captive to back down. And he'd accused the boy of lacking wisdom. He himself should have foreseen this end.

With fumbling, near-numb fingers, he took off Timval's purple cloak and wrapped it around himself against the cold of the evening, which he felt acutely in human form without his core of dragonfire to warm him.

He looked up to meet the eyes of Donnel the shepherd boy. He stood not far off, at the top of a rocky outcropping. The boy's sling dangled in one limp hand. He was staring at them, wide-eyed, his face slack with shock. Vorgon didn't know if it was himself in human form or the body of the dead hunter that disturbed the boy more.

"Donnel, you saved my life," he called. "Thank you."

The boy did not answer. He only stared blankly at the body lying on the ground.

Vorgon's heart went out to him. No one so young should ever have been exposed to such ugliness.

"Have I killed him?" the boy asked in a near whisper.

"No," Vorgon replied. The boy continued to stare down at the hunter's body.

"Donnel!" he said, sharply enough that the boy flinched and looked at him. "You didn't kill him. I did. With his knife. You see?"

The boy hesitated a moment, then nodded.

"You saved my life. Now I need you to listen."

The boy began to approach him, but Vorgon held up a hand. "Stay there. I will deal with this. You need to listen to me."

Donnel nodded again. His eyes were very wide. "You changed into a man."

"Yes. Now, listen to me. You must run. Leave this place and do not return."

"But—"

"No buts. I expect you to obey. If more hunters come to your camp asking about their comrade, tell them nothing. Don't talk to them at all, do you understand me?" He held the boy's gaze, keeping his expression stern. Maybe he could finally get Donnel to obey. "Promise me you will not speak of this."

"But why? If they're scared, they will leave you alone."

"They will not. They are chasing gold, and they'll never stop. Promise me you won't go into Shademere until they're gone. Stay at the shepherd camps. If more men come looking for me, don't go near them. Promise me."

The boy nodded. A tear slipped from one eye and curved down his cheek. "I swear it."

Vorgon was too far from him to wipe the tear away, but he found himself reaching for the boy all the same as if he could somehow comfort him. "Listen, brave one. I owe you my life. I will always be grateful to you and I will find some way to repay you."

The boy's face immediately brightened. "Will you let me fly on your back when you are a dragon again?"

Vorgon threw back his head and laughed. Donnel had so much of the human spark that dragonkin admired: the bravery, the verve, and that endearing curiosity. Even though humans were tiny and breakable, there was much to admire in them.

"I promise." He made his expression serious again. "But not until these troubles are past. Until then, you must do as I say. Stay far away from me and from these hunters. Do you understand?"

The boy nodded, though he clearly didn't relish the idea. Finally, he turned and disappeared from the ledge.

Vorgon turned back to the slain hunter. Something inside him stirred in pity at the sight of the fallen human. Brave, foolish, over-proud. So young. Now he would never have the chance to learn wisdom.

"I'm sorry this happened, young one," he said softly. "You were rash beyond measure, but no one can ever say you were not brave."

He stood again and sang *Korshalla Dossa De'vurkos*—the dragon song known as *Setting Red Sun*, a dirge of mourning for the fallen. His voice rang strong, dark and lonely through the gorge. His song carried out onto the wet grass of the plains on the back of the wind. Finally, Vorgon arranged Timval's body on the stones, laying him out respectfully, removing the knife from his heart and laying it over his breast under his crossed hands. He laid the sword carefully beside him. Then he removed the purple cloak from his shoulders, feeling the cold wind bite into his human flesh, and draped it over the hunter's body like a shroud. This way, his companions might find him and finish laying him to rest in his homeland.

His heart heavy, he shifted back into dragon form and took flight, leaving the mournful scene behind.

CHAPTER THREE

Rycard spotted Timval's horse grazing the fields a dozen or so miles from town. It had been a beautiful morning until then, the sun bright, the air crisp, the sky so blue it appeared painted on the heavens. But the sight of the riderless horse was nothing short of ominous.

Rycard rode atop Redmane with Charza at his side as they closed in on the horse. Timval's mount whinnied in greeting and trotted to meet them through the tall grass still wet with dew. Dezarie reached him first. She took his reins, patted him, and whispered soothing words as she led him back to where they waited.

Rycard scanned the sky for the dragon but spotted nothing. The muddy ground had made it easy for them to track Timval's horse, chasing his trail from Shademere into the foothills. Charza also had his scent, so it was only a matter of time until they found him.

"Not a good sign," Gansen said, staring at Dezarie as she held the bridle of Timval's horse and led it back to them. Gansen turned his glare to Yero. "You should've gone with him, you bastard."

Yero's expression darkened. "He didn't want me to come. You all heard him. And Rycard told him to be careful. Bloody hell, how was I to know he'd do some damn fool thing?"

Gansen's fists clenched. "Because he was a damn fool, that's how."

"That will be enough," Rycard said. "If there is blame to be shouldered, then I will take it. But until we know for certain, we keep our hopes high and we believe Timval still lives."

"Without his horse?" Gansen grumbled. "The dragon ate him."

Rycard fixed him with an icy look, staring the other man down. Gansen finally simmered down to muttering to himself, which was the best anyone could hope for.

"Axton, Deacon, and Dezarie, keep tracking," Rycard said loudly, grateful his voice did not betray the turmoil of the emotions inside him. "The rest of you, let's move out."

He hardly slept last night. When Timval had not returned before nightfall, he'd led the other hunters on a quick ranging around Shademere, hoping to find him. They had found nothing except his tracks into the hills, which would be impossible to search at night. Especially with dragons about. They'd returned to the town, none of them speaking much, and had set out again at dawn. All last night, his stomach had been a churning wreck of cold dread.

It was worse, now that they'd found Timval's horse.

It was all his fault for sending the brash young adept off alone. He should've insisted that Yero go with him. Then again, if he had, they might be searching for both Timval *and* Yero right now.

What had the fool gotten himself into? Damn it, he'd been clear in his orders. Timval was only to track the dragon to find its lair, then return.

Had he stumbled too far into the lair? Been seen by the dragon? Killed?

That was assuming Timval had fun afoul of the dragon and not something else...like a Boa Visk patrol. The fiery young man might've said something unwise, believing himself safe under the gardzar's contract. No one was ever safe around the Boa Visk.

They set forth again, spread out across the grassy field with Charza in the lead, nose to the ground. Dezarie rode behind the dog, using her magic to follow traces of Timval's tracking spell, already mostly faded. Whenever she lost the thread, they either relied on Axton and Deacon to read the signs of Timval's horse in the rain-softened earth, or followed Charza's zigzagging trail. By midmorning, they had followed the signs to a gully in the foothills between two rocky slopes, where a stream flush with rainwater and snowmelt threatened its banks as it wound down into the plains.

They didn't need Axton or Deacon to point out the clumps of grassy earth and upended rocks where Timval's horse had spooked and run. It no longer mattered. From here, they could clearly see the body laid out beside the stream, shrouded in Timval's purple cloak.

"Bloody hell," Gansen grumbled. "I told you the fool was going to get himself killed."

"You said eaten by the dragon," Yero said. "Clearly, he's still in one piece."

"Enough." Rycard was too tired to curse. His heart sat in his chest like a frozen stone. No one said another word as they dismounted, leaving the horses with Gansen to guard them at the bottom of the gorge. Rycard ordered Charza to stay with the horses. The dog circled the ground once then curled up beside Gansen.

For whatever reason, that made Rycard feel worse about his young mage adept's death. If Timval had only obeyed half as well…

As Rycard and Dezarie carefully made their way into the gorge, Axton and Deacon swept wide behind them, while Yero and Brockon circled up the slopes to provide cover from above. The dragon was nowhere to be seen, but the ground held plenty of signs he had been here. Burned rock. Scorched gravel. He'd been here recently.

Rycard dismounted and knelt beside Timval's body. He pulled back the purple cloak. The young man's skin was very pale, grayish, but the death rigor had loosened. A bloody wound to his chest. Stab wound. Another wound to his head. A blow of some kind, but not something that likely would've killed him. Not a mace. A rock perhaps? The hilt of the knife that killed him?

His body was carefully arranged, a fallen warrior sent off with respect to the afterlife. There was blood on Timval's knife blade too…and the blade roughly matched the size of the wound. Stabbed with his own blade?

Clearly, he wasn't killed by the dragon. Nor the Boa Visk.

That made no sense.

Dezarie crouched next to him, her expression grim. "What do you think happened?"

"I don't know." He nodded to the flattened grass, the depressions, and large four-clawed tracks and burned areas that had to have come from a dragon. "The dragon was here, I'm sure of it."

"There are traces of magic here as well. A powerful spell discharged." She pointed to the scorch marks all around a cluster of rocks. "Why would the dragon burn those rocks, but not burn Timval? That's the only evidence of fire damage, aside from a few tiny burn marks that might have been made by embers."

"A warning?" Axton suggested. The short, barrel-chested hunter was keeping well clear of them so as not to disturb the ground as they searched for anything they could track.

Rycard glanced from the scorched rocks back to Timval's body. Axton had to be right. The fire-blasted rocks did seem like some kind of warning shot. An arrow over the head to make an attacker think twice. And the rocks were to the right of the gorge. From all the signs and tracks, the battle had taken place with the dragon facing toward the bottom of the gorge, and Timval having come up that way after losing his horse. If the dragon had wanted to burn the mage adept, he had a clear shot.

And none of that explained why the body had been laid out with such care...almost respect. Nor did it explain the knife wound.

He and Dezarie carefully scoured the ground once

more, paying special attention to the area around Timval. Four sets of tracks in the defile. Timval's boots, the dragon tracks, and two other sets of tracks he puzzled over. Small, rigid tracks that looked like the boots of a child or a small woman, dotted with some sort of treads. Then another, from a man's bare feet.

The man who'd stabbed Timval? Or perhaps it had been the woman?

After a careful search, he found a smooth stone nearby with a little blood on it. The stone was far enough away from Timval that Rycard didn't believe it had been splashed by his blood when he'd been stabbed. When Rycard held the stone against the wound on Timval's head, it seemed to roughly match the bruising. Again, odd. The final thing they discovered was a very fine scattering of blue dust over the ground most disturbed by dragon tracks. The dust felt slightly warm to his touch, although that could've been the morning sun.

"Is that what I think it is?" he asked Dezarie. With the death of Timval, she was their last mage adept and most likely to know.

She pushed it with her finger and held some of close to her eyes. "Traces of magic... One of his spell stones. The remains of it anyway. A binding stone perhaps?"

Rycard sighed. The little fool. "Timval said he had the

means to force the dragon to take human shape. Form bindings. This must've been what he meant."

"It explains the bare human footprints we found. He got close enough to use the stone. But why did the dragon allow him that close to begin with? And why lay his body out like that?"

Rycard shook his head. The whole thing was very odd. "Another warning, this time to us?"

"So he forced the dragon to change form," Dezarie said as she knelt beside Timval's body, staring at his pale, still face. "The dragon killed him, and then laid him to rest?"

Rycard shrugged. It was the only thing that made sense.

"It would be a dangerous thing to do in human form," Dezarie went on. "He couldn't know if there were other hunters closing in…" She looked around and her gaze settled on the stone Rycard had found. "Unless he *did* know. If this dragon has the friendship of the farmers or shepherds, perhaps they warned him? Helped him?"

Rycard let out a long breath. Why couldn't Timval have just done what he was told? "We will return and bury him where he's fallen," Rycard said, standing again. He whistled for Charza. His dog quickly padded over and sat close to him as if trying to give comfort. "Right now we have no spades to dig him a grave, and we must pursue the dragon before the trail grows any colder."

Gansen unslung his two-handed war ax and rested it before him, his hands gripping the long shaft. For a moment he bowed his head as if in prayer. "His soul has returned to the stars with honor for his bravery," he finally said, looking down on Timval's body before shaking his head. "I don't understand why the thing that cut him down took the time to show him respect, but I will show his killer the same respect. After I split the bastard in half."

"I've heard dragons were the closest to the gods before they were banished from Starhold," Deacon said softly. Deacon had the look of a monk, shaved head, kind eyes, a quiet nature. The bowman rarely spoke, but when he did speak, Rycard listened.

"They were said to be beautiful creatures of learning, grace, and power. If we do hunt a dragon from the great clans of legend, it would not surprise me if he took the time to honor our comrade."

"Doesn't matter," Axton said. "It killed one of us; now we kill it."

Rycard raised a hand. "We were hired to bring it back alive. If we kill this dragon, the Boa Visk will not be pleased." He let the rest of the implications dangle there and watched as each face around him caught his meaning. He hadn't revealed how up to their necks in quicksand they truly were on this bounty, but he could not have his hunters killing the dragon in revenge for Timval. Otherwise they all would pay.

"This dragon might have already died," Gansen said, his voice tight. "It may have bled out from the wounds the Boa Visk inflicted."

"For all our sakes, I hope not." Rycard pointed farther up the stream. "From the signs, it looks as if the dragon stopped here to recover and heal from the attack on the stronghold. There doesn't seem to be another blood trail—"

Shouting broke out on the foothill slopes above, cutting him off. Rycard reached for his blade as the rest of his hunters drew their weapons and spread out, peering around uneasily for the source of the threat.

A moment later, Yero appeared at the top of the gorge, dragging along a small shepherd boy. The boy was yelling and twisting in Yero's grip. He kept trying to kick the hunter in the shins and struck out wildly with his staff.

Yero dodged a near blow to his head from the staff and dumped the boy in front of Rycard. "Seems we have a spy."

The boy was glaring at Rycard but didn't even glance at the dead body. That was a surprise. Rycard thought the sight would be troubling for a young boy. Unless he already knew it was there.

The boy also had a sling attached to his belt.

Anger boiled inside Rycard as he reached down, grabbed the boy's leg, and lifted it to see the sole of the boy's worn leather boot. The boy wrenched away, but he'd seen what he'd needed to see. The soles had tread—little metal nubs—that would help with climbing rocks. They matched the tracks he'd spotted around the streambed.

"Where did you find him?" he asked Yero.

"Hiding up the slopes." He pointed toward the rocky mountain slopes covered with evergreen trees where the foothills ended. "Saw him as soon as I started climbing. He tried to run, the little rat."

Rycard studied the shepherd boy. He might've been anywhere from eight to ten years old. His clothes were wet at the knees and grass-stained. The boy glared at him, showing his teeth as though he were half-feral.

"Did you kill this man?" Rycard demanded, pointing to Timval's body.

"Let me go," the boy snarled and tried to bite Yero again. "Let me go, you bastards!"

Axton was squatting near the stream, washing his big hands in the cold flow of water before splashing it on his broad, rough-featured face. His voice was just as cold as the snow runoff. "We're the bastards, but this runt killed a man who was trying to save his filthy people from a dragon."

"He wasn't trying to save us," the boy yelled. "He just

wanted gold. The dragon never hurt us. He doesn't hurt people."

"Someone hurt my man here," Rycard said. He reached out, grabbed the boy's chin, and turned his head so he had to stare at Timval's body. "Look at him. He's dead. Look at him!"

Tears came to the boy's eyes. "He was trying to kill our dragon!"

Rycard let him go and stepped away, closing his eyes and turning his face up toward the sun. *Our dragon?* The warmth of the sunlight did little to ease the pounding in his head. This whole thing was such a tragic mess.

Or perhaps the boy was speaking the truth. Perhaps Rycard should open his ears and listen for once. Read the signs like any good tracker. The dragon had attacked the Boa Visk stronghold but hadn't attacked the houses, mill, or fields. Yes, a few homes had been damaged, but that could have been due to spreading flames, drifting embers and sparks. Here, where Timval had fallen, the dragon had clearly loosed fire...but not at the hunter. It had been a warning.

Was the dragon acting as some kind of guardian for the land or for the people in the valley?

That would certainly explain why the boy would think of him as *their dragon*. It also meant they would see his hunters as betraying fellow humans to the Boa Visk for gold.

With a curse, he scrubbed his hands across his face and turned back to the mess he'd found here. When had hunting monsters become so hellishly complicated?

"What now?" Gansen asked. "Do we drag him back to the Boa Visk?"

"They'll hang the boy," Deacon said softly. "His blood would be on us."

Axton made a show of spitting through the gap in his teeth. "If we don't hang him first and save them the trouble. He killed one of our own. And it had to have been an ambush. Timval was green as spring grass, but he was powerful."

"No one will hang," Rycard said through clenched teeth. "But we can't let him go either. He was clearly part of this." He looked into the boy's eyes again. "Here's what the signs tell me. My man here faced the dragon, forced it to shape-shift into human form with his magic. But you ambushed him. Attacked him with a stone from your sling. The dragon—the dragon-man—killed him with his own knife. Is that how it happened?"

The boy didn't answer, only glared.

Well, the boy had a spine at least, that was certain. Rycard had to respect that.

He turned to Yero. "Bind his hands. He's coming with

us for now."

"What if he tries to bite me again?" Yero protested.

"Then keep your hands away from his mouth." There was no way he would turn the child over to the Boa Visk. Even if he'd played some role in Timval's death, the tracks and signs were clear. He had not stabbed Timval.

"Easy for you to say. You aren't the one he wants to chew on."

Rycard ignored Yero and made sure the boy's attention was on him. "We aren't going to hurt you. But I want you to give me your word. No more biting or trying to escape. And you stay silent or I will be forced to gag you."

The boy said nothing, but the distrust never left his eyes.

Agreement or defiance, Rycard didn't care. As long as the boy obeyed him. There were no bare human tracks leading out of the gorge, so the dragon must have shifted back into dragon form and flown away. Which made his task far more difficult.

"Let's move out. We search the canyons, caves, anyplace that could hide a dragon. We search them one at a time if need be. Keep your eye on the sky and your weapons at the ready."

"I say we leave the boy here," Gansen said. "We don't need him shouting out and letting the dragon know we're coming."

"No," Rycard said. "If we leave him here, he'll just run to spread the alarm. Besides, the dragon won't attack us if we have the boy."

He walked back to Redmane, but first he took a few moments with Charza. His dog eagerly licked at his face, his tail whipping wildly back and forth as Rycard knelt beside him and rubbed his head. When he stood again, Charza whined, watching him with those big soulful eyes.

"It's all right, boy," he murmured.

Then he turned to his men. "Come on. Let's get this over with."

The mood of the company was black as they rode out. He could feel it swirling around them like a dark aura. This hunt had barely begun, and already he wanted it over with. All he had to do was survive this final hunt and he was done. If he hadn't been certain of it before, he damn well was now. No more monsters. No more losing hunters. No more bloody Boa Visk. He would find a quiet place far from all these troubles if it was the last thing he did.

But it probably wouldn't be. The dragon would probably kill him first.

* * *

The noon sun warmed Vorgon's scales. Since dawn, he'd watched the valley from a mountain slope swathed in mist. Now the mist had mostly burned away, and the sun high overhead kept the shadows short. He remained in dragon form, staying low to the rocks and hidden by the pines. It was easier to hide as a human, but he needed to be able to take flight or to defend himself at an instant's notice.

After all that had happened, he'd decided not to risk returning to his lair in Blackgap Canyon. He had already made several mistakes, underestimating the human hunter and showing too much restraint, and it had nearly cost him everything. He'd dragged an innocent boy into the mess as well. For that, he would never forgive himself. But what was done was done.

Long ago, when he'd left the Isle of Rasella, he'd been called a fool for returning to the continent of Anzin after the Boa Visk had driven dragonkin from the land. Vaemor, the northern kingdom of the dragons, had fallen. The air had been filled with smoke and ash and the stench of warfare. The Boa Visk had surged like a dark tide from the north, eager to bring down the dragons, slaughter them and twist their magic into something powerful and evil.

The flight, the retreat from Anzin all those years ago, remained carved in his memory. So did all the emotions: the fear and shame of fleeing an enemy, the burning desire for revenge, the realization that the dragonkin were abandoning all of Anzin to the Boa Visk. Worst was knowing that all the races watched as the sky filled with retreating dragons flying west to the ocean, aware of the despair they must have felt.

At the time he'd believed it cowardly to abandon their homeland to cower on the Isle of Rasella, ringed by wide seas, jagged reefs, high cliff walls and the mountains surrounding it. When he'd returned to Anzin, he'd thought time had not changed that belief. Now here he was, hiding, cowering, having changed nothing for the better. It weighed heavily on him. It enraged him and broke his heart at the same time. He'd thought he could be different from his brethren. It hurt to discover he was not.

No. He wasn't going to hide here any longer. Let them come. He would face them like a dragon. He had a right to exist. He had a right to be free.

He spread his wings, ready to spring into the air and take flight, when he spotted the group of riders coming over a rise in the valley below.

He narrowed his gaze and focused, allowing his dragonsight to zoom in on the group from miles distant. As he'd feared. Hunters. Eight of them, all armed, all on horseback, leading one horse without a rider, and a dog trotting out in front. One of the horses had two riders...

It was Donnel. The boy had his hands bound and was held in place by the hunter in the saddle behind him. Vorgon's dragonfire seethed inside him, sending a blast of steam past his teeth. For a moment he could not move as all his thoughts broke apart into shards of panic and dread.

How had they found the boy? Doubtless they'd tracked Donnel into the foothills.

He was a fool. Instead of laying the dead man to rest in honor, he should've incinerated the entire area. Started a fire that would've hidden all tracks and destroyed any evidence of their foolish hunter adept and how he perished.

This is what he got for mercy. The boy taken prisoner to suffer in his place.

The bitter taste of self-loathing filled his mouth. He would not be so foolish a second time.

Vorgon launched himself from the mountainside, his wide wings beating the air as he used magic to manipulate the air currents, giving himself more lift for his heavy mass. Deer fled his shadow, bounding down mountain slopes. On the foothills and plains below him, sheep and goats scattered in all directions. Roaring with the deep piercing rumble that shook the treetops, he streaked toward the riders.

The group of hunters saw him coming and spread their formation out in near perfect unison. They shouted to each other and drew their weapons.

He flew low over them, spooking their horses and ruining their formation as their mounts shied in terror. One man at the front of the group managed to keep his horse under control. He was shouting orders and gesturing with the blade in his hand. This one had to be their leader. The one who'd sent the foolish young adept to his death. The one who'd captured the boy Donnel.

Vorgon banked hard, feeling the pull of the land against his mass and the rush of air as he came around again, tightening his turn with magic that controlled the winds. He couldn't use fire against them. Not when Donnel was in their midst. He came at them again, flying even lower this time, flying at his highest speed and meaning to seize the rider who was holding Donnel prisoner.

The rider was too quick. He saw him coming and kicked his horse hard. The beast leaped away. Vorgon's talons closed on empty air.

Magic flared around one of the riders to his right. Vorgon cursed and veered off. Another mage adept. A female. She loosed a trapping spell at him—whirling energy meant to ruin the airflow around his wings and gut his own magic.

But her attack wasn't the same as the binding stone that had caught him yesterday. This was no physical object. He tapped his own power and shattered her magic. As her spell failed, the rebound of energy had her reeling in the saddle.

An arrow nearly caught him in the wing, but he swerved off, dodging two more arrows. He came around again in front of the scattered and disorganized group of riders.

They were using the boy against him, keeping him front and center to prevent Vorgon from using his fire or his magic. Frustrated, he drew up sharply, wings thrown wide, roaring defiance. When he landed, his feet hit the earth hard enough to shake it.

"Take him alive," their leader shouted. Vorgon focused in on him with his dragonsight. Hard eyes, harsh features, the hunter had the look of a man who's seen his share of danger. He wore chainmail armor with boiled leather and a dark gray cloak that looked as if it had seen better years. Everything about him seemed worn and hard. But there was no masking the battle-intensity blazing in his eyes.

Vorgon threw back his head, loosed another ear-shattering roar, and followed it with fire, keeping the flames high in the air in warning.

The hunters spread out around him. One of their archers leaped from his horse and edged forward, staying low to the ground with his bow in hand.

"Release the boy!" Vorgon roared, using the combined weight of command and magic to amplify his voice, to shake them in their boots. His voice had their horses dancing and pulling at their bits again in panic. The riders were forced to dismount, but the one holding Donnel still kept a blade free. The dirk wasn't at the boy's throat, but the man had his arm around him, pinning him tight. The threat was clear.

The leader dismounted as well, and he bounded forward with his sword and dagger drawn. His dog never left his side, teeth bared, growling low in his throat at Vorgon. The man kept a wary distance but was tense, as if ready to spring in any direction to avoid a stream of fire. Foolish human. If Vorgon wanted them all dead, they'd be ash by now.

"You speak with a human voice," the leader said.

"I do," Vorgon growled. "Now leave the boy and go." He let a small tongue of flame lick past his lips in warning.

The human was not put off by his display. "This boy killed one of my men," the leader said. "He's coming with us to face justice."

"No!" Vorgon roared. Larger flames slipped past his jaws in his fury and dread. "There is no *justice* under the Boa

Visk, fool. Release him and go. This is not your land. You are not welcome here."

The leader stepped toward him, blade in hand. "And it seems neither are you, or we wouldn't have been sent to collect you."

"This is my home," Vorgon roared. "I am Vorgon Graydalon, third of the Tahkeshin, of the dragonkin descended of Torodon, who served the god Danjenma before the closing of the doors to Starhold. I returned here from the Isle of Rasella after the scourge, to protect my homeland, long before humans even walked this valley. *You* are the trespassers here."

"And I am Rycard Serod, of the Splitchain Hunters, with a bounty letter that says differently." Rycard pointed at Donnel. "This boy means something to you?"

"He is a child. He did not kill your man. Let him go."

The hunter tilted his head. His expression was tight, unfriendly. Harsh. His face was scarred and stubbled with a few days' growth, tanned and lined by the sun, with pale gray eyes that seemed cold and hard, but it possessed a stark beauty, like a desert landscape. There was a strength to this man, from his words to the way he carried himself, that Vorgon would not underestimate.

As he spoke, his hunters continued to spread out along his flanks at a safe distance. Farther than Vorgon could sustain a stream of flame. But not too far for their arrows.

"The signs don't lie," Rycard said coldly. "The boy was involved in Timval's death. He hit him with a rock. But there is no need for further violence. I'll be happy to release him to his family...provided you surrender."

"You ask much for the release of one human child. There is nothing to stop me from burning you to cinders and leaving your bones for the wolves."

The hunter made a show of shrugging. "Kill us and the Boa Visk will only send more hunters. Or they'll come here in force and burn the entire valley, driving you out, murdering all the humans in their path. I have a feeling you know their tactics, know how they subjugate and rule. The same as I suspect you care more for the humans who live here than you're letting on."

The hunters had formed a ring around him. The archers nocked arrows, just past the range of his fire. They thought they had him. They did not. It would take nothing for him to launch himself into the air and fry them all.

But even if he succeeded in defeating them all and rescuing the boy, he couldn't take the chance that their leader, this Rycard Serod, was correct. The Boa Visk would send more hunters, would pursue him until there was nowhere left to hide and no more humans to defend. And they would eventually gain what they sought. His blood, to augment their evil magic.

It was clear that no other path lay before him. Donnel and the humans would perish, in any case.

Perhaps they had him after all.

"If I surrender to you, how do I know you will keep your word and let the boy go?" He tried to keep his voice strong, even menacing. In his heart, though, he knew the truth of it. He would not harm these men if it meant safety for Donnel and his people.

Rycard sheathed his blade and took another step toward him. His stride was strong, confident. One of his men shouted a warning, but Rycard dismissed the caution with a curt wave of his hand. "The boy will be set free. We will speak nothing of him to the Boa Visk. I pledge this upon the honor of my ancestors."

Vorgon hissed out a breath of steam. "Your ancestors may have had honor, but you have none, using a child as a shield to protect you from dragonfire."

He sensed the rage from the other hunters at his words, all except Rycard, who only nodded. "You are right. It was ill done. But you have already killed one of my men; I do not wish to lose any more. These hunters are my family, and I'll do what I must to protect them, the same way you're protecting the child."

The tension in the air grew even stronger. The hunters

watched him, weapons out, smelling of fear and determination both. Donnel stared at him, his big eyes wide, tears on his cheeks, looking very young and very afraid.

"I yield then, Rycard Serod. Keep your word. The boy must be safe."

"No!" Donnel screamed. "No! No! They'll kill you, dragon!"

He looked at the boy, feeling warmth in his heart for him. The concern and sorrow on the child's face touched him deeply, even though he bitterly wished he had never been the cause.

"Do not worry about me, young one," he said softly, holding the boy's tear-filled gaze. "Run home and stay there until these men are gone. Promise me you will do what I say."

At first the boy shook his head wildly, denying that he would obey. Vorgon only looked at him, willing him to understand, to overcome the emotions and impulsive reactions of boyhood and take his first difficult step as a man. Regret poured through him, that a child's innocence should be stolen so abruptly. But if the boy could have the chance to live out the rest of his life, find a mate, find some happiness, then it was worth the sacrifice.

The boy closed his eyes, tears leaving wet tracks on his face, and finally relented. "Yes. I...I'll do as you say."

Vorgon gave him a wan smile that sent two of the archers pulling back on their bowstrings. He knew obedience wasn't the boy's strength.

"Promise me," Vorgon said.

The boy hesitated and looked up at him, clearly trying to figure a way out of his promise. Eventually, he realized there was none to be had and heaved a heavy sign of resignation. "I promise."

"Good." Vorgon turned his gaze back to Rycard. "Order your men to allow the boy safe passage through the hills."

Rycard nodded. "We'll let the boy start walking toward the hills. But my bowmen will fire if you decide to double-cross me."

"Understood."

Rycard said nothing for a few moments, then his expression hardened and he went on. "When the boy is a dozen meters away—when he reaches that gap by the two pines—you shift into human form."

Vorgon felt a roar of anger and frustration building inside him, but he fought to keep his temper. "Human form? What foolishness is this?"

Rycard's expression grew annoyed. "Don't play games with me, dragon. We know you can take human form."

"That's a myth. A tale told by old women at the

fireside."

"We found your footprints in the dirt by where you killed our man. Or did he stab himself in the heart? Or wait. Perhaps the boy stabbed him."

"It's no myth," one of the hunters said. He lowered his bow slightly to speak in his soft, low voice. "According to the histories, it was a curse inflicted by Odari Un, a trickster god. The curse—or blessing according to some—was said to be the reason the dragonkin were expelled from Starhold millennia ago and lost their place as steeds of the gods."

Vorgon held his tongue. The archer spoke true.

The leader Rycard spoke again. "Agree to transform into your human form when the boy reaches the two pines, and we'll set him free. Otherwise, we have no deal. The boy comes back with us."

Vorgon looked over at the boy. So young. So brave.

No sense in drawing this out any longer. He focused his concentration and shifted. Energy from his fiery core wrapped around him in a whirlwind of light-fire. His spirit-essence form changed from a huge dragon into that of a man, the energy inside him even more compressed, denser as his mass changed. A moment later he stood before them in human form with the grass blades around him still trembling from the flare of power.

He looked Rycard in the eye. "I have kept my word.

Now keep yours."

Rycard signaled to the hunter who held Donnel. The hunter cut the ropes off the boy's wrists. Donnel immediately started toward him, but Vorgon shook his head and pointed to the hills. The boy hesitated, his face revealing the war of emotion within him. Then, tears still glistening on his cheeks, he turned and ran. He didn't look back.

That was good. That was as it should be.

The hunters closed in on Vorgon warily. He waited for them, part of him darkly amused by their caution. This shape was so much weaker than his true form. Although he still had his magic, he had no other weapons or armor. A single arrow could destroy him.

Rycard reached him first, his dog at his side. From the dog's expression, he didn't trust Vorgon any more than his master did. That gave him a small measure of satisfaction.

"I'm sorry it had to be this way," the hunter said.

"The choice to bring the boy into danger was yours alone."

To his credit, the man made no excuses. He only nodded, his expression grim. The other hunters encircled Vorgon, weapons drawn, arrows nocked. One of them, a woman, stepped forward with a pair of shackles. Even from here he could feel the spells forged into the metal.

"Put out your hands," she said.

He did. She clamped the shackles on his wrists. When the unnaturally cold metal touched his skin, the runes etched into the surface flared red, walling off his magic. He could still feel the raw power inside him, but it was as if a glass barrier kept him from touching it. He gritted his teeth against the frustrating sensation, against the need to touch the magic again, even as his every effort was thwarted. But when he calmed his mind a little, he realized that not all of his power was locked away. A small part of it remained in his grasp. But it felt like being submerged in water and given only a reed to breathe through.

"Those shackles will keep you from shape-shifting or using any destructive magic," Rycard said. "Be grateful we didn't slap another kind on you to sever you from your magic completely. But I know that would kill you, and killing you is not my goal. Just know that I won't hesitate if you force my hand."

The man's voice was harsh, even angry, but Vorgon could hear the slight note of relief in his words. He was right. As a being with magic so tied to his soul, cutting him off from it completely would kill him. Still, what little he could still feel kept him alive. And it lifted his heart a little to realize this man still feared him.

Rycard's dog circled him, sniffing warily. Then the dog hurried back to his master's side, partially hiding behind

Rycard with his tail between his legs. The dog was wiser than any of these human hunters.

"Somebody get him some bloody pants," one of them said crossly. The burly man with the bushy beard was glaring at him in disgust.

The woman who'd shackled him only laughed at the other hunter. "What's wrong, Gansen? Jealous that his cock is bigger than yours?"

"Don't make me pull mine out and compare," Gansen growled.

"Gods forbid. You'll scare the sheep."

"Be still," Rycard snapped. "We still have to bury Timval." He gave Vorgon a hard look. "You will watch."

Vorgon nodded solemnly. "I will watch. The hunter was brave. I will help honor the passing of his soul."

That gave the other man pause. His eyes narrowed and his mouth tightened, but after a moment he only turned back to his hunters and began giving orders.

"Axton and Gansen, ride back to town. Have Owen bring one of the wagons with the tents and shovels to the stream where Timval fell. If the Boa Visk trouble you, tell them that we're still tracking the dragon. Nothing more."

The two riders headed off. The remaining hunters gathered their spooked horses and found a pair of roughspun trousers and a spare cloak in their packs. Vorgon dressed, but his feet and chest remained bare. The horses were still skittish, smelling something inhuman about Vorgon's scent. Rycard attached a thick rope to his shackles and had Vorgon walk alongside his horse with the rope secured to the saddle. Rycard's dog stayed on the other side of the horse and kept giving Vorgon glances he would've sworn were suspicious.

They set off across the fields, heading east, angling toward the mountains and the narrow gorge where Vorgon's actions had sealed his fate.

Donnel, at least, had vanished from sight.

CHAPTER FOUR

They buried Timval Deyswift beside the stream where he'd fallen. The sun was setting fast, turning the sky red and purple behind the dark storm clouds gathering in the west. The air had grown cold, and wind shook the grass and made the evergreens sway.

Rycard's hands were dark with ground-in earth and his clothes soaked and muddy by the time he finished digging the grave. He had done most of the work after Owen finally arrived with the wagon. Rycard had refused to take a rest or let others take his place until the grave was finished. He felt he owed the boy that much. But now Timval had been laid inside his grave. They buried him with his weapons and his spell stones so that he might take those things to guard his spirit in his journey beyond this life. Gansen and Brockon filled the grave, hurrying to beat the approaching storm. There would be no way to reach Shademere before dark, but perhaps they could at least finish this business and make camp before the rains hit.

Rycard looked over at their prisoner, standing at the stream's edge where Dezarie and Deacon guarded him with weapons ready. The dragon. But human. The creature reputed to be gone from the land for generations, if they ever existed at all.

Clearly, they did.

His gamble had paid off. The largest bounty they'd ever seen, for a creature he wasn't even sure existed. A move born of desperation—for his company, for himself. He wanted to be happy. But the sound of the dirt being shoveled into Timval's grave stole whatever feeling of victory he might have felt.

The dragon's human form stood a bit taller than Rycard and was a little broader in the chest. He had the muscles of a warrior, just as Rycard did. His light brown hair was longer than Rycard's, lifted by the wind that rustled through the pines. His face wasn't that of a warrior, though. He was prettier, his cheeks smooth, without stubble, and free of the lines and scars that painted Rycard's harsh features from years in the weather and squinting into the sun. His eyes were strange enough to be unsettling—large and golden, the same as the dragon's. But it was their intensity that Rycard found disturbing. When that gaze turned to meet his own, the sense of power and presence from the dragon raised the hair on Rycard's arms.

Even in shackles, he wore an aura of power and nobility. He stood there like a king among peasants, though he never sneered, never showed the slightest outward disdain. It was clear he was no friend, but his dignified demeanor was…unexpected. Rycard hadn't known what to expect, but the quiet fearlessness Vorgon displayed was not it.

He wasn't sure what he'd expected, but it certainly hadn't been a handsome, noble creature such as Vorgon, with an inner strength that pulled at Rycard, somehow. Drew him.

Rycard looked away from him, unwilling to follow those thoughts where they might lead. The dragon would likely be dead within a week.

Typical of his luck. Always drawn to the ones he couldn't have.

"Grave's all filled in," Gansen said. "Will you say a few words for him?"

Rycard turned to his men. He was exhausted and sick at heart, his hands cold, his body filthy. Part of him—a selfish part—didn't want to say these final words of farewell to one of his hunters. That part of him only wanted to leave here, to fill his belly with hot food and find the blissful emptiness of sleep and forget about this. The next day would be here soon enough...and he already dreaded it. But Timval deserved more than that, no matter how foolish and reckless he'd been. So he'd speak over the grave as his comrades listened, as the shadows deepened, and the storm closed in.

He stepped to the head of the grave, looking down at the little cairn of stones his men had built to mark the site, while his company filed in around him. "May his spirit find its own star. One that matches the brightness of his heart. He fell as he lived, brave and determined. Let us honor him. Let our memories of him be good, the words we speak of him be true, so that when we fall in turn, our brothers and sisters will do us the same honor." Rycard knelt on the cold, rocky ground and set a final stone on the cairn. "May you find peace."

"May you find peace," the others repeated.

He stood again, his body aching from today's hard use. His heart felt like one of these river stones, cold and heavy in his chest. Charza nuzzled his hand and whined, staring up at him with big eyes. He smiled sadly, grateful for the comfort as he stroked the dog's head, although the weariness in him only grew deeper. He turned away, intending to head down to the camp they'd raised at the base of the defile, but Vorgon stepped forward.

"I would like to sing for him," Vorgon said. "If you will allow it."

Gansen put his hand on his knife. "You make a sound, monster, and I'll cut out your tongue."

Rycard raised a hand, silencing Gansen with a look. He turned his attention back to Vorgon. He scrutinized his face, trying to understand what the dragon intended. Some kind of trickery? A spell? Honoring a fallen foe? Or was he simply trying to win favor in some futile hope of clemency?

Vorgon stared back at him evenly with those mesmerizing golden eyes. "Will you allow me to honor him in my way?"

"If you want to sing," Rycard finally replied, pulling his gaze from Vorgon's face and focusing on the muddy ground of Timval's grave, "then I will not stop you."

Gansen shook his head, scowling. "I can't believe you're letting him—"

"Peace, Gansen. The gods approve of those who honor the spirits of the fallen. We will not stand in the way of something sacred."

Rycard looked back at the dragon. Vorgon's gaze was locked on him, so intense it seemed to burn along his body like dragonfire. A rush of adrenaline surged through him, and he had to will himself to remain still. Then the dragon stepped forward until he stood beside Rycard at the head of the grave.

Vorgon closed his eyes and began to sing. His voice was strong and resonant, deep but smooth and melodic, one of the most beautiful sounds Rycard had ever heard. Rycard didn't understand the language, but the words spilled forth in a mix of sorrow and hope that needed no words, both melancholy and uplifting. The song echoed down the gorge and up into the hills as the sun finished sinking behind the horizon. When Vorgon finished, the silence seemed to ring over the gorge as if part of the song itself. No one said a word. Even though he hadn't understood the words, something in the song, or perhaps Vorgon's voice, affected him deeply.

One by one, his hunters turned away from Timval's grave. Vorgon still stood beside him with his eyes closed as if in silent prayer. Rycard reached out and touched his arm, intending to steer him back to their camp.

As soon as he touched Vorgon's skin, images flooded his mind and swept away his thoughts like a tidal wave, replacing them with things he'd never seen, never experienced before. The images were so vivid, so real, it was as if he were drowning in a memory.

He was looking down on the land from hundreds of meters in the air, flying fast and buffeted by cold, roaring wind. At first he thought he was staring through the eyes of a bird, until he caught a glimpse of his wing and realized he was looking through the eyes of a dragon as he soared high over the mountains with the sun at his back.

His heart lurched in terror. He was so high up, moving so fast, and the vast expanse around him was daunting. The mountains retreated, replaced by fields and a town. His stomach jumped into his throat as the dragon he seemed to be suddenly dove straight for the town. He was focused on a stone fortress in the middle of the town square. Tiny figures ran in all directions. His mouth opened and fire shot out, partially blocking his view with flames of blazing light and heat. As he swept over the stronghold, he glanced back and saw he'd left the stone burning as Boa Visk beat drums to signal the alarm. His chest tightened as he looped around hard to attack again.

Then the images changed, jarring him. Now he was flying over open waters toward a land he'd never seen, where big, gray waves broke against cliffs hundreds of meters high and spread in either direction as far as he could see. Mountains rose around him, and fields, and massive herds of lumbering, four-legged sidon grazing placidly below. Huge flocks of birds gathered in trees taller than any tower Rycard had ever climbed. More dragons wheeled in the sky, circling a citadel that, amazingly, floated in the air on a current of magic flowing up from a massive hole in the ground. He flew toward this floating citadel, his heart filled with joy. Dragons flying overhead roared out greetings to him, while others, in human form and dressed in elegant garb, walked the parapets of the floating citadel and gathered on the wide balconies.

More memories flooded his mind, faster now. Fighting a skrealing beast on a mountainside and defending a terrified shepherd who scrambled to get his panicked flock away. The face of another man—no, another dragon, in human form— beautiful, bold, striking, looking at him with golden eyes, seeming to see into the depths of him until he leaned close enough to kiss... That kiss, stirring the heat of passion in his body, the warmth of love in his heart. Then flying at night, with the moonlight bathing the land in a silver glow and countless stars overhead. Hands, not his, turning the pages of a book as a fire burned in a hearth. More images and memories, too many for him to fully experience, left him reeling.

The memories cut off all at once when Gansen grabbed his arm and wrenched him away from Vorgon. The pull nearly sent him tumbling into the mud. It took him a few seconds to focus, to find himself again after the onslaught of another creature's memories. His head was dizzy and his limbs felt weak.

Gansen drew his dagger, his eyes full of murder as he stepped toward Vorgon. Vorgon stood his ground, watching Gansen calmly as if the man wasn't coming at him with drawn steel.

"Stop," Rycard ordered. He coughed, gritted his teeth, then said again, "Stop, Gansen. I'm okay."

Gansen obeyed, though he kept his dagger out. "What happened? Did he attack you? Some kind of spell? Even with the shackles?"

"No. It was nothing." Rycard didn't know why he lied. Perhaps because he didn't know if what he'd experienced had been an attack, or some kind of...sharing, strange as that sounded. He still felt a little drained and disoriented after the sudden onslaught of memories and how amazingly real they'd felt, only to have them abruptly end. His stomach still felt as if he'd been flying. His mouth still felt that kiss.

"You certain, Rycard? He didn't try to take over your mind with sorcery, did he?"

"Nothing like that." He realized his hunters wouldn't be satisfied with a simple denial. He wasn't sure he was, either. It had been some sort of power, that much was certain, and it had happened even while the dragon was shackled. Some sort of telepathy that didn't rely on magic? Whatever it was, he had to warn them against touching Vorgon directly.

"When I grabbed him, something happened… It was as if the shackles reacted to me." He seized on the idea and went with it. "It was so cold it shocked me. I couldn't move."

Dezarie frowned. "Those shackles shouldn't work on someone who has no magic."

He turned to her with a smile that felt completely unconvincing. "Perhaps I'm a great mage and haven't realized it yet. Either way, no one touch him skin-to-skin in case the shackles are somehow dangerous to us. We have to be careful."

Vorgon was watching him intently, but he didn't say a word to affirm or deny Rycard's story. Rycard wished he could ask about what he'd seen. And then another idea occurred to him. If he'd shared in the dragon's…what? His mind? His memories? Then what, if anything, had Vorgon seen in his?

Vorgon didn't speak. But those expressive golden eyes said they'd seen something. They pulled at him, and Rycard found it difficult to turn away.

Rycard finally tore his gaze away from the dragon. Perhaps this was part of the dragon's magic, some kind of seductive allure to draw its enemies to their doom, like a siren's song. He'd have to be wary of this beautiful, enigmatic creature until they turned him over to Malak Telk and collected their bounty. Then they could all go home.

He turned back to his company. "We've laid our fallen comrade to rest. Let's finish getting the tents up and get some food on the fire, and then we can raise a skin of wine in memory of Timval before the rain starts." And in celebration of the impossible—taking the dragon alive.

"And the dragon?" Gansen demanded.

"Chain him in one of the tents. And for the sake of the gods, keep your hands off him."

* * *

Much later that night, Rycard filled a plate with a soupy mix of beans, rice, and salted bacon and took it into the tent where they'd chained the dragon. He'd ordered his men not to go in there, in case they fall victim to whatever charm the dragon used to seduce its prey. Mostly, though, he wanted to bring dinner to the dragon himself. He had questions he wanted answered.

Charza followed him, wagging his tail and carrying his favorite sidon leg bone in his mouth. When he got to the tent, he nodded to Deacon, who was standing watch outside.

"Go get some dinner. I'll watch him for a while."

The quiet archer didn't need to be told twice. He just nodded his shaved head in assent and made a beeline for the big kettle over the fire. Rycard pushed through the tent flap, holding it open for his dog and being careful not to spill any of the food.

Vorgon sat in the middle of the tent, eyes closed, legs folded beneath him, his arms in front of him with the shackles binding his wrists. He appeared to be sleeping. Gansen had chained his shackles to the thick center tent pole that had been set into the ground. A small brazier and a camp lantern bathed the tent in a mellow golden glow. The tent itself smelled faintly of smoke and mildewed canvas.

"Are you awake?" Rycard asked, letting the tent flap fall closed behind him.

Vorgon's unforgettable eyes snapped open. His piercing golden stare locked on Rycard with an intensity that made him suddenly uneasy.

"I was only clearing my mind."

Rycard held out the plate. "I brought you dinner. Don't know if your kind can eat beans and rice. We were out of fire-roasted villager."

Vorgon's eyes seemed to heat with momentary anger, then he looked away and took the plate with both hands. "Thank you." After setting it on his lap, he picked up the fork and began to eat, awkwardly with his wrists bound together.

Rycard watched the dragon's every motion. He found himself surprised that the dragon was so graceful in his human form. It seemed strange that a creature could be both powerful and terrifying, and beautiful and graceful, all at the same time.

Vorgon took a forkful of food and glanced at Charza, who stood at Rycard's side. His dog had lost his initial fear of the dragon but remained on guard. "Your dog is brave."

Rycard rubbed Charza behind the ears. "He is." Rycard pulled a stool over and sat down, keeping a safe distance from the dragon as he continued to eat. Charza curled up at his feet, but didn't take his eyes off the dragon. Or maybe it was his food.

Rycard had so many questions he wanted to ask, but he wasn't certain he should voice them. If he were wise, he'd stay far away from the prisoner and simply dump him in the hands of the Boa Visk and have done with it. Every moment he spent in this creature's presence might make that harder.

Finally, Vorgon finished his meal and set the plate aside. He met Rycard's gaze candidly. Those golden eyes were intelligent and curious…but still unnerving.

"Don't be afraid," Vorgon said softly. He raised the shackles and shook them gently so they clanked. "These hold me, but I'm also bound by my word."

"You're telling me you wouldn't try and escape if you could? Because I don't believe that for an instant."

"A dragon's word is a sacred thing. I won't try to escape from you. But I won't give my word not to escape from the Boa Visk. They are not worthy of my honor."

"You'll forgive me if I don't test your word by removing those chains," Rycard said. "I don't trust anyone's honor."

The dragon gazed at him with those big, golden eyes. "That's a hard way to live, my friend."

"We're not friends."

The dragon's expression did not waver. "No. I suppose we are not."

A silence sprang up between them, growing longer and more uncomfortable. Rycard cast around for something to say to break the building tension. "Are you cold?"

Vorgon only wore the trousers they'd given him along with the patched cloak, leaving his chest bare. It was an impressive chest, all sleek muscle and hard abdominal ridges. The body of a warrior.

"Dragons are never cold, even in human form, unless we're hurt. I don't need clothing to keep warm."

"Ah." The thought of Vorgon's form without clothing was distracting. He'd already seen the man naked. His body was beautiful, stunning, even marred by the still-healing wounds of his recent battle with the Boa Visk. Perhaps even more so because of them. The thought caused a shiver of primitive attraction that annoyed him.

What in the name of the gods was wrong with him? This was no friend, no potential lover. This was a creature who had already killed one of Rycard's men. A powerful being that might've killed them all had things gone differently. His band of hunters might have been able to destroy the dragon with Dezarie's magic and their long bows...maybe. If they'd had a terrain advantage and had attacked from suitable cover. But taking the dragon alive without Timval's binding stones? The fact that they'd done so began to seem more and more miraculous the more he learned of this dragon.

Vorgon leaned back and sighed. "I can see the questions in your eyes, Rycard Serod. Ask them. Soon you will no longer have the chance."

Rycard had questions, all right. But he didn't know which question to ask first. "What was it you sang? At Timval's grave?"

Vorgon's eyebrows rose. "You surprise me. I would've expected you to ask about the visions I gave you."

Rycard shrugged. "It was a toss-up."

Vorgon's lips rose in a small smile. "It is nothing secret. The song is *Korshalla Dossa De'vurkos*—a dirge, a song of mourning and honor for the fallen. The words, when translated, roughly mean setting red sun. It was the second time I sang it for him."

Rycard narrowed his eyes. "After you killed him."

"After he attacked me, and I killed him, yes." Vorgon looked at him a moment, then took another bite of his meal.

Rycard watched him eat, thinking how at odds this man seemed with the dragon that could have burned them all to cinders. "Tell me how Timval died."

Vorgon gave a bitter smile. "He was brave...but foolish. Many young males are—dragons, humans, it doesn't matter. I was the same, once. But I'll tell you how he fell, so that you might pass the knowledge to his kin. Perhaps it might play some small part in dulling their sorrow."

Vorgon placed his plate on the ground beside him and let his hands rest loosely in his lap. "He tracked me to the gorge. I was lying there, healing my wounds from the Boa Visk. The boy was there. The shepherds had sent him to bring me some sheep to aid my recovery. I tried to intimidate your man into leaving. He surprised me with the binding stone."

Rycard sighed but remained silent. As he'd suspected, Timval had disobeyed his order simply to track the beast to his lair, and instead had decided to capture him single-handedly.

"The stone bound my magic and forced me into my human form. He had a knife, unsheathed, and I assumed he meant to use it. The boy distracted him with a rock from his sling, and I took the opportunity to defend myself."

There was no lie in his golden eyes. No waver or hesitation in his voice. Every intuition inside Rycard told him the dragon spoke true. It was impossible to hate the creature for what had happened, although part of him wanted to do exactly that.

"I told him to stay away from you," Rycard said when the dragon was done telling his tale. "He'd always been headstrong, but he'd never disobeyed a direct order before. Not so blatantly."

"His heart yearned for glory. He wanted to bring me back to the Boa Visk and be the hero. I don't think even the gold they promised to pay for me mattered as much to him as being a hero."

Rycard snorted in contempt. "Heroism is for fools. Hunters work for money. A man has to eat. A man needs boots without holes worn through the soles. Food for his dog and his horses and his troops. In that order."

Vorgon watched him, those big eyes unblinking. "You feel guilt, working for the Boa Visk."

"I feel nothing," Rycard snapped. "The Boa Visk's gold spends as well as any other. I don't have the luxury to be idealistic about whose jobs we take. My men have no floating castle to return to after a hunt."

Vorgon nodded, conceding the point. "Fair enough. This is a hard world. I learned as much when Vaemor, the high kingdom of the dragons, fell to the Boa Visk."

Rycard remembered one of the scenes he'd seen in Vorgon's mind. Of fire, and of battle. "One of those memories—was it of your attack on the Boa Visk stronghold?"

Vorgon nodded again but said nothing.

"Why attack the Boa Visk in the first place?" Rycard pressed. "You're no fool. Surely you realized you'd be kicking a hornet's nest."

"This is no single day's battle. It began the moment the Boa Visk first arrived in force to enslave the humans who've lived here peacefully for generations, and send their gold and goods back to the Undlev Empire."

Interesting. So he'd been right in thinking the dragon felt some sort of loyalty to the humans who lived here, in opposition to the Boa Visk. "We have nowhere to go tonight. I would hear the tale, if you'll tell it."

"Very well," Vorgon said, leaning his head against the tent pole behind him. "You mentioned the image of the floating citadel that I shared with you. It was a place called the Isle of Rasella, where dragonkin had fled after the Boa

Visk overran Vaemor, our home on the continent of Anzin. I did not want to run and hide. I returned to Anzin, and to this valley in the borderlands of Shomogar. At first there had only been nomadic humans moving through, most of those shepherds or goatherds. This of course was centuries ago. Eventually, a group of refugees fleeing the wars arrived and raised farms, then founded the settlement of Shademere around the common market, back when there had been trees reaching from the river to the mountains. It was peaceful then. They spared a few goats and sheep; I protected the valley from the occasional nomadic raider or monster from the wildlands. Though they could have protected themselves. The people were really quite fierce, having survived the wars further south and living rough with herds of helpless prey to protect. Still, the Boa Visk arrived in force with slaves and dark magic and built their stronghold."

Rycard reached out a hand and idly stroked Charza's head, which had worked its way into his lap.

"At first I left the Boa Visk alone," Vorgon continued. The dragon's voice was smooth and melodic, beautiful and easy to listen to. "I'd hoped their victory over the outlying kingdoms might have tamed their lust for more blood, more power. I stayed far from the eastern side of the valley where they built their fortress because I saw no way to destroy the Boa Visk without risking the humans they held captive, their farms and fields and homes. I believed I was doing the right thing by showing restraint, by keeping my hatred for the Boa Visk, who'd destroyed dragonkin's homeland, contained. But my restraint did not matter. Evil cannot be appeased. Evil must be defied, must be fought with every breath, lest it spread and destroy all that is good in the world."

Rycard studied the dragon's face as he spoke, and a realization hit him. The dragon seemed to see the people of this valley as his, as if he were their lord and responsible for their well-being. That was something he never would've expected.

No. He wasn't going to let the dragon soften him. He'd killed one of Rycard's men. A man they'd just buried.

A man the dragon sang for, twice, at his graveside.

Bloody hell. Why was this getting so complicated? The dragon's problems with the Boa Visk were not his concern. He had a thousand problems of his own. And all of them were to be solved in the morning when he turned the dragon over and collected the bounty.

"They slaughtered an entire camp of shepherds in their attempt to capture me," Vorgon went on. "The Boa Visk haven't had access to dragon blood in hundreds of years, since they slaughtered the dragonkin in Vaemor. Those of us who fled to the Isle of Rasella have destroyed every fleet they've sent in their quest for more dragon blood."

"Why do they want dragon blood?"

"With it they forged a powerful dark magic, but without it, they cannot. If they could do so again, they would be even more powerful than they already are." He paused. "It was I whom the Boa Visk were after. By not destroying them when they first arrived, they became too many to stop. So in essence, it was I who cost those shepherds their lives at the hands of the Boa Visk."

"I'm sorry," Rycard said, looking Vorgon in the eyes and meaning it.

"As am I. At first I tried to draw the garrison away from the town and the humans after they murdered those innocent shepherds." Vorgon looked away, staring off toward the camp lantern and its flickering flame. Although he had the face of a younger man, twenty-five, twenty-eight at most, at that moment his eyes seemed centuries older.

"I lured the Boa Visk into ambushes and burned them," he continued. "At first it worked... But whichever Boa Visk gardzar rules the garrison is either too cunning or too much of a coward to keep risking his men in the field. Instead he began ordering the townsfolk slain. He had his soldiers leave the bodies of a new-wed human couple and their elderly father for me at the place called Tablestone, near the Hardene cliffs. At first I thought the Boa Visk meant the humans to be some kind of twisted sacrifice—an appeasement for my wrath. But then I realized the Boa Visk had uncovered the truth. They knew I avoided killing humans, so they decided to do it for me. Taunted me with the bodies. It was a challenge I could not refuse."

"You attacked their stronghold."

"I had no choice but to try to destroy them once and for all. They anticipated my attack. They were waiting for me, armed with bows, scorpions, and catapults. Even kovohl wielding dark magic."

"You were wounded in the battle. I saw the scars."

"Acid burns and a scorpion bolt. A few arrow wounds. None of them were enough to kill me outright. Combined, they were sufficient to drive me off before I destroyed all the Boa Visk. The wounds forced me to land. Forced me to enter a healing trance to stop the blood loss. That was when the shepherd boy, Donnel, found me near the stream."

Rycard shook his head. "Does the boy mean something special to you? I don't understand why you would sacrifice everything for him."

"That is my business and my choice. I don't need to explain it." His expression hardened and his eyes flashed before he stopped, took a deep breath, and sighed. "He is an innocent, Rycard Serod. If you tell the Boa Visk of his role, they will kill him, his family, and all his tribe of shepherds. If you know the Boa Visk, you know I speak the truth."

Rycard did know the Boa Visk. Vorgon spoke true. The Boa Visk were known to do far, far worse. He recalled the words he'd exchanged with Vorgon at the streambed. It irked him that the dragon believed he would actually have turned the boy over to the Boa Visk. It irked him more that he'd used that as a bluff to get Vorgon to surrender.

"I would never have harmed that boy, you know. We hunt monsters. We don't murder children."

Vorgon gave him a disbelieving look. "You used him against me readily enough. And you have an interesting definition of monster if you take the side of the Boa Visk over the one who's always protected the humans of the valley against them."

Rycard found he could not argue against Vorgon's point. No monsters were worse than the Boa Visk. But the last thing he needed was to let the dragon soften his resolve by playing on his emotions. "My opinions don't matter. You're a bounty. Nothing more."

"Fair enough," Vorgon said. "Disappointing, but fair enough. Still, I doubt you would have found me again if it weren't for Donnel. It was arrogant of me to underestimate your abilities. I should've burned the entire gorge to destroy all evidence of what had happened." He lifted the shackles to make a point. "Seems I'll pay a high price for that arrogance."

"Why was the boy there to begin with?" Rycard asked.

Vorgon closed his eyes. His words were gentle but weary. "That boy... I warned him, but he does not listen. He probably believed he was doing the right thing, spying on you, making sure you didn't begin tracking me again. The guilt he must feel now, after how this turned out... It shames me that I've brought so much pain to him. And now I'll never have the chance to keep my promise to him."

"What was your promise?"

Vorgon smiled, a wistful smile that would have been beautiful if not for the note of regret around the edges. "He wanted to fly with me."

That immediately turned Rycard's thoughts to the visions after he'd touched Vorgon skin to skin. "When I touched you, after your song... Those were your memories, but how did I see them? *Feel* them? The shackles should have prevented you from touching your magic..."

Vorgon looked at him with those large, intense eyes. "I am a creature of magic, after all. More magic than flesh in some ways, and more magic than your humans understand. When a dragon touches another dragon, or even another creature, we can open our souls to one another for an instant outside of time. It is an old magic, called *kahnsay* in the tongue of the dragonkin. It was created and bound to the dragons after their exile from Starhold and the Chaos Wars that followed, when dragon fought dragon. The magic was created as a way for dragons to make certain of each other's intentions, to know enemies and identify friends, without the risk of lies or misplaced trust."

"Why didn't the shackles prevent you from using this…kahnsay magic?"

Vorgon shrugged. "I don't know much about your human magic. It seems you humans know even less of mine."

A frisson of unease ran through Rycard's bones. What other magic did the dragon have access to? He began to wonder if all this had been just a bit too easy.

"I allowed you to see inside me," the dragon said. His eyes narrowed and heat crept into his voice. "But I was also able to see inside you. Handing me over to the Boa Visk for execution will not be easy for you. You hide behind the excuse that you were only hunting a monster, that your need for gold outweighs what you know is right. You know this is a lie, Rycard Serod. You know that by turning me over to the Boa Visk, you are dooming the people of this valley."

"These people were doomed the moment the Boa Visk conquered their lands," Rycard shot back. "Where did the dragons go, damn you? I saw it in my mind. An island, far out in the ocean. Far away from here, where the skies are clear and blue and you can live your magical little dreams.

Cowards, all of you. Well, to hell with your little floating fairy tale in the sky. Here there's only war, subjugation, plague, and death. Don't judge me or the decisions I make to keep my men free and fed for one more day."

"I don't need to judge you. You judge yourself. I saw it in your mind."

Rycard struggled to rein in his temper. Charza raised his head and stiffened.

"If you're so intent on saving the people of the valley, why not get the rest of the dragons to help you? An army of dragons might actually stop the Boa Visk. But your kind flew away like frightened little birds."

Vorgon did not immediately respond. He was staring at the shackles on his wrists, his jaw clenched so tightly Rycard could see the bunched muscles at the base of his jaw. When he finally spoke, his voice was eerily calm. "You are right. We did flee. When the Boa Visk first came swarming out of the Broken Sea onto our shores, the dragonkin fought them. We drove them back, destroying their fleet, turning the tide red with their blood. But more of them came. And more. And still more. They had strange, powerful magic and rode monsters they controlled with their power. They had assassins who could walk undetected, even by dragonsight. The war was savage. They killed us by the hundreds and turned the magic in our own blood against us...and against the other races fighting to stop them. When it looked as if Vaemor was doomed to fall, the dragons abandoned Anzin to deny the Boa Visk the power of our blood."

"Spare me your excuses. Your kind fled to save their necks. We humans weren't so lucky. We had no fortress island to hide on, no wings to carry us away."

"And that's why I came back." Vorgon's eyes seemed to heat as he spoke, as if they were made of fire. "I left my people and made this my home. I wanted to make this valley safe—for myself, for the humans who lived here. And I was doing that." He looked Rycard up and down. "But that is no longer a possibility, now, is it? You have decided for us all."

"Screw you." Rycard stood, his thoughts all a-tumble in his mind. "How dare you imply I'm somehow responsible for what happened here. What power do I have to stop it? The world is merciless. It will march right over everyone and never even pause to spit on their broken bodies. I've lost two men to the plague in Landilar and another man today. I have people who rely on me, people who've given up any claim to farm or fish or otherwise support themselves to risk their lives hunting monsters, protecting the people the only way they knew how. Just like you. Your talk of wars and ideals is all pointless. The kingdoms have all fallen. The humans have lost. The rebellion in Shomogar is in its death throes. Plague and pestilence are everywhere. The rumors of victorious human armies in Tyrdenva don't matter either. It's only a matter of time until the Boa Visk regroup and smash them all. With or without their dragon blood magic."

The dragon just looked at him with those strange, golden eyes.

Rycard stood and strode out of the tent. The sooner he was free of this dragon, the better. He had his own problems. And getting the promised gold from Malak Telk without the Boa Visk killing them all was at the top of his list.

Outside the air was cooler. The night stars glittered brightly to the east, but overhead, rain clouds had moved in. The campfire cracked and popped, sending up drifts of embers. Charza went bounding off toward the fire, but when Rycard didn't immediately follow, he stopped and looked back, his ears twitching.

Even when out of Vorgon's presence, the dragon remained with him, like a feeling in his mind. Rycard felt hot and angry, as much at himself as at Vorgon. He was right, damn him. But what the hell was he supposed to do? Starve? Join the villagers in their despair and hand his company over to the Boa Visk?

This was a job like any other, dammit, and they needed this job. It was a monster hunt, nothing more. If he was feeling torn up and confused by Vorgon's words, by those golden eyes, wise, intense, and sad, by the resonance of his voice…it was only because he'd let himself be seduced by the monster.

If every monster they hunted could shift into a beautiful man with the words of a poet, they'd all say the same.

There was nothing more to it. They needed the money. They'd never get another job before the rains turned to ice storms. Already it was later in the year than he liked. They were half a continent away from home and winter was coming.

And Malak Telk had been clear. If they failed to bring him the dragon, they'd be killed and left for the buzzards.

Two of his wagons and both drivers were still at the Shademere Inn, and he was certain the inn was being watched. The Boa Visk had let them bring one supply wagon out, but escaping with the other two before the gardzar found out would be next to impossible. Not only would he be forced to abandon his men to the Boa Visk, he'd have to cut the wagons loose—all their supplies, weapons, even the company's history tomes—and make a run for it on their horses, with no food, no money, nothing but mud and rain, leagues and leagues from their winter camp.

He had no choice. He was as powerless as Vorgon.

Rycard finally went to sit beside the fire, staring into the coals. They reminded him of Vorgon's beautiful, golden eyes. Charza put his head in his lap, and Rycard stroked him absently. For the first time in a long while, he had no idea what to do. When the clouds began to drizzle, he ignored the drops for as long as he could. Eventually the drizzle turned to rain. He sighed and went with Charza to find his tent and hope sleep would at least give him peace.

It did not.

* * *

Dawn came too soon. Vorgon had slept badly and was already paying the price. They'd kept him chained to the tent pole all night, allowing him only one chance to stretch his legs, relieve himself, and end up soaked by the rain. Trying to sleep while sitting chained to a pole was uncomfortable, but it would've been pointless to wrench the pole from the ground and collapse the tent on himself, possibly starting a fire in the process. The shackles that bound him felt like ice from the mountains pressed against his wrists. No matter how hard he'd tried, he'd been unable to find any sense of inner peace. Rain pounded the tent canvas, loud and repetitive, not soothing as it usually was. Worries plagued him whenever he shut his eyes. Not simply worries about what the Boa Visk would do to him when the hunters handed him over, but lingering worry for Donnel and the rest of the people in the valley.

But those weren't the only things that made him irritable and uncomfortable.

They gave him bacon and hardtack for breakfast. One of the other hunters, not Rycard, brought Vorgon's food into the tent and left. He knew Rycard wouldn't come. He'd baited him last night. He shouldn't have. But he'd needed to know something about the man—something he suspected— hoped for, at least. But he hadn't been able to see any indication of it in Rycard's thoughts and memories.

He ate alone, listening to the sounds of the hunters breaking down the other tents and preparing to move out. He often heard Rycard's baritone rising above the other voices, giving orders and sometimes trading jests with his hunters.

The leader of the hunters was no friend. Vorgon had made certain of that with his foolish baiting last night. He was a hunter—a monster hunter—hunting a monster.

Him.

There was nothing else to it.

But what he had seen in Rycard's mind complicated

things. While he'd insisted Vorgon was nothing more than a bounty, it was a lie. This was no simple love of gold or pursuit of glory. The pressures and responsibilities of leading his band of hunters weighed heavily on the man. Their livelihoods, their lives, were in his hands. And he felt those lives were all in danger.

The kind of pressure Rycard felt was not something Vorgon was familiar with. His lineage had never been of the high blood. He had never led or ruled any of the dragonkin, nor had he ever desired to so. He preferred to fly alone. And yet…didn't he also feel responsible for the humans in this valley, the lands he saw as his own ranging ground? Wasn't that part of the reason why he'd gone after the Boa Visk again and again?

He finished his food and waited for them to do whatever they planned to do with him. He tried to feel neither bitterness nor resignation about this fast-approaching end. The brief moment of thought-binding had showed him that Rycard truly wouldn't have harmed the boy, despite his bluff. Vorgon could acknowledge that the hunter had been in a difficult spot, caught between a dragon and the Boa Visk.

Still, the man had some sense of honor and empathy. Rycard knew love and grief. He loved his animals, the dog and his horse. He cared for his hunters, and grieved the loss of the one Vorgon had slain. He'd had past lovers, all men, including one four years ago whom he'd felt intensely passionate about...until something had happened that Vorgon hadn't been able to see. They shared that much at least, as Vorgon also preferred the company of males, and he could certainly sympathize with love that seemed like forever, and then one day, wasn't.

What he felt for harsh, aloof human hunter was foolish and impossible.

He saw a man standing strong under the yoke of impossible pressure, loyal and honorable, a man who would die for his men if the choice had to be made. He saw a man harshly beautiful, strong, austere, forthright.

A man who made him ache to touch him.

What he'd needed to see for himself, though, was whether Rycard felt similarly about him. Because there had been no thoughts of him in Rycard's mind.

He wasn't sure why he'd thought baiting the man would make him show his hand. All it did was drive him away.

And make the man that much more eager to deliver him to the Boa Visk.

The tent flap opened and one of the hunters, the quiet archer, came to unchain him and take him to the wagon. The hunter wore gloves and was particularly careful not to touch him, which Vorgon found amusing. They'd believed

Rycard's lie about being touched by the magic of the shackles without question, even when the woman—their adept—pointed out the flaw in that logic. They were loyal to him, that much was clear.

The hunter loaded him onto the back of the wagon, chained him to one of the posts, and set out. The day was gray and overcast again, the ground soft with the night's rain, the air damp and the wind carrying a chill hint of coming winter. Rycard met his gaze for a moment as he drew alongside the wagon on his horse, then looked away, his mouth set. Vorgon felt a brief shiver of happiness at seeing him, but it petered out when he saw the ice in Rycard's expression.

Rycard nudged his horse into a trot and passed the wagon, riding up to take the lead at the head of their column with his dog alongside. A pair of riders rode in front of the wagon, a few behind, and two riders ranged far out on their horses, protecting their flanks. The humans were tense, clearly on edge. No one spoke much. The only sounds came from the creaking wagon, the horses' hooves sinking into the wet earth, the jangle of tack, and the wind murmuring through the pines.

It was early afternoon when they cleared a rise in the muddy road and the town appeared in the distance. A slight smoky haze lingered over the rooftops, while the nearby stream looked like a ribbon of steel cutting through the fields. In the distance to the north, a wide column of troops advanced toward the town. The head of the column had already spread out and was beginning to fortify a position for encampment. Vorgon didn't have his dragon sight, but even with his human eyes he could tell by their armor, pennants, mounts, and weapons that they were Boa Visk.

Rycard immediately signaled a halt. The riders reined in, and the wagon clattered to a stop. The dog ran in a circle before sitting down at Rycard's stirrup, waiting for the next command.

"What in the darkest hell is this?" a hunter—the one called Gansen—said and spit into the mud beside him.

Rycard didn't answer, staring instead at the mass of troops encamping. There were perhaps four or five hundred. As they watched, at least a dozen huge beasts—rendlich, each with a Boa Visk warrior on its back armed with a carska spear—broke from the sentry lines and came thundering in their direction.

Vorgon's blood turned to ice. Heavily muscled and draped in armor, the beasts' long tales and long, toothed jaws gave them the look of crocodiles. Or deformed dragons.

"Hunters," Vorgon said sharply, talking to all of the humans but staring straight at Rycard. "Those rendlich will rip you to shreds. Remove my shackles. I'll destroy them so you escape."

The hunters shifted uneasily in their saddles, looking between him and Rycard. Even though Rycard didn't look his way, Vorgon could read the worry and tension in his face. He looked like a man on a burning ship in an ocean full of sharks.

"Hurry!" Vorgon said.

When Rycard didn't answer, one of the archers hesitantly broke the silence. "What if he's right?"

"I *am* right, hunter," Vorgon said, willing, praying for Rycard to believe him, to trust him even though there was spilled blood between them. He could save them, but only if they freed him. "Look at those banners, those sigils. That is the kerrsgard, the holy warriors of the dynasty. Whatever deal you had with the Boa Visk is over. This town's gardzar will not outrank the leader of those troops."

The rendlich and riders had covered over half the distance to them as they pounded across the fields. Horses could outrun the heavy, powerful beasts, but the hunters would have to abandon the wagon.

Rycard stood in his stirrups and addressed his men. "This changes nothing. We follow the same plan as before. I still have the bounty letter. We take the dragon to the gardzar, we get paid, we leave. I want everyone on their best behavior." He scanned them, glowering. When he met

Vorgon's gaze, he narrowed his eyes. "Especially you."

Vorgon held his gaze. "Then we are all dead."

The rendlich and their riders drew closer. The impact of their feet shook the ground and made the horses dance and pull at their reins. Rycard's dog stood beside his stirrup, ears back, teeth bared, and letting out a vicious growl as he watched the creatures charging toward them. The Boa Visk reined in hard, the claws of the rendlich digging into the soft earth for traction as they came to a halt, blocking the road with their spears lowered, ready to run them through.

The hair on Vorgon's arms and the back of his neck rose at the sight and smell of the rendlich. His stomach roiled in disgust. Rendlich were twisted perversions born of dark magic and corrupted dragon blood. Their kahn, their soul breath, their essence, was both familiar and deeply wrong. Each of the beasts was wider than the wagon and twice as long to the tip of its spiked tail. Green scales, iridescent with red as they moved, covered them from their heavy, ridged brows to their huge, three-toed feet. Thick muscles writhed beneath that scaled skin, and their teeth were as sharp as any dragon's. Yellow eyes with oblong pupils stared at them with brutish hunger. The Boa Visk rode atop armored saddles, bristling with spare carska spears. A small red and black banner sprouted from the back of each saddle, covered in Boa Visk writing beneath the crimson moon of Vosk.

Vorgon had killed the garrison's rendlich when he'd driven the Boa Visk from the fields back to their stronghold. His fists clenched as he eyed the rendlich and their riders. Disgusted rage seethed inside him. He cursed the shackles that trapped him in this weak form, stopping him from burning them all to ash.

"This isn't going to end well," the female hunter muttered from her saddle. She'd kept a watchful eye on him for the entire ride here, staying near the wagon. Even though he wore binding shackles that separated him from his magic, he could still sense her own. And he was close enough to read the fear on her face.

"Unbind me," he ordered her. "I will help you destroy them. I swear it by the gods, yours and mine."

She glanced at him and scowled but didn't free him. He hissed out a frustrated breath. The hunters spread out, shifting from a loose column to a wide front facing the Boa Visk blocking the muddy road.

The Boa Visk riding the biggest rendlich gestured with his long spear and grinned his sharp yellow teeth at them. "Rebels, you are hereby ordered to surrender your weapons and submit to the sacred authority of the High Undlev. The first of you to tell me where the rest of the rebels are who attacked this town will be allowed to live. So be quick."

Rycard approached the Boa Visk who'd spoken, his

expression fully controlled. Vorgon admired his poise. He only wished he didn't have to. If the stubborn man had only listened, Vorgon might've saved them. These kerrsgard seemed to believe human rebels had attacked Shademere and not a dragon. If he'd been able to shift to his true form, they'd have been caught by surprise. He could have routed them, allowing the humans to flee.

He didn't understand why this hunter, who seemed wise enough in other ways, was so determined to damn himself and his men over the promise of Boa Visk gold.

"We aren't rebels, we're mercenaries," Rycard said. "My dealings were with gardzar Malak Telk. We were hired to bring this...rebel leader to him."

Vorgon couldn't help a sour smile. So now he was a rebel leader? One with golden eyes that looked nothing like a human's? And now the hunters were mercenaries. Well, at least Rycard wasn't an absolute fool, although Vorgon wished these chains were off his so he could drop the hunter off a cliff for not listening to him. Or perhaps he'd be merciful and simply drop him into a lake. An icy one.

"Mercenaries or rebels, the blood priest's authority supersedes the gardzar's. The kerrsgard is in control here now. You humans will surrender your weapons and come with us. Defy us..." His grin widened. "And we'll feed you to our rendlich."

The hunters kept still, waiting for Rycard's call. Vorgon hoped the foolish man wouldn't condemn them all. Once unleashed, the rendlich would tear the hunters and their horses limb from limb.

"Some of my men and my wagons are still inside the town," Rycard replied carefully. "If Malak is no longer in command, then let me deliver this prisoner, get the rest of my men, and go. We have no other business in your town."

"You will all be brought before the riqqud do'dan, the blood priest known as Hadrak Carn." He nudged his mount forward, making a clicking sound in his throat. It was some kind of signal for the rendlich, because the beast began to drool and lick its long purple tongue over its huge fangs. "You can come quietly, or you can die."

Rycard, sitting stiff in the saddle, had no choice but to yield. "Take us to this blood priest, then."

CHAPTER FIVE

"Now this is a pretty picture," Gansen said to Rycard as the Boa Visk kerrsgard herded them into the fortified encampment being constructed outside of Shademere. "My mother always warned me to never trust a lizard. These crocodile bastards are going to keep our gold and our weapons and leave us right and truly buggered."

One of the Boa Visk riders glanced their way. He snarled something in his guttural tongue, but the meaning was clear enough. Silence. Threats. Rycard had once heard the language of the Boa Visk had twenty different words for "murder" and seventeen for "war." He'd never heard of one for justice.

As they were escorted through the camp, Rycard focused on counting the number of kerrsgard warriors, how many bows they had, how many spears. The number of slaves the Boa Visk had brought. How many rendlich. The disposition and layout of the camp, from weapons caches to food stores. No detail was unimportant, because he couldn't escape the dread that he would be trying to fight his way out of here very soon.

Gansen leaned toward him and whispered, "We should've listened to the bloody dragon."

He didn't bother to reply. They had been caught between the hammer and the anvil with no good options. Vorgon might've been telling the truth. He had been true to his word so far—that he would not try to flee from Rycard. And it was clear he hated the Boa Visk. But if Rycard had removed his shackles, the dragon could just as well have flown off to save his own skin from the Boa Visk. He'd been clear in the tent that his promise not to flee was made to Rycard—and that he owed the Boa Visk no such promise not to escape. And at that point, it was clear they'd all been the Boa Visk's prisoners.

Even had Vorgon stayed and fried every last Boa Visk from the air, it would still have spelled their doom. Without the Boa Visk, what would Rycard have been left with? One woman and nine men—eight men, now—plus their horses and a dog to feed and provision over the winter, trapped in some provincial borderland town half a continent away from their winter camp. No work. No gold. They'd all starve to death, if they didn't freeze to death or die of the plague beforehand.

Rycard continued his inventory of the kerrsgard encampment. The more he saw of this new kerrsgard army that had crossed the northern mountains from Undlev, the faster his hopes dried up. The kerrsgard were warrior elite, some mix of soldier priest and fearless berserker sworn to shed blood for Vosk, their crimson moon god. A force five hundred strong at least, settling in for the long haul.

The kerrsgard's human slaves were furiously digging trenches around the camp, fortifying it. Beyond the trenches they'd encircled the camp with an earthen wall full of sharpened stakes. Other slaves were busy raising tents and driving banner poles into the muddy ground. Everything was filthy with mud, which made Rycard feel the slightest bit better. Even the Boa Visk couldn't escape the mud.

The rendlich riders had taken all their weapons and thrown them in Rycard's wagon. They had kicked Vorgon out and made him walk. An iron chain ran from his shackles to loop through a metal eyelet on the saddle of one of the rendlich. Vorgon's expression was frighteningly cold, his movements stiff and curt, as if he were only seconds from tearing his way free and killing everything near him.

Rycard tried not to look at him. Whenever he did, all he felt was that he'd made the worst mistake in the world.

The Boa Visk seemed to believe Vorgon was merely a human rebel. Rycard was determined they believe that for as long as possible.

Rycard looked over at the dragon. Vorgon turned and caught his gaze. The icy fury in his eyes was as sharp as a stab in the heart.

Rycard looked away. He couldn't bear to face those eyes.

The Boa Visk kerrsgard ordered them to dismount and tie their horses to a hitching post erected along a row of barracks tents. The one in command glowered at Charza, and a chill ran up Rycard's spine at the malice in his orange and black eyes. He pointed at the hitching post. "Tie the mammal pet here."

"My dog comes with me," Rycard said. "He's a hunter, same as the rest of us."

The Boa Visk commander licked his teeth. "He's food or sport, same as the rest of you. Now leave him." He did not offer threats. He didn't need to.

Rycard glanced around. This was no low-ranking door guard to be backhanded. He'd never succeed in pulling a weapon on a kerrsgard. If he even reached for one, everything would collapse into bloodshed, and they'd never get out of here alive. But neither did he feel comfortable having Charza out of his sight.

Vorgon spoke up before Rycard could reply. "Perhaps if one of the slaves watched the dog—"

The commander darted over to Vorgon and punched him so hard his head rocked back and he staggered a step, but he stood his ground and leveled the same cold stare at the Boa Visk.

The commander waved a hand and three guards appeared at his side. "Tie the pet. Or you can keep him at your side as you're fed to the rendlich."

Rycard grabbed a rope from the wagon and squatted beside his dog. He tied the rope around his neck and ruffled the fur around his face. Then he tied the rope to the hitching post and pointed to the horses. "Charza, stay."

The dog obeyed, but fixed him with a look so expressive he would've sworn Charza was worried for him. As he stood, he caught Vorgon's gaze. His throat and chest felt strangely tight when he nodded his thanks to the dragon. He didn't know why Vorgon had tried to intervene, but he was grateful for the attempt.

The Boa Visk led them single-file deeper into the encampment. They finally stopped at a massive, black and white tent guarded by a dozen heavily armored Boa Visk.

Instead of herding them inside, the commander ordered them around back.

The slaves had cleared a wide space nearly eighty meters across. A massive cage on huge wheels sat in the clearing, hitched to a team of six rendlich. Inside the cage was a creature Rycard had never encountered before. It looked like some kind of twisted, corrupted version of a dragon. Its black scales and the sharp spines bristling from its body glistened with slime. The neck was shorter, the tail thinner, and the wings seemed wider and closer to the head. The head itself was too large for its body, with a wide snout and a mouth brimming with three sets of teeth. Steam poured from its throat, seeping out between the jagged fangs. Its eyes were huge, easily as big as a shield, and were a strange amber color with black vertical slits for pupils. Its curved claws were the same shape and size as a Boa Visk gutting knife. The beast showed none of the grace or majestic beauty of a dragon. It only seemed twisted and unsettling, a mocking attempt at recreating a dragon by a madman plagued by nightmares.

A sudden cry caught Rycard's attention, and he glanced back to see Vorgon staring at the monster in the cage in horror. His face was contorted with revulsion so deep it seemed to have shaken him to the core.

Rycard took a step toward Vorgon, reaching out for

him as if he could somehow comfort the dragon. Anything to take the stricken, horrified expression off his face. It wrenched his heart to see his distress so clearly.

One of the Boa Visk guards shoved him roughly backward. "Stay where you are."

Rycard checked his steps and stayed where he was. It was just as well. He wasn't sure why he'd reacted the way he had. The dragon wouldn't want comfort from a man who'd taken him prisoner and brought him to his death.

"He is beautiful, is he not?" a purring voice asked, startling him.

He turned in the direction of the voice. A Boa Visk was stepping out of a black and gold palanquin that had been set down behind them by six human slaves. He was unlike any Boa Visk Rycard had ever seen. He'd never seen one of their blood priest warriors before, but judging from the elaborate silk robes, the vestments, the bloodred gloves, and the gold and black torc around his neck, he thought it a safe guess this had to be one of them. Most unnerving was the mask he wore—gleaming black obsidian, gold mesh covering the eye sockets, and with an exaggerated, twisted mouth full of dagger-blade teeth. Stylized ruby tears of blood dotted his cheeks and circled the engorged lips.

The Boa Visk kerrsgard immediately bowed their heads and saluted. The blood priest scarcely deigned to notice them, accepting their salutes with the slightest wave of his gloved hand as he walked to the cage.

"There is nothing like him on all of Anzin," the blood priest said. "He is called a draegkal, a new breed of weapon, fashioned specifically to my desires."

He raised a red-gloved hand and several slaves immediately stepped up to the cage door and hauled back a massive iron bar. The door swung open. The draegkal shoved its way out of the cage, glared around with those enormous, slit-pupil eyes, and emitted a screech that grated its way down Rycard's spine and raised goose bumps on his skin. The slaves scattered. Vorgon, however, did not even blink. He stared at the draegkal as though he could scorch it to ash with a single look.

At another gesture from the blood priest, a squad of Boa Visk pulled a small catapult into the clearing along with a wagon full of sheep, bleating in terror as they were drawn closer to the beast.

"Time to feed, my beautiful," the blood priest sang out, and the draegkal screeched and launched itself skyward.

The Boa Visk at the catapult loaded a panicked, flailing sheep into the bucket of the catapult and released it into the air. The circling draegkal swooped down to snatch it cleanly in its jaws and swallow it whole, like a snake.

"I control him with my will," the blood priest said, his

hands lifted as if in worship. "He is of the ancient dragon blood, but we have perfected him. He is an extension of my desire, my dominion."

He pointed at one of the human slaves. He didn't say a word, but the draegkal swept down and breathed a stream of bright green flame that engulfed the slave.

The heat was so intense that Rycard felt it from a dozen meters away. The poor man barely had time to throw his arms over his face before he was blown backward and pinned to the ground by the force of the dragonfire. The other terrified slaves scattered. When the fire stopped, all that was left of the slave was charred bones.

"Gods be damned," Gansen muttered and turned away. The slaves cowering at the edges of the clearing all lowered their heads. There was one sob, quickly stifled.

Rycard did not turn away. He stood, unable to move as the implications became clear.

Neither human, nor dragon, would escape the Boa Visk's reach.

The blood priest raised his hands and began to sing. His harsh language rang out across the clearing. The draegkal screeched again and landed. The blood priest waved him back to his cage with a flick of his hand.

Rycard gritted his teeth, wondering how all of this had gone so wrong, so quickly.

"I am the riqqud do'dan, Hadrak Carn, singer to Kelshek, the Conquering God. I prefer to begin my devotions by feeding my beautiful cherished one." The blood priest turned his masked face to look over Rycard's company. He couldn't see the blood priest's eyes through the gold mesh covering the eye sockets of his grotesque mask, and that unnerved him.

"Now that I have your undivided attention," Hadrak Carn went on, "I expect you to always bless Kelshek, the Conquering God, with the truth. Now, where should we begin? Perhaps you humans can explain why you were roaming about our lands with all those weapons."

Rycard stepped forward and bowed deeply. "Forgive us for bothering you, Riqqud Do'dan. We were hired by Gardzar Malak Telk to catch a man believed to be a rebel and a danger to the Undlev Empire."

Hadrak walked across the clearing and stopped in front of him. He clasped his red-gloved hands behind his back. That twisted, empty-eyed mask stared right into his face. "The one in shackles, was he your prey?"

"Yes, I need only deliver him to Malak to fulfill our charge." He bowed again, hating that he was cowering to this creature. But he had the lives of his hunters to consider. "I deeply regret disturbing you. If you'll allow me to see Malak Telk, I can settle our deal and we can be out of your way."

"Malak Telk is dead. He was the first one I fed to my pet."

Rycard's blood went cold inside him. "Then perhaps whoever has been put in charge?"

Hadrak silenced him with a wave of his hand. "It matters not. All humans are rebels. You will all be dealt with accordingly."

"With respect, we have done nothing other than fulfill our duty to the Boa Visk gardzar—"

"The gardzar who nearly lost this land to the rebel humans? Rebels who burned his fortress to the ground and routed his garrison? The same gardzar who blamed it on dragons, which we exterminated hundreds of years ago? Your request is refused." The blood priest gestured toward the monster back in his cage. "I have brought my beautiful one to burn this ugly place into submission. It will look far more interesting in flames." He turned his black mask to the kerrsgard that guarded them. "Chain them all."

Rage and fear exploded inside Rycard. "Wait—!"

The Boa Visk commander who had led them here drew his blade and pointed it at him. "Shall they be put with the other slaves?"

The blood priest turned his eerie, eyeless mask to the commander. "Have you need for more slaves?"

"No, Riqqud Do'dan."

"Then send them to be fed to the rendlich for their evening meal."

"What about this one's mammal pet, great one?" the commander asked, bowing his head and lowering his eyes but keeping his sword ready. "And their horses?"

"Feed them all to the rendlich," Hadrak Carn said, sounding annoyed as he turned on his heel and strode toward his palanquin.

"No!" Rycard screamed. He shoved aside the commander's arm, pushing the blade out of the way, and charged at Hadrak Carn. The blood priest didn't even bother to look behind him. Three armored Boa Visk charged in front of Rycard, cutting him off.

He slammed his fist into the face of the closest one, breaking teeth, knocking his helm off, and sending him staggering. With a curse, he snatched at the hilt of creature's sheathed blade, but the other two Boa Visk attacked him at the same time, hammering him to the ground. He hit the muddy earth hard enough to drive the wind out of him. He gasped, sucked in air like a drowning man, and tried to roll as they began kicking him with their heavy, studded boots. One boot clipped his head and the world began to spin. The sound of his hunters yelling and cursing seemed very far away.

In the distance, as if swaddled in cotton, he heard

Charza barking wildly.

Charza… He tried to get back to his feet, but another kick to his side sent him onto his back. He turned his head, trying to see where that bastard Hadrak Carn had gone.

Across the clearing, the slaves scrambled under the palanquin poles and lifted it onto their shoulders. Hadrak Carn's black mask with its horrible empty eyes and painted bloody fangs stared out the window as the slaves carried the palanquin away.

He tried to crawl toward the sound of Charza's barking. A boot connected with his head and black spots flared into his vision.

And then Vorgon was there, shielding him with his body. The dragon stared down into Rycard's eyes with his golden ones. "We'll save your friends, Rycard," Vorgon whispered as the Boa Visk slammed him with the pommels of their swords and the hafts of their spears. He winced with every blow, but he didn't stop shielding him. "And your dog. Trust me."

Rycard didn't know why, but he did. He seized onto Vorgon's words like a drowning man as the darkness washed over him.

* * *

Vorgon landed hard on the dirt bottom of the pit. The Boa Visk kicked Rycard in after him, and the man tumbled in to land half on top of him, crushing him with his unconscious weight. The cold, earthy-smelling mud at the bottom cushioned him somewhat from the impact.

Above him, the Boa Visk guards cursed and mocked them both before slamming down a wide cage-like roof built of lashed saplings. The grid of crudely hacked poles lay about four meters over his head. The sides of the pit were muddy and wet for a meter down from the top, before becoming dry, hard-packed earth in the middle, and then changing back to mud at the bottom.

His injuries weren't as nearly bad as they could've been. Bruises, no broken bones. The pain throbbed and pulsed in his body, but he could ignore it, and so he did.

He sat up and turned Rycard over. His heart froze in his chest for a moment, as he thought at first he was dead. But a small, shallow breath escaped Rycard's lips. What little skin that was clear of mud or purpling bruises appeared very pale. His eyes were closed, and blood stained his lips. As Vorgon stared at the injured hunter, a gut-churning mix of rage and anguish swept through him. He placed his hand on Rycard's chest and leaned close to his face. Shallow breathing, but regular, and a steady heartbeat. His surge of relief was so strong it left him breathless.

He shifted closer and lifted Rycard's head out of the mud. Gently, he laid the man's head on his lap, carefully brushing away what mud he could. Rycard's eyes remained closed. He tried to share his mind and memories, to read those of Rycard, to feel for his injuries. But in Rycard's unconscious state, all was murky, like walking through a thick, gray fog.

Vorgon had made the man a promise. He would help save his hunters and the dog Rycard loved. He couldn't let the man down. His word had been given, and a dragon kept his word.

The glimpses of cloudy sky through the cross hatching of the overhead bars told him he still had some time. The blood priest had said the dog and horses would be fed to the rendlich at their evening meal, but he couldn't risk waiting too long. Pressure to do something and do it *now* crushed down on him. The damned shackles on his wrists were the problem, separating him from his magic and preventing him from transforming to his true form, strong enough to choke the raging river of his magic down to a trickling brook.

He stared at the metal bracelets, loathing them, hating

how they felt against his skin, so unnaturally cold as if they leeched not only his magic but his heat as well. The shackles might keep him from shifting back into his true form, but they hadn't separated him from the kahnsay magic that allowed him to share his thoughts and memories with Rycard when he'd first touched him.

If the shackles hadn't blocked his kahnsay magic…was there any limited amount of other magic he could reach?

What if he tried to reach his magic some other way…if he could touch something, some other soul not bound by the restraints?

He gently placed his hands on Rycard's face, over the worst of the bruises there. A groan slipped from the man's lips.

"I'm sorry," Vorgon whispered, knowing the touch had hurt him, but Rycard did not regain consciousness.

He sought out the spark of magic that allowed the thought-channeling *kahnsay* power, opening himself up to it fully instead of shielding it. This subtle power, more spiritual than physical energy, was hindered a bit by the crovmane metal of the shackles, but none of the spells forged into them were at all directed at that type of power. He reached for the kahnsay, and felt it.

It felt as if he stood in a field swallowed in fog, searching for Rycard yet unable to see very far into the distance. He sensed him near, though. He placed his other hand on Rycard's face, pressing delicately against the bruised skin. The fog thinned, and he could see, in a metaphorical sense, Rycard's body vaguely through the mist.

Rycard moved slightly but remained unconscious.

Gently, Vorgon pressed his palms flat against both sides of Rycard's face. The closer he was to Rycard, the better he could see him. He bent his head as far as he could toward Rycard's. When he was within the field of Rycard's aura, close enough that their soul-breath, what the dragons called their *kahn,* intermixed, the strength of the kahnsay was stronger than the dulling effect of the crovmane in the shackles. If only Rycard were conscious and he could see past the grey fog that swirled through his mind.

Rycard's flesh felt cold and clammy. Not a good sign. Vorgon concentrated, focusing his powers, allowing his spirit-mind to flow inside the other man's kahn and body, searching out the harm done to him. The shackles still interfered—the spells forged into the crovmane were more than adequate to separate him from his healing magic, all but for the smallest trickle. Injuries his dragon magic could've easily healed without the shackles were now engulfing him, as if he were swimming through mud.

He understood the human body very well. He found injuries, bruises, contusions, broken ribs. Blood in his kidney that worried him. But those he left alone. He found Rycard's concussion. That was the place to start.

He willed his power to his hands, to the swelling in Rycard's brain, to the pressure that kept consciousness at bay. It was like stretching to reach something just a hair out of reach, touching it but not being able to grasp it. He tired quickly, and it wasn't long before he'd exhausted his will and had to rest.

He slumped against the side of the pit. Even without the shackles interfering, it would've taken plenty of strength and concentration to fully heal the man. But now Rycard was breathing easier and his skin no longer felt clammy. Vorgon brushed the hair back from Rycard's face. The hunter had a hard face, lined and scared, with stubble shadowing his jaw. Some of the bruises were gone where Vorgon had held Rycard's face in his hands.

Rycard stirred, moaning again. His eyes fluttered open. He slowly sat up, holding his head gingerly.

"How do you feel?" Vorgon asked.

The hunter massaged his temples. "I've felt worse." He wiped his cut lip and looked at the blood on his fingers. When Rycard looked up at him again, his expression was unreadable. "You healed me."

"Not completely, no."

"Why?"

"The shackles prevented me from—"

"No, no," Rycard said impatiently. "I meant why did you even try?"

Vorgon gazed at him, wondering why the answer was unclear, when he felt as if he had all his emotions written on his face. He forced himself to regain some self-control. "You were hurt," he said simply.

Rycard blinked, then frowned. "But the shackles—"

"I am dragonkin," Vorgon said with a surge of vehemence. "You humans don't know as much as you think."

Rycard pressed a hand to his ribs and flinched.

"Several of them are broken," Vorgon said.

Rycard glared up at him. "I gathered that."

Vorgon watched Rycard in silence as he assessed the extent of his injuries. He wasn't sure why he was so drawn to this man who wanted to feed him to the Boa Visk. All he knew was that something about him, something inside him, glowed like a precious thing that Vorgon ached to touch.

"What about my men?" Rycard asked without looking at him.

"I don't know."

"And Charza?"

Vorgon sighed. "I don't know. I think we still have time to free them if they're to be the evening meal, but how much time, I don't know."

Rycard looked up at him. *"We* have time? Why would you help me after all this?"

Vorgon just looked at him, hoping the man would see the sincerity in his eyes. "Would I have healed you if I hadn't wanted to help you? Seems a waste of every ounce of strength I had fighting through the fog of your bruised brain just to let you and your men die."

Rycard considered him, his face expressionless. "Thank you. For the healing."

"You're welcome." Vorgon watched him as he looked around their prison, at the ground, the walls, the crisscrossed tree-bough cage four meters above that separated Rycard from his men the way the shackles separated Vorgon from his magic—strongly, but not completely.

"If you remove the shackles, I will help you free them."

Rycard looked over at him. "I wish I could. Only Dezarie can release the spell that keeps them bound to you."

Vorgon felt his heart sink. But at least Rycard had said he wished he could.

It didn't matter. There would be no bounty for Rycard's men with Malak Telk dead. The blood priest had made that clear. Perhaps the only reason Rycard was willing to remove his shackles now was so Vorgon could save his hide.

That didn't matter either. As long as Rycard was safe.

"These pits they're keeping us in," Vorgon said, "they aren't made to hold us for long. If you get out and find her, get her here and take these off, then I can shift. Once I shift, I can get us all out of here."

Rycard's brows lowered in disgust. "If I get out? With broken ribs and the gods know what else? How do you propose I do that?" He stood gingerly, favoring one of his legs and leaning into one of his sides as if trying to find the source of what pained him there. As he did, something seemed to catch his attention, and he stared at the wall of the pit as if something fascinating were etched there in the dirt.

Vorgon watched him, still sitting in the mud with his back to the dirt wall, feeling drained from the healing. He needed to conserve the rest of his strength, which he was having little luck regaining. "What is it?"

Rycard ignored him, and gazed up at the lashed-together tree trunks. "Sloppy," the hunter muttered. He undid the buckle of his sword belt with its empty sheath—they'd taken the sword of course—and with the empty sheath, began to gouge out a small pit about knee high in the dirt wall.

"What are you doing?" Vorgon asked as Rycard began to dig a second little pit, a little higher and to the right.

"'Climbing out," Rycard said.

Vorgon felt a smile press across his lips. The change was remarkable. Only minutes ago, Rycard had been lying here helpless, seriously injured, doubting himself. Now he was back on his feet and focused on his task—saving his people. Vorgon couldn't help but feel a surge of admiration for him.

He worked surprisingly quickly for using such a crude tool, and for being unable to fully raise his left arm because of the broken ribs. He climbed as he dug, gouging out the next handhold or foothold, losing his balance and falling a few times, but never staying down for long. It wasn't long before he reached the top.

He pressed his face to the tree-branch cage top to peer through the holes. "They have guards nearby," Rycard murmured, glancing down at him for a moment before shifting around to look in another direction. He carefully balanced himself by grabbing one of the crooked sapling trunks, wincing in pain. It moved slightly. Rycard looked down at him. Then he climbed back down, dropping into the mud and splashing them both.

"Sorry," he said softly. "Are you well?"

"I've been dirty before, human."

A smile flickered across Rycard's mouth, there and gone again. If Vorgon had blinked, he would've missed it.

"I meant are you hurt? You took as many blows as I did."

"I wasn't badly hurt. Perhaps it was the shackles. They didn't believe they needed as much force to subdue me." He shrugged and gave Rycard a tight smile. "I suggest we take that as a gift from the gods and find a way free of here."

"On that, we're in complete agreement," Rycard said. "I managed to get a pretty good view of where we are. Two guards nearby. They look bored, the arrogant bastards. There are a few more sentries, but they're cooking on a brazier and not paying much attention. There must be at least one more cage pit nearby. If it's the same as this one"—he pointed up to the lashed-together sapling trunks—"it's just set on top of the hole. It's not secured or weighted down. I should be able to just move it and climb out."

"What's your plan?" Vorgon asked.

"Plan? You think too highly of me, dragon. The only plan I have it not to get eaten by that…that thing we saw."

"The abomination." Vorgon's voice came out as a low, rumbling growl filled with loathing and threat. What the blood priest had named a draegkal was not a dragon, yet it had been formed by dragon blood, dragon flesh, all twisted, and profaned into some new kind of monster. And monster it was. Vorgon had looked into its eyes and had seen none of the intelligence, empathy, or wisdom of the dragonkin. All he'd seen in its eyes had been hunger and rage.

"You hate it, don't you?" Rycard asked, watching him closely.

"I hate it…but hatred is easy. I pity it almost as much as I loathe it. But that won't stop me from destroying it if I can. It is a thing that should not exist." He tried not to shudder with revulsion. "Our time is draining away quickly. If the soldiers are cooking over a brazier, that means they're settling in for the evening meal. It won't be long before their monsters get theirs as well."

Rycard took a deep breath, staring up at the top of the cage. "So here's the plan. I climb out. The guards see me and immediately attack. Instead of fighting them, I reach Dezarie, tell her what I need. Then I run like hell, as far and as fast as I can, drawing them off. She gets to you, releases the shackles. You turn into a dragon and kill everything that looks like a Boa Visk. We escape with my people and my dog and the horses and live happily ever after. And if we pull that off, I'll buy you all the ale you could ever want. Hell, I'll even rename my dog after you."

"You said you didn't have a plan," Vorgon said, his voice grave.

"I'm quick on my feet."

Vorgon sighed. "That isn't a plan, it's a half-mad delusion. Do you realize everything that could go wrong?

What if you can't find Dezarie? What if she can't get out to reach me? What if they kill you the moment you climb out? What if you can't run worth a damn with your ribs broken?"

Rycard's smile lingered longer this time, though it had a hard edge to it that Vorgon didn't like. "You want those shackles off or not?"

Vorgon sighed again as Rycard turned and began climbing the wall. He waited at the top for a moment with his face near the wooden bars, watching. Then he heaved himself up, slipping between the edge and the top of the cage with a momentary flinch and hiss of pain as his movements tugged at his broken ribs. But he didn't stop. The soft earth around the edge of the pit began to rain down on him as Rycard's muddy legs disappeared from view.

Shouts of alarm rang out from the guards. Vorgon's heart leaped in his chest, and he got to his feet, staring shakily up at the gray sky overhead. His vision blurred slightly. He wasn't ready to be moving yet after sapping his strength fighting the drain on his healing power. He raised his shackled hands together to one of the handholds and tried to climb, but he only got one foothold up before he fell back down. Until he had these shackles off—and could use his magic to regain his strength—he was trapped.

He slipped back down to the muddy floor and rested his back against the wall. He hoped Rycard's *plan* worked as he'd hoped.

A roar of voices sounded from above. This was it, then.

"Everyone out!" Rycard shouted over the raised voices of the guards. "Dezarie! *Dezarie!*"

"Here! Rycard, *here!*"

"Get those shackles off our prisoner! Everyone else out! Get to the horses! Go to Timval!" Then, sounding farther away and a little out-of-breath but still full of fight: "You snake-faced bastards can't even catch a human?"

The Boa Visk were yelling for his blood now. More shouting and sounds of chaos broke out above, but Vorgon could only stand there waiting with his heart in his throat, peering up at the gray sky visible between the branches of the cage top. A moment later, the top was shoved aside and Dezarie's face appeared.

A burst of relief hit him, so intense it left him breathless for a moment. She dropped into the mud beside him an instant before a spear shot down at her, barely missing her and burying its head in the mud at her feet.

Vorgon scrambled to his feet.

"Give me your hands," she snapped. "Hurry."

He did so just as three Boa Visk with long black spears appeared at the edge of the pit, glaring down at them as if daring them to climb up.

He felt the surge of power from Dezarie's hands as she gripped his shackled wrists, then something snapped around him as the spells powering them were broken and the metal shackles fell open. They dropped to the mud with a wet, clanging thump. His powers flooded back to him like a tidal wave, so forcefully that he nearly fell over.

He felt so alive, so strong as his magic thrummed around him like a living thing, its power coursing through him and within him and around him. As he looked up at the uneasy faces of the Boa Visk guards, he felt the incredible ache in his bones to shift into his true form.

He said softly to Dezarie, "Do as your leader has ordered. Gather all the hunters and get to the horses. Don't fight unless forced. Ride hard for Timval's grave."

"What about Rycard?"

"I'll find him."

With that, he bounded up the side of the pit using the holds Rycard had made. As he neared the top, one of the Boa Visk lunged, stabbing at him with the spear. Vorgon flicked one hand and the spear darted away in the opposite direction, then fell into the pit. Before the second guard could reach him, he hauled himself over the edge and gave in to the beautiful urge.

He shifted back into his dragon form and launched himself into the air. Oh, the freedom. The power. The magic and life. How he loved this. He reveled in the perfect excitement and joy of being a dragon, his true form, once again. Cool air rushed past his face as he cut through it. He roared with all his might, shaking the ground and sending the Boa Visk scattering like leaves.

He beat his wings, using his magic to create thermal updrafts to push him higher, faster. The encampment below him was in utter chaos. Boa Visk and human slaves scrambled in every direction. Shouts and screams filled the air. The sounds pleased him. The fear of his enemies sent a thrill racing through him. He would teach them more fear before this day was done.

The hunters were still helping each other out of the holes where they'd been imprisoned and fighting with the guards. A Boa Visk archer put an arrow through one man's back, the one called Axton, dropping him as he climbed out. He roared again and sent a stream of fire down to envelop the Boa Visk archer who'd killed Rycard's man and burned the sentries around him. Vorgon's heart was overcome with sadness, knowing Rycard would mourn the loss of another of his men.

More guards began shooting arrows and throwing spears at him. He swung around, circling away from the hunters, burning down any Boa Visk in his path as he drew their fire, allowing the hunters to make their way toward their horses through the chaos, fire, and smoke.

He used the same magic that helped him manipulate air currents for flight to help deflect arrows and crossbow bolts. A few still found their mark and hit hard enough to bite through his scales. He ignored the pain. Minor wounds did not matter. He worried about Rycard, the half-brave, half-mad hunter who'd provoked the Boa Visk into chasing him. He had to find him, but first he had to protect Rycard's comrades until they reached his dog and the horses.

A group of kerrsgard soldiers wheeled out a ballista to fire on him. He engulfed it in flames, burning the crew along with it. When a smaller catapult hurled stones his way, it ended up the same.

A challenging screech split the air near the center of the encampment. He knew that unholy sound. He banked hard, turning back to the area where the draegkal was caged.

Two Boa Visk stood near the cage, fumbling with the bar that sealed the door.

For a moment his heart soared. He wanted nothing more than to tear that foul creature to shreds and purge it from the world.

Then he realized that joy would have to wait. He couldn't protect the hunters and find Rycard if he were engaged in aerial combat with that abomination.

He zeroed in with his dragonsight, focusing on the

cage, and raked it with fire, killing the Boa Visk struggling to free the draegkal before they succeeded. His flames left the bars glowing red-hot and the draegkal shrieking in pain and frustrated rage. But it remained locked in the cage.

Billows of black smoke rose into the air from the fires that burned here and there below him, making it harder for the archers to shoot at him, but also making it harder for him to see his targets. The rendlich had scattered in terror at the fires, trampling through tents as they fled toward the fields, adding to the chaos and destruction. The human slaves were running toward the safety of Shademere. He took great care not to harm any of them. He hoped they managed to escape in the turmoil.

The hunters made it to the horses. Some of them had found Boa Visk spears and used them as they fought their way past the few Boa Visk who tried to stop them. Vorgon continued to fly overhead as the hunters quickly retrieved their weapons from the captured wagon, cut the horses free, and swung into the saddles. Vorgon kept a sharp eye out for Rycard's dog, but he was nowhere in sight. Vorgon cursed, dread turning his insides cold. He'd made a promise about the dog, and it wasn't here. Rycard would be heartbroken over the animal. Vorgon would not let that happen.

Below him, the hunters had mounted their horses, but instead of riding hard out of the camp, they milled about uncertainly. He realized they were waiting for Rycard, who was nowhere to be seen.

He put himself into a fast dive and threw his wings wide at the last second, slowing his momentum and coming to a graceful landing, near enough to see the hunters but not close enough to send their horses into a blind panic. More smoke billowed across the camp filling the air with the scent of char and death, briefly obscuring the soldiers from his view.

"Go!" Vorgon roared at the hunters. "Take Rycard's horse and his weapons and go! I will find Rycard and get him out."

One of them—the big one with the two handed ax—rode closer and yelled, "What about Charza?"

"I will find the dog as well. Now go while you still can! We'll meet you at the place of the fallen!"

The hunters set off, riding hard for the hills, the two archers putting arrows through the Boa Visk who came upon them as they passed. Four kerrsgard horsemen, all archers, rode up from behind the ruined fortress. Vorgon bellowed his rage and spit enough fire to incinerate them all, but two arrows flew before the archers fell. One of them hit its target, and another of Rycard's men—the wagon driver—fell from his horse and landed dead and still in the road.

Vorgon's heart sank with remorse. He'd been a

moment too late.

And still no Rycard. A surge of fear and dread washed through him. He wheeled around again, searching desperately through the smoke for Rycard.

He found him near the northern part of the camp. He was holding off three Boa Visk swordsmen with a spear. His dog fought by his side, snapping at the flanks of the warriors if they tried to outmaneuver his master.

The tide of relief sweeping through him nearly stole his breath. But the three Boa Visk were too close to Rycard for dragonfire. He'd have to destroy them another way.

He drew in his wings and dove sharply, landing hard close behind the swordsmen. They wheeled around to face him, but not before he clamped his jaws around one and snapped him in half. He ignored the brief explosion of fear and pain from the warrior's mind. The Boa Visk had a foul-feeling kahn, but there was nothing about the Boa Visk that wasn't foul.

Rycard drove the spear into the back of one of the two remaining Boa Visk who gazed up at Vorgon, aghast. The third one turned and ran. Charza snapped at his heels until Rycard called him back to safety.

Vorgon turned toward the fleeing Boa Visk and charred him to a cinder as he ran. Then he turned back to Rycard.

The hunter was bleeding from half a dozen wounds, though none of them appeared life threatening. His skin was pale, and he was breathing hard. He leaned heavily on the spear as he craned his head to look up at Vorgon. The expression on his face was a mix of relief and awe. Finally, a small smile broke through. "It's about time you got here."

Vorgon smiled back.

Rycard stepped backward, nearly tripping over Charza who darted behind him.

Vorgon laughed. "I'm sorry. My smile is rather…intimidating."

Rycard seemed to realize the teeth weren't aimed at him and relaxed. He reached a hand out to pat Charza's neck. "Easy," he murmured, but the dog wasn't convinced. Rycard looked back up at Vorgon. "Wow. You're…impressive."

Vorgon felt a surge of happiness at Rycard's words. "As are you. Three against one…"

Rycard's gaze moved over Vorgon's scales. "You have arrows stuck in—"

"They're nothing. We have to catch up with your company. They're heading for the burial site as you ordered. Get on my back."

Rycard's eyes widened at that. "What about Charza? I can't leave him."

"Let me worry about your dog. Get on!"

Rycard hesitated a moment more, then tossed the spear aside and staggered over to him. Vorgon stretched out a wing as a foothold to help him climb onto his back. Rycard wrapped his arms around Vorgon's neck to hold on. His arms just barely reached around him, but the man was accustomed to riding, and Vorgon felt the pressure of Rycard's legs as he squeezed tightly to keep his seat. "Don't do any fancy maneuvers," the hunter said.

Vorgon chuckled. "I promise."

Charza was running around him in circles, barking and trying to reach his master. Gently, Vorgon reached out one of his taloned feet. The dog darted away.

"Tell him to be still. I won't hurt him."

"Charza, sit and stay," Rycard said. The dog obeyed.

Vorgon grabbed the dog in one of his taloned feet, taking great care not to hurt it. It squirmed a moment in his grasp, then Vorgon opened his mind and sent him images of safety and warmth and comfort, memories of his happiness at seeing Rycard safe just moments ago, the feelings of...whatever it was he was starting to feel for the human hunter that sat astride him.

The dog calmed immediately, and Vorgon received the image of lying beside Rycard before a crackling fire, sleepy and content.

That was an image he would be happy to make his

own.

He secured his grip on Charza and beat his powerful wings until he was airborne again. A few more Boa Visk archers appeared, but their arrows flew far from their mark. He soared away from the town and the burning encampment, flying as gently as he could for the gorge where Timval was buried.

Rycard clung to him tightly. Charza was barking and squirming uneasily, but still safely cupped in Vorgon's grasp.

Rycard's thought burst into Vorgon's mind. *"It's beautiful."*

Vorgon didn't think the thought had been intended for him, but he caught it anyway. He was a little surprised that Rycard's thought had come to him unbidden, without Vorgon actively using kahnsay magic to open a link between them. He did so now. A flood of emotions rushed into his mind from Rycard. Pure wonder at the ground moving below him. Exhilaration at the motion of flight. Amazement at being alive. But he was also worried and in pain. Worried about his hunters, of their chances of escaping the valley alive. The pain came from the wounds he'd suffered, running and fighting with the Boa Visk, and his broken ribs. Most of the wounds weren't critical, but one slash at his side had split through his armor. Vorgon hadn't seen that wound at first, but the pain from it was deep and black, thrumming constantly inside Rycard's mind. He had lost a lot of blood.

That concerned him. He would have to get Rycard to safety before he lost the strength to hold on. But through all that, Vorgon felt something else. Elation and joy at seeing Vorgon again, relief that he too was alive, appreciation of the beauty of his true form, and a similar, but different, appreciation of his human form.

Lust.

Desire.

Stunned, Vorgon closed the link.

He wasn't sure why the thoughts scared him. They were nothing he didn't feel for the human in return. Perhaps it was because it seemed so out of character for the hard, harsh hunter to feel something so tender as desire.

He couldn't help the rush of feeling that overcame him. Feeling he very carefully shielded from Rycard.

Then he thought about Rycard's fear for his hunters. That was something he could soothe. He opened the link again. *"Most of your friends made it to their horses,"* he thought to the man. Thinking directly to one another was preferable to shouting against the roar and rush of air as they flew. That was how the dragons and the dragonriders of old had become one with each other in the air. Back in the days before the humans had been driven from Vaemor. Long before he'd been born.

Rycard flinched when Vorgon's thought entered his mind. For a second, his grip loosened before he clamped down again twice as tight. *"You...your voice is in my mind?"*

"We can share this way, yes. It is part of the kahnsay magic. The same way I shared memories with you the first time you touched me. This close, we share kahn. Soul breath. Our auras mingle."

"Thank you. Thank you for saving my people. And my dog." A churning swirl of emotions turned inside him. But the clearest and strongest was a deep gratitude. *"And for saving me."* And then, that other feeling again. Vorgon was certain Rycard hadn't intended to share that.

He suddenly felt the need to lighten the mood. *"I promised you I would save your dog. I think he just peed on my claw."*

He felt Rycard's laughter in his mind, but it was faint and far off. Consciousness was deserting him. *"Where are we going?"*

"We are going to meet your hunters. How badly are you hurt?"

"I'm fine."

But that was a lie. Rycard could keep no secrets when they were linked this intimately. His thoughts were already getting fuzzier, slipping into grey around the edges.

Vorgon picked up speed. He needed to reach Timval's

grave, and he needed to reach it soon.

CHAPTER SIX

Rycard ended this miserable day by falling off the back of a dragon.

Luckily, Vorgon had already landed. By the time they'd reached the stream in the gully where Timval was buried, Rycard had already begun to fade in and out of consciousness. It had been cold higher in the air, which had helped keep him awake. But as Vorgon descended, Rycard began to feel warm. And sleepy. He knew he had to stay awake, that right now sleep was the enemy, so he fought the exhaustion, concentrated on the pain from his wounds. Anything to keep himself awake and aware. He kept focused on a few goals, and that helped as well. He wanted to pet his dog again. He wanted to see his hunters again, know they had all escaped the nightmare he'd led them into. He wanted to beg them for forgiveness, but he had no idea where to even begin.

After Vorgon landed in the gully, he'd tried to carefully climb down from Vorgon's back, but the ground seemed to spin away from him and he felt himself landing hard on his face with a pained *"Oof."*

He lay there now, Charza licking his face all over. Rycard managed a weak laugh. He blinked his eyes against the big fat droplets of rain that had just begun to fall. Only a few at first, but then more and more. He sighed. Most of the fattest raindrops seemed to be aimed right at his face.

A pulse of power made all the hair on his forearms and neck stand up straight. Vorgon came back into view, human-sized and man-shaped again. And naked. Rycard could no longer hear his thoughts—which had been strange and frightening, but also intimate on a level he'd never experienced before. He'd felt the dragon's honor, sensed Vorgon's concern for them. His fierce protectiveness and his fearless nature.

Rycard was too exhausted to even pretend to look away from Vorgon's body. It was a nice body. Covered in well-shaped muscle, strong and proud. His body was also scarred and covered with wounds, some half healed, some new. Burns scarred their way along his left side, his hip, to his thigh. More old scars on his chest. The worst of the new wounds was his side where an arrow had punctured him. The hole still seeped purple-red dragon blood. Vorgon was looking at him, his expression deeply concerned. His eyes shone that striking, golden color that had startled him at first, but which he found mesmerizing, wishing to gaze into forever.

Rycard opened his mouth, intending to somehow express his dismay at Vorgon's wounds and the blood running down his side. Instead, what came out of his mouth surprised him. "You have a beautiful…"

He snapped his mouth shut just before he said cock. "Eyes. Beautiful eyes."

Vorgon knelt next to him in the rain. The expression on his face was tight with concern and weariness. "You're hurt worse than I thought."

"So are you." He flinched as a raindrop hit him right in the eye. He was sick of all the rain. Why couldn't he have traveled to this cursed place during a drought? "Why did you change back into a man? I'd have thought you'd be done with that shape for a while."

"I would be, but I have a stronger connection to you when I'm in this form. It will be easier to heal you this way. Or at least I can mend the worst of your wounds so you won't bleed to death. After that, I'll be forced to rest. And so will you. We'll be at risk, especially until your friends come."

"They're not here yet?"

Vorgon smiled down at him. "Horses can't outride a dragon."

Rycard closed his eyes. His hunters and the horses. This fool's errand had put everyone at risk. Gansen had been right when he'd said it was foolish to work for the Boa Visk, to hunt a dragon.

To hunt this dragon. This beautiful, noble dragon with the big, beautiful cock.

He laughed stupidly. He was fairly certain he hadn't said that out loud.

Vorgon looked down at him with concern in those big, golden eyes.

Eyes he almost sold to the Boa Visk.

The warm feeling he felt looking up at Vorgon turned sour. "I don't deserve your healing," Rycard said. "I'm the one who got you into all this to begin with."

Charza started to lick his face again.

"Enough, Charza. Your breath smells like a latrine."

Vorgon laughed gently. "Your dog loves you."

"Of course he does. He's a dog."

"Then allow me to heal you…for your dog's sake."

Rycard opened his eyes and looked at Vorgon kneeling beside him. His throat was tight, as if some invisible hand had clamped around his neck. He didn't have the right words to say. No, it was more than that. He didn't trust his words. His head felt muzzy and thick, and he wasn't sure if he was awake or dreaming. So instead he closed his eyes and nodded.

When Vorgon laid his hands over his wounds, pain ripped through him and he inhaled sharply. His eyelids flew open again, and he had to grit his teeth against the flare of agony.

"Easy now," Vorgon murmured.

"I was going to say the same to you," he grunted in reply.

Vorgon touched his side again, touched the sword cut he'd taken. Warmth spread through him, seeming to radiate outward from the wound. He'd been a little too slow dodging that blade. Hell, he'd led six of the guards on a merry chase through the camp while trying to buy Dezarie and Vorgon time. He'd even managed to kill two of them with a stolen spear. A third had run away when Vorgon had taken to the skies. The remaining three hadn't been in a very forgiving mood. Even when Charza came bounding to his side, growling and snapping at the Bo Visk, he'd still been certain he was a dead man. Three on one was terrible odds, even with a dog.

Then the dragon had filled the sky above him, and

suddenly he'd felt a flash of hope.

Looking back, he couldn't believe they'd actually survived the chaos at the camp. The fires, the insane blood priest and his horrible draegkal. The fear and desperation...and the intensity of battle when they had nothing left to lose. The insane plan-that-wasn't-a-plan. Vorgon had been right. It shouldn't have worked. He had no idea how they'd pulled the whole thing off.

"It helps to know a dragon," Vorgon's thought pressed into his mind, and Rycard realized he'd drifted into a haze of his own thoughts as the dragon healed him. *"Now, be at peace while I close this wound."*

Another burst of pain flared deep in the sword cut, then slowly faded. Then more pain burned around his ribs, seeming to sear deep into the bone before also fading. Rycard let himself drift, unaware of how much time had passed. Finally Vorgon drew back after healing his wounds and his broken ribs, exhaustion written in every line on his face.

"There. That is all I can do for now. At least you won't bleed to death."

"Well, that's a comfort," he said, lifting a trembling hand to stroke Charza behind the ear as the dog panted his foul stink-breath into his face. "For the dog at least."

Vorgon smiled as he stood again. Rycard caught another eyeful of the naked man and let himself linger on the sight. Now that the pain had faded into the background, his cock stirred to life. Rycard tried to think the sensation away. Knowing that Vorgon was drawn to males didn't help. Those memories from Vorgon... Of him kissing another man, both dragons in human form, delighting in the soft, silken feel of skin pressed against skin and the heat of desire. Part of him wanted to reach out and stroke his hand along Vorgon's cock, to stir it to life with touch. Gentle at first. Teasing. Coaxing. And when he was hard, he would take him in his mouth—

He shook the thoughts away with a curse. A fool. He was acting like a foolish young man mooning over his first crush. He didn't understand it. He didn't understand any of this. Why Vorgon didn't fry him to a cinder after what he'd done was the biggest question of all. Why would the dragon risk so much for humans who had thrown him in chains, stripped him of his true form, of his magic? Sent him to die at the hands of the Boa Visk... How could any creature be so...forgiving?

Vorgon walked away from Rycard and Charza until he had enough space to shift back into his dragon form. Light and energy wrapped around him. The brightest of it glowed near Vorgon's heart, as if all the energy had been compressed into one place, and then it spread wide, flaring from his heart to envelope him. The light gradually faded, leaving him changed from a man into his huge dragon form, stunning in its power and beauty and grandeur.

Rycard remained lying on the wet ground. He wanted to get up and wait for the rest of his Splitchain Hunters, but he couldn't seem to summon the strength. He might not bleed to death, but that didn't mean he wasn't bone tired from the last couple of days. Charza had snuggled up right alongside him, as if trying to keep him warm. He gently stroked his fingers through the dog's brown and black fur.

Vorgon came over to them, moving with surprising grace for something so big. He carefully settled himself beside them, curving his beautiful blue and white neck, body, and tail around them to enclose them in his heat. It felt like lying next to a fireplace full of glowing coals. Without a word, Vorgon spread one of his wings over Rycard and Charza, making a canopy that protected them from the rain.

Rycard found the gesture absurdly touching. Careful to keep the silly grin off his face, he looked Vorgon in one of his big, golden eyes and said, "Thank you."

Vorgon blinked slowly and gave a curt nod. "Tell me of yourself while we rest and wait for your friends. Tell me the tale of Rycard Serod."

He blew out a breath of air. "That's not an interesting tale, I'm afraid."

The dragon raised one of its ridged brows. "I'm not

certain I believe that."

"The lives of men are boring, short, and always consumed with finding something else. Searching for it. Fighting for it. For love. For gold. For glory. It doesn't matter, because when you find it, it's never enough. There's always something new to need."

"You are quite cynical, Rycard Serod, for a creature so young."

"And why aren't you the same? For a creature so old?"

"I am young for a dragon. But there were years when I was the same. But bitterness is like an acid, burning me even when my fires did not. I simply made a choice not to be that way."

"Easier said than done."

"That is true. But also because life constantly surprises me and renews my hope. The shepherd boy... The shepherds gave me food when I was wounded, watched over me while I slept. You. We began this journey as enemies. Now we are here."

Rycard opened his mouth to say something, perhaps how the dragon was an even bigger fool than he was. Instead, he slowly closed his mouth again without saying a word.

The dragon continually surprised him. He upended all

Rycard's preconceptions, his assumptions of what a dragon would be like. The dragon was dangerous, without a doubt. But…perhaps Vorgon was simply a better man than Rycard. Because if their roles had been reversed, Rycard had a difficult time believing that Vorgon would've sold him to the Boa Visk for gold. So why was a huge predator showing him this kindness in return? He'd expected aggression, dominance, challenge. Not healing. Not…a wing over his head.

It simply did not make sense. How could he have gotten everything so wrong? He took a deep breath, feeling a twinge of pain from some of his minor wounds, and let it out slowly. Wrong or not, he wanted to learn more. He owed it to Vorgon.

"Tell me something about the dragons," he said.

"What would you hear?"

"Anything. Everything."

For a while, Vorgon was silent, thinking. "I'll tell you of the distant past, long before these human kingdoms had their names or their borders."

"Are you that old then?"

Vorgon chuckled. This close to the dragon's broad chest, the chuckle sounded more like the rumble of thunder. "This was long before my siring. A time of legends. Vaemor was the greatest kingdom in Anzin in those days. A time when dragons and men lived together in peace. The time of the kahn song. The age of the dragonriders, those who lived in the sky. They were mighty warriors, mixing magic and dragon fire, donning magic-charged armor that made them near invincible, wielding bows with shafts that could not miss and lances that could crack mountains. That was the age of Torodon, said to have once been the steed of Danjenma, the most powerful of the gods, before the fall of dragonkin and our exile from Starhold, home of the gods."

Rycard yawned deeply. The heat was making him tired—the heat and the steady, melodious sound of the dragon's voice. "The dragons were kicked out of heaven? Why?"

"That's another long, sad tale. The god Odari Un was outsmarted by Torodon, but he wanted revenge. So Odari Un tricked the dragonkin by giving them the ability to change into humans. He claimed the form would give us power, allow us to create unparalleled works of art and learning, to bring peace, to find entirely new ways to express our love. The dragonkin eagerly accepted. But the gods saw humans as little more than cunning animals—dirty, stupid, unworthy of flying the gods across the skies. For that reason, the god Danjenma expelled us from heaven, for we were no longer pure enough to serve as their steeds. Odari Un mocked the dragonkin, calling the gift he'd given a curse. But time has proven it both a curse…and a blessing."

"Gods," Rycard grunted. "Half the time they're worse than the devils. What do you believe? Is it more curse or blessing?"

Vorgon laughed gently. "You do speak your mind, human. I've come to think it is neither. It simply is. A human form is only an aspect of the dragon, while the dragon is an aspect of the human. Both can do wonderful, powerful, life-changing things. Each has a strength, each a weakness. Each has a time. I would not be the same Vorgon without the ability to shift between human and dragon, and I believe I would be less. Does that answer your question?"

Rycard nodded, absently stroking Charza's head, feeling weary, yet strangely content here with the dragon's heat keeping him warm and his dog at his side.

"But where was I?" Vorgon said, talking to himself. "Ah, Torodon ruled Vaemor, and the land around it knew peace for a thousand years. Humans formed alliances with Vaemor, became a part of dragonkin society. This saw the rise of the dragon riders and powerful magic that could rival the gods. It was said that was why the gods closed the gates to Starhold—they feared the alliance of humankind and the dragonkin."

The dragon paused, staring at the stones at the head of the gravesite. When he started to speak again, Rycard noticed that melancholy had crept into his words. "It was an age of peace and learning. Until a man, one of the Council of Nalyn, grew greedy for power. He and other human nobles tried to overthrow Torodon. They even drew dragons into their plots. They were thrown down after a furious battle that destroyed much of the northern lands. The traitors were killed, but the damage was already done. The dragon king decided all humans could no longer be trusted. They were exiled from Vaemor and the dragon riders were no more. That marked the beginning of the long decline. The humans spread into the south, past the Drahahn Mountains, and the dragons sealed up the passes, ending all trade. The humans became numerous, while the dragons grew ever more isolated. Torodon died at a great age, having led the dragonkin through a millennia of peace, but the dragon kings who followed were not as wise and powerful. During the reign of King Lovos, the Boa Visk suddenly arrived from across the sea on ships like knives, dragged by sea monsters at incredible speeds. Untold thousands of them. The war raged for years. I was born during this war. I was raised to fight in it. But the arrival of the Boa Visk meant doom for Vaemor."

Vorgon stopped talking. Rycard craned his head around to look at him, wondering if he'd fallen asleep. But he was merely looking off across the grasslands spreading the valley to distant mountains below low, dark clouds. The rain tapped on his wing and ran off the sides in little streams to patter on the grass. Rycard realized this was difficult for the dragon to share. It wasn't simply history for him. It was memory.

"What happened then?" Rycard asked softly.

"There is little more to tell. The Boa Visk could be slowed but not stopped. Defeated but not destroyed. Eventually the dragon king decided to flee with all his people and abandon Vaemor. It had been devastated by the constant warring. When the dragons left, we scorched the earth behind us, turning everything to ash and dust, burning off the lakes, setting all the plains afire, burning the forests."

"The Harrowing Wastes. Beyond the mountains. That's what created them? The tales always claim the Boa Visk corrupted and broke the land."

"They did, in a way. But we played our part in it. The dragonkin fled to the Isle of Rasella. The island is protected from the Boa Visk because of the high cliffs and deadly reefs that surround it, preventing their ships from landing. Only creatures that fly may land there. Their ships we easily destroyed at sea."

A thought suddenly occurred to him. "Is that why you hated that blood priest's monster—the draegkal? Because if the Boa Visk can suddenly fly like the dragon riders, your island is no longer safe."

"You have a quick mind, Rycard Serod," Vorgon said softly. His voice sounded tired. "Now, you should sleep while you have the chance."

"I enjoy hearing you talk," he protested, even though another yawn crept up on him.

"None of the tales of dragons have happy endings."

"No one's do. I want to hear them anyway."

Vorgon paused for a long moment, seeming saddened or weary of heart. Finally, he began to speak again. This time he talked of the Isle of Rasella. The floating citadel, and the magic that flowed through every stone. Yet it wasn't long until Rycard drifted into sleep. He lost himself in the deep, soothing rumble of Vorgon's voice, while the dragon's wing kept the worst of the rain off them, and his dog stayed curled at his side.

All his dreams were of flying. And of making love to a man with mysterious, golden eyes.

* * *

The dog began to bark, waking Vorgon from his rest.

He raised his head, searching for the cause of the dog's warning, and saw only three shepherds approaching. They followed the stream, walking on the rocks and using their staffs to steady themselves. Donnel wasn't among them. Vorgon was a little disappointed. He would've loved to see the boy again and make sure he was okay, but it was safer if he stayed away.

Beside him, Rycard scrambled to his feet. He had no weapon, but he clenched his fists and faced them warily.

"Peace, Rycard," Vorgon said. "These are friends."

Rycard didn't reply, although he settled his hand on his dog, calming him with his touch.

The oldest of the three shepherds stopped and bowed. His weathered brown face was heavily wrinkled, especially around the eyes from squinting into the sunlight. He wore the hood of his dun-colored cloak drawn up over his head. "I am Weldros. We've come to tell you riders are approaching, driving their horses hard. They are human." His gaze shifted to Rycard. It wasn't friendly. "They are hunters."

"My men," Rycard said. "Thank the gods. Any sign of pursuit?"

The shepherd didn't answer. Instead he looked back at Vorgon, his eyebrows raised in silent question.

"They are friends," Vorgon said simply.

The shepherds didn't seem to like this much. It

amused him how protective the shepherds and goatherds felt toward him...especially considering the number of sheep he ate. He did strive to confine most of his hunting to the mountains, especially around the borders where monsters often strayed from the wildlands. Monsters always provided a far more invigorating hunt than sheep anyway.

"We saw no one else," the shepherd replied. "They will be here soon. We only wished to warn you, Vorgon Graydalon."

"I thank you for your warning. I shall never forget how the shepherds have been a true ally to me. Especially Donnel. How is the boy?"

The old man's face broke into a smile. "Donnel is doing extra work around the camp as punishment for not obeying your command to stay clear of the hunters. He confessed it all to us the moment he ran into the camp. He is deeply ashamed of the trouble he has caused. As are we."

"No shame," Vorgon said. "Donnel proved to be a brave friend. Without his help, things might have ended badly."

"I will tell him you said as much. It will lift his spirits as he scrubs the dishes. Again." The man paused as if suddenly hesitant to say something further.

"Speak your mind, Weldros."

The old man leaned on his staff and drew himself up

straighter. "We have watched you war with the Boa Visk for the people of this valley. We are humbled. We've come to tell you that our people stand with you, ready to aid you if you call. Our bows and slings are yours. And we shall raise our staffs to defend you against those who murdered our people."

"You honor me, human." Vorgon spoke true, but there was a sadness he did not express. What hope did a bunch of peaceful shepherds have against the Boa Visk? Against their brutal kerrsgard? "You have done more than enough already. I do not wish to see more innocent blood spilled."

Weldros nodded and leaned on his staff. "As you wish. But know that there are also many in the town of Shademere itself who stand with you as well. This land is a kettle near boiling. If you choose to lead, many will follow."

Vorgon nodded because he did not wish to offend the man or belittle his offer. But he had never been a leader—of dragons or men. He certainly did not know how to spark a revolt. The last he'd heard, the human rebellion in Shomogar was concentrated far to the south, away from the borderlands, and was faring poorly. Shepherds were not soldiers. Townsfolk were not warriors. While their loyalty to him was humbling, Vorgon would not be the one to lead them to their deaths.

"I shall keep your words in my heart, Weldros," he

answered gravely.

The shepherd glanced toward the sun and squinted. "We must take leave. Farewell, Vorgon Graydalon. I am leading our flocks south of the valley, on the far side of the mountains. The Boa Visk will be full of wrath after all that has happened. We would stay out of their path. Yet, you will know where to find us if you have need."

"Thank you. I will do all I can to protect you and your people. May peace find you."

All three shepherds bowed to him, then turned and made their way up the rocks of the gorge and into the foothills. In the distance, Vorgon could hear the faint sound of hooves approaching at a canter.

Charza began running around in circles eagerly, looking back at them as if hoping they'd all go running out to meet the hunters. But Vorgon wanted to stay in the cover of the rocky slopes around them for as long as possible.

Rycard was watching him intently. "Why does a dragon care so much about shepherds?"

"Why shouldn't I care?"

"They aren't your kind, for one. Even humans pay no attention to them."

"That's a shame. They are good people, kind to those in need, and they live close to the land."

Rycard shook his head and whistled for his dog as he

started walking away alongside the stream. "You continually surprise me, dragon."

"Is that a good thing, or a bad thing?"

Rycard said nothing more, simply stood with his back to Vorgon at the end of the gorge where the stream cut out into the valley grasslands. The dog sat at his side, slapping his tail against the dirt in anticipation of the hunters' return.

CHAPTER SEVEN

Rycard let Charza run off to greet the horses as the first five riders appeared at the mouth of the gorge and rode toward them. Gansen, Dezarie, Brockon, Yero, and Deacon, who was also leading Rycard's horse, Redmane.

The hunters rode into the gorge and swung down from their horses, Charza barking and darting from one to the other to receive a scratch behind the ears. Rycard looked back at the mouth of the gorge for Axton and Owen.

No one else appeared.

"Where are Axton and Owen?" he asked, hurrying to take Redmane's reins from Duncan and stroking her neck and muzzle, getting a snicker and a butt of the head in return. He glanced up at Duncan, who looked over at Gansen and cleared his throat nervously.

Rycard followed his glance to Gansen, then to the rest of the hunters. They were looking at each other, at their feet, everywhere but at him or the dragon behind him.

He glanced back. Vorgon had stepped back, keeping a safe distance so as not to frighten the horses. He looked back at his hunters.

"Where's Axton?" Rycard asked, his voice strangely quiet. "And Owen?"

Gansen frowned at him. "They're dead. They didn't make it out of the Boa Visk camp."

Rycard closed his eyes and tilted his head back. He rubbed a hand across his eyes. Two more of his men to bury. Two more dead because of his foolish decision to take Boa Visk gold.

Vorgon spoke from behind him. "I'm sorry. I should have told you, prepared you for this. I couldn't find a way to bring it up."

"We had to leave their bodies," Dezarie said, tears shimmering in her eyes. "It was all we could do to get away. We had to leave them behind."

"I understand," Rycard said. "It was...chaotic. I'd hoped everyone had escaped."

"As had we all," Vorgon said. "Given the odds against

us, we should be grateful the losses hadn't been higher."

Gansen glared at the dragon. "Don't speak to us of gratitude, dragon. The only gratitude you should be feeling is that you still live. None of this would have happened if it hadn't been for you."

"Enough," Rycard said. "He is not to blame. It was my decision to come here. Now we figure out our next steps."

"We have your weapons," Deacon said, holding his sword and dagger out to Rycard. "I grabbed them as we escaped. But we had to leave the wagon behind. There isn't much food left. Just what we have in the saddlebags."

Rycard took his steel almost reverently. "Thank you." He slid the sword back into the empty sheath on his belt and the dagger back into its own. "Were you followed?"

"No…" Gansen answered, though his expression was troubled.

"What is it?" Rycard asked. "Your face tells it plain enough. What else?"

"We thought they'd come after us with the rendlich, but there was no sign of pursuit for miles and miles. Maybe they were all run off by the dragon. So we headed up into the hills to get off the plains, and that slowed us some. But we had to hide in the trees when we saw that…that Boa Visk dragon—"

"That's no dragon," Vorgon snapped. Rycard turned

to look back at him. A wisp of steam slipped past the dragon's teeth and swirled in the air before him. "It's an abomination."

Gansen's eyes widened and he stroked his beard quickly. "I meant no offense."

"The dragon knows that," Rycard said, throwing a glance his way that clearly said *stop scaring everyone*. "Go on. You saw the draegkal. Was the blood priest on it? The one with the mask?"

"Someone was riding it. We couldn't tell who. It circled high overhead, hunting us, no doubt. We stayed under the trees on the slopes, searching out westward trails. Headed here, just like you told Dezarie."

"It didn't track you?" Rycard couldn't help looking up to scan the sky.

"I don't think so," Gansen said. "It headed west and south, while we stuck to the forests on the slopes."

Rycard glanced at Vorgon. "Can you kill it?"

"I *will* kill it," the dragon growled. "But a fire-breathing monster and a kovohl dragonrider who can use spells to divert my own fire and magic will be a powerful adversary. And after this recent healing, it will be some time before I'm strong enough to fight anything."

"So what do we do now?" Brockon asked. The lean archer had his arms crossed over his chest and refused to look Rycard in the eye. Rycard didn't like the mood that seemed to swirl around them.

"We lost the wagon we left at the fort," Brockon continued. "Urson and Salcan are still trapped in Shademere with the other two wagons and all the supplies. If they're even still alive."

"We can't go back there," Gansen said quickly. "We barely made it out alive. We go back there and we're dead."

"Why not, Gansen?" Dezarie snapped. "We have a dragon. You saw how he burned anything that got close to us."

"Having a dragon didn't help Axton and Owen, did it? Yero's spear broke off in a rendlich. Rycard looks like he's been chewed on by something twice as big and three times as angry. And we have exactly one mage adept. You. And you're here to track things, not kill an army of kerrsgard and rendlich. Let alone that…thing."

"The kerrsgard were already regrouping," Deacon said, his voice low enough that Rycard had to concentrate to make sure he didn't miss any words. "Now that they know there's a dragon here, they'll bring more kerrsgard. Or worse. An army."

Rycard shook his head. "We won't leave our men behind. Dezarie's right. You saw what the dragon can do."

"Aye. We saw." Gansen eyed Vorgon warily. "But

what makes you think he'll do it again?"

"I will help you get your men out of Shademere," Vorgon said.

Rycard turned to look at him. He wished the dragon had changed into his human form, so that his men would be more apt to trust him.

"That's madness," Gansen said. "We barely escaped with our lives when we had the element of surprise on our side. If we go back for Urson and Salcan, now that the Boa Visk have had time to regroup and are probably expecting us, how more many will we lose?"

Dezarie glared at him. "You'd leave them to die the gods know what kind of deaths at the hands of those monsters?"

"It's a damn, cursed shame what might happen to them. But the fates turned on all of us equally. We came here to do a job that we all knew was too good to be true. We were greedy fools to get mixed up with the Boa Visk. Now we've got a second chance. And I'm sorry Urson and Salcan aren't here—I am bitter sorry. But the sad truth of it is that if we go back, we'll all be dead."

Rycard couldn't believe the silence that fell around them. No one said anything to disagree.

"We were fools," Gansen continued. "Now we have nothing. Three men dead, two back in Shademere that might already be dead too, and no wagons or supplies. We've got the clothes on our backs and whatever we have in our saddlebags to get us all the way back to the winter camp, with plague and ice storms in between. And a bloody monstrous Boa Visk dragon"—he turned a sour look at Vorgon—"Sorry, *abomination*—that might or might not have seen the direction we headed off in. This job is over. We failed. Now all we can do is run as hard as we can and pray they don't come after us."

Rycard glared at him. Gansen had always been a complainer, but he'd always been loyal. He was the last one Rycard had expected to give up. "Go then. The rest of us will head back to Shademere for Urson and Salcan."

Vorgon stepped up beside him, sending the horses skittering back a few steps. "I will help you save your friends. Then you will help me drive the Boa Visk from this valley."

Gansen laughed. "Oh, aye. The six of us against the entire kerrsgard and their pet monsters. There's good odds."

"You said you were greedy fools to mess with the Boa Visk," Vorgon said. "Now you have your chance to fight for something better."

Rycard closed his eyes for a second, head slightly bowed, before he turned back to his hunters. As much as he hated to admit it, Gansen was right. Rescuing his men was one thing. Going to war against the Boa Visk was entirely another.

"We're not warriors, we're hunters," Gansen said. "And I won't fight someone else's war. The dragon's the reason we were here in the first place. Him…and you. Chasing the Boa Visk gold. That's blood gold, and it's our blood on it." He grabbed his horse's reins and mounted. "I've had a bellyful of this. I ride for Lindermain. I'm not waiting until morning."

Rycard did not try to dissuade him. He felt saddened to his core, but he would not try to convince Gansen to stay against his will. He'd already done enough damage to his company. He would not force Gansen to do anything he was so clearly set against.

"The rest of you, make camp," Rycard said. "Whatever we have in the packs will have to suffice. We'll ride for Shademere in the morning."

For a few moments, no one said a word. Then Brockon mounted his horse and maneuvered him over to stand beside Gansen. Rycard stared at him in disbelief. His heart sank in his chest as the implication of Brockon's move hit home.

One by one, all of them mounted up. Rycard felt his blood run cold with dread, with heartbreak, as they each headed over to stand with Gansen. None of them would meet his eyes.

Dezarie was the last to make her choice and looked the unhappiest about it, but she mounted up nonetheless.

Rycard fisted his hands at his sides to control the emotions roaring through him. Betrayal. Anger. Isolation. Sadness. That most of all, a deep, deep sadness.

"Come with us," Gansen said, the unhappiness pouring off him in waves. "Don't end up like him." He gestured toward the small cairn of river stones marking Timval's grave.

"Yes, do come," Dezarie said as a few of the other hunters nodded. "Come with us, Rycard. We'll work as caravan guards or barkeeps or whatever we have to until spring, then we can forget this ever happened."

Rycard gazed at their faces, the faces of the four men and one woman left of his company. He huffed out a small breath of derision. His company no longer.

"No." That was all he said. The only thing that needed to be said.

"Then we wish you luck," Gansen said and turned his horse in the direction of the flatlands below them.

"May the gods watch over you," Yero said, but he didn't meet Rycard's eyes as he turned his horse.

The rest of them murmured words of parting, turned from him, and followed Gansen out of the gorge.

Dezarie shifted in her saddle to look back at him.

"Please come with us," she called. "You know how to find us."

Rycard could not answer.

She raised one hand in a final gesture of farewell and faced forward again.

After a moment, Rycard lifted his hand in a return salute, though she had already turned away.

Charza whined and took a few steps to follow the horses, then back to Rycard, and forward again, looking from him to the horses, clearly waiting for him to follow the hunters. Rycard's throat was too tight to speak and tell him to stay. If the dog wanted to follow the rest of the company, it would serve Rycard right. He'd brought this upon them. And himself.

He watched them ride away until they crested a rise and disappeared from sight. Charza circled back and sat down beside him, looking out at the emptiness, his brown and black fur fluttering in a gust of cold wind that blew down through the gorge.

"Come, Rycard Serod," Vorgon said. "We will go to my home where we'll be safe. Then we can eat and talk on how we plan to save the two still in Shademere."

Rycard glanced at him. He'd momentarily forgotten the dragon was there. He sought for words but found none. What good would words do, anyway? He looked back to the flatlands, staring off at the fields where the only sign of his hunters was a faint trail in the grass, pressed down by their passing.

* * *

The Splitchain Hunters were finished. The truth of it backhanded Rycard, left him reeling and stunned as he rode Redmane through the lengthening canyon shadows. They were on the western side of the Eddrassa mountain range, the slopes orange-red around them in the setting sun. Every time Redmane's hoof hit the stony canyon ground, it echoed sharply off the surrounding cliffs. Charza trotted along at his stirrup, occasionally straying off to investigate some small animal or other, but always circling back to his side.

He'd spent half his life with the hunters, coming under their red and black flag as a young, brash hunter out of Sand Creek who thought he knew everything. He'd ridden with them for over a decade, worked his way up the ranks, and eventually took over the company when Faemred sheathed his sword and retired his command.

And now it was done. Nearly a hundred years the Splitchain Hunters had survived, through wars and plagues and the Boa Visk.

His stomach felt sick, as if someone had kicked him in the gut. His hunters, his friends. He couldn't blame them either; that was the worst of it. He'd brought them to the borderlands, dealing with the Boa Visk despite the dangers, so he'd been the one responsible for bringing them to their end. The heritage of the Splitchain Hunters had been entrusted to him by Faemred, and he'd destroyed it.

Vorgon waited for him on a rocky outcropping beneath the top ledge of the canyon. "Welcome to Blackgap Canyon, hunter. We're almost there." His deep dragon voice echoed down the canyon and back up again, startling a flock of birds into flight.

As they traveled farther into the canyon, the stillness deepened and the echoes seemed to last longer. Vorgon landed on another rocky outcropping high above the canyon floor.

"Since my horse and dog don't have wings," he called to the dragon, annoyed, "how do you expect us to get up there?"

The dragon gave a short, rumbling laugh and swiped at something with his leg. A rope ladder tumbled down the cliffside and swung there, tapping lightly against the stones.

"Your horse will be safe here," Vorgon told him. "There's good grazing along the stream bed. No wolves or other predators ever venture this close. This is my hunting ground after all."

Rycard dismounted and grabbed his saddlebags, then led Redmane a short ways away, down to the small clearing a few meters from a stream running a jagged, wandering course through the bottom of the canyon. He pulled off the bridle and slung it over his shoulder, looking around him at the austere, rocky beauty of the little clearing. Redmane put his head down and nibbled at a tuft of grass poking up at Rycard's feet. He unbuckled the girth and lifted the saddle from the horse's back, then gave him a gentle slap on his neck. He set the tack down on the rocks and headed back to where Vorgon waited. Charza barked up at Vorgon as if vexed that the dragon was out of reach.

Vorgon leaped from the rocks and floated down to him, wings spread wide to slow his descent. After landing, he carefully took hold of Charza and flew back to the ledge. The dragon released his dog safely onto the outcropping. Charza turned in an excited circle, as if taunting Rycard far below.

The dragon flashed a grin full of sharp teeth as his golden eyes sparkled. "Like I said, it's good to know a dragon."

"Maybe if you're a lazy dog." He raised an eyebrow at Charza, who scratched his ear with his back foot and ignored him. Rycard allowed himself a small smile and grabbed his saddlebags again, slung them over his shoulder, and began to climb the rope ladder.

When he reached the top, he pulled up the ladder behind him and studied the quiet scene below him. The wide canyon had nearly vertical cliff walls and a winding stream that trickled over rounded rocks and sandbanks. Above them, the shoulders of two mountains rose up high. From here, he could still see Redmane grazing twenty or so meters below. The canyon was deep and remote, and it wouldn't be easy to discover.

"What now?" he asked Vorgon. He hadn't intended for his weariness to bleed into his voice, but it was unmistakable. They were on a ledge with a pile of rope ladder and seemingly nothing else but rock. A cold wind blew through the canyon, rifling Rycard's hair. "This might do for a dragon, but it's going to get awfully cold when the sun goes down."

"Patience," the dragon replied. He swung his long neck around and faced the cliffside at the end of the outcropping. Rycard felt the push of the dragon's power—like a sudden gust of warm wind—as he spoke a word in a tongue Rycard did not understand. The rocks that had appeared so solid only an instant before wavered and misted away. When they were gone, an opening nearly ten meters across appeared in the cliffside.

"Follow me," Vorgon said, his long tail swaying slightly side-to-side as he folded his wings back and entered.

Rycard followed him into the darkness. Charza padded along at his side, stopping to sniff along the cave floor and then scurrying to keep up. This was no natural grotto or cavern. He'd seen plenty of those in his time, because many of the monsters he hunted made lairs in caves. But unlike natural gaps in the rocky cliffside, the sides of this tunnel were nearly as smooth as glass, as if the rock had been melted, or dissolved. The floor was also smooth but uneven.

It didn't take long until the darkness grew even deeper, and Rycard struggled to see through the gloom. A moment later, the dragon spoke another strange word and the stones—a near-perfect illusion or some warding spell he didn't understand—blocked off the cave's entrance again and drowned them in complete darkness.

Rycard stood still. "Doesn't the darkness bother you?"

"It does not bother me. Put your hand on my side and I will guide you."

He did so, feeling the heat coming off Vorgon's smooth scales. At least the chill air of the cave wouldn't bother him as long as he stayed near the dragon. "How do you see in here?"

"Dragons have a second eyelid. It allows me to see without light. I can tell the walls and the ground from variations in the temperature from the stone and the air. Do not worry. There will be light once we go deeper."

Gradually he realized he could see again. The smooth walls were dusted with something…a plant? Algae? Spores? He wasn't certain, but it glowed a faint blue. In the total darkness, it cast enough faint bluish light to see by. Eventually they reached a huge door made of a strange wood that also glowed. Instead of blue, the wood glimmered with an orange-yellow hue like flame. The door itself was circular and set on massive steel hinges that groaned and swung wide at a single word from Vorgon. A different word this time, and a slightly different pulse of power.

Past the door, the tunnel narrowed again, splitting off in several directions with strange lamps mounted on the smooth stone walls. The lamps seemed to be filled with mirrors and more of the powdery substance emitting the same blue light he'd seen earlier. The air grew steadily cooler and smelled of stone and earth, and something else he'd smelled from time to time, some mineral he always associated with caves. Soon the tunnel grew so narrow that Vorgon shifted in mid-step, changing from dragon to human form as easily as blinking.

It startled Rycard enough that he jumped and was immediately irritated with himself. "Why change now? Why not widen this tunnel?" He glanced at the naked Vorgon standing beside him, then made himself look away.

"I prefer to be outside when in dragon form. The freedom and flying—I'm sure you understand. But inside, I feel more comfortable in my human form. More maneuverable in tight spaces."

Vorgon wound his way through a maze of tunnels. Rycard tried not to notice the broad back, the strength of him, the firm buttocks, the well-formed legs. In the dim blue light of the narrow passageway, the burn scars along his side and leg seemed to fade almost to nothingness.

They reached another door, this one human-sized and built of the same glowing wood. Vorgon opened it for him. He spoke another word and the rooms inside lit up with dozens of lamps along the walls and in stands. The slightest breath of air pushed against his skin, telling him there was a flow of fresh air through the tunnels, a ventilation shaft or breeze tunnel, because the air didn't have the stale, heavy feeling of deep caves.

"Welcome to my home, Rycard Serod," the dragon said, smiling and watching him with those golden eyes.

Rycard peered around him. Shelves and shelves of books lined the walls, all neatly arranged. A spirwood table, beautifully carved, with matching chairs. Sculptures carved out of sandstone. Elaborate candleholders. Banners on the wall with a device he'd never seen before. A black dragon and a white dragon facing each other in front of a rising sun. Tapestries covered the walls where there were not shelves of books or banners and displayed scenes from Gondellan myths. Rugs and carpets from Arnoth and Yiddoni covered the stone floor. There was even a huge map of Anzin laid out on a different spirwood table.

Along one wall ran a fireplace with a carved mantle. Everything was impeccably neat, perfectly arranged. The colors all complimented one another, the darker colors balanced by explosions of brighter hues, all in carefully arranged harmony.

"This is beautiful. I'd imagined something else entirely."

Vorgon's handsome, regal features showed amusement. "Something more like a lair? The bones of my victims lying around in the dust? Perhaps a treasure hoard?"

Rycard laughed. "Something like that, I suppose. But this…this is beautiful."

Charza immediately trotted over to the cold fireplace, curled up, and favored him with a look that seemed to ask how long it would be before he did something useful and made a fire.

Vorgon smiled at the dog and spoke another word in his strange tongue, and the fireplace flared to life. Then he turned back to Rycard, seeming pleased by his reaction.

Looking around him, Rycard was staggered he ever believed this dragon anything close to a monster. Vorgon was a warrior, yes, but his home spoke of other, surprising sides to him that Rycard wouldn't have guessed. This balance of form and color was something he expected from an artist...

"How did you get all this here?" he finally asked. "Did it come from Rasella?"

"Some of it. The banner. Many of the books. I built the tables myself. Other things I've picked up from markets and brought here over the years."

Rycard gave him an odd look. "How did you carry all of this?"

He shrugged as if it was not a big deal. "I fashioned a harness and pack to carry supplies. We don't have to haul everything around in our claws for hundreds of miles."

Rycard's neck heated with embarrassment. He'd imagined something very much like that. Vorgon the dragon flying off with a table and chairs for his cave.

Vorgon arched an eyebrow at him. "The things from Anzin...some of them I hired wagons for. But I didn't buy them while in dragon form, for the sake of the gods.

Although if I had, it might've earned me an advantage when haggling over the price."

Rycard laughed. "I like it a great deal. It's not often we—I—find myself in such luxury." He had lived on the road with the hunters for much of his life. At best, they'd stay a few weeks in an inn, mostly they camped on the trail of whatever they hunted. Their winter camp was a rough barracks, although it was clean and warm. That was about as much could be said for the luxury of a hunter's accommodations.

The winter camp he'd never return to.

"I'll make us some food if you're hungry," Vorgon offered.

It was strange being here in this cavern hideaway. Stranger still to have a creature hundreds of years older—a dragon of magic and power who'd already healed him twice and singlehandedly routed the feared Boa Visk—ask him about sharing a meal. Standing naked as if clothes didn't exist. Rycard was no prude, there was no room on the road for modesty, not even with a woman in the company. But now he found himself very pointedly trying not to let his gaze trail over the man's body, past those scars, the defined ridges of his abdomen, and lower. The absurdity of it all made him laugh awkwardly.

Vorgon tilted his head to the side and raised an

eyebrow. "Is that hungry laughter or not-hungry laughter?"

"I'm sorry. All this is overwhelming." He blew out a long breath. "I think maybe I'm simply exhausted. So much has happened so quickly. Now I'm the guest of a dragon who saved my life and whose cave is more regal than any palace I could have conjured in my deepest dreams. I didn't even believe dragons were real, a few days ago. But here you are. Talking to me. Completely naked."

The dragon's eyes flashed, and his lips curved in a smirk. "I'll go put on some clothing. It was not my intention to be a…distraction. After that, we'll eat. Join your dog by the fire, get warm. Perhaps you can heat water for tea."

"A fireplace deep inside a cave," Rycard said. "How does that work?"

"I've bored out ventilation shafts. A chimney cuts up through the rock."

"Won't the smoke give away where we are?"

Vorgon nodded as if in approval of his question. "A hunter's thought, and a good one. But I use seasoned wood, no bark, and the airflow means the fire burns hot and clean. The chimney curves back slightly into tree cover, which helps diffuse any smoke that does escape. If we're careful, there should be minimal smoke."

"I'll start it then."

"And I shall return as soon as I dress," Vorgon said,

turning to head through a doorway.

Rycard watched Vorgon striding away from him deeper into his living quarters and couldn't help admiring him once more. He'd already chosen a few favorite features on Vorgon's human form. His broad, well-muscled back. Thick, powerful thighs. Tight, muscular buttocks.

What was he doing? Ogling a creature that wasn't even human. A creature he'd come here to hunt...before things came to pass the way they had. Was he mad? What right did he have to feel anything—attraction, lust, pleasure, even amusement? Three of his men were dead, another two were trapped in a town held by the Boa Visk, suffering the gods knew what. The rest of his hunters had fled south and abandoned him. And he was here with a dragon who had killed one of his people, peeping at his muscled arse like a horny teenager. His lust was wasted. It was wrong. He cursed himself for it. Right now, he had no right to feel it, especially not for Vorgon. He didn't have a right to smile. He didn't have a right to laugh. He'd ruined everything, for everyone.

He bent down to the fireplace, noting the kettle that hung from a metal arm beside the fire. He raised the lid and saw it half full of water, so he swung the arm out over the fire to heat the water for tea. Tea with a dragon. He was mad.

Charza whined and bumped him, his tail wagging and

slapping Rycard on the side.

"You hungry, boy? What do you say we stop the self-pity song and have something to eat?"

Charza licked him eagerly, nearly killing him with dog breath. He grinned and did his best to shove the dark thoughts deeper into his mind where he wouldn't have to deal with them. At least for now. He closed his eyes and felt the warmth heat his clothes, his face, and tried not to think of anything else.

* * *

Vorgon cooked a mutton stew with carrots and potatoes and dried herbs, and roasted bones until their marrow was soft and melted. He was proud of how it came out, and Rycard seemed to like it as well. Rycard also liked eating out of his porcelain bowls with spoons made of real silver, seated in front of the fire instead of at the table. Charza got some of the meat and a thick marrowbone to chew on, clutching it between his paws and fighting to get the last of the marrow out with his tongue.

Vorgon smiled as he watched them eat. The idea of the human—and a dog—sitting by his hearth made him feel happy, somehow. He was never lonely, not for human companionship, anyway. But having Rycard sitting beside him in companionable silence, sharing his meal and a mellow-tasting ale brewed by a Shademere alewife, made a happiness settle over him that he hadn't expected to feel.

They didn't speak much as they ate. Most of the light came from the flames in the hearth as they jumped and flickered. He'd always found the motion soothing, the light almost mesmerizing. Then again, he felt a particular kinship with fire.

Charza was lying near Rycard's feet, snoring softly. Rycard had his boots up on a split log on the stack of firewood. He sipped the ale and stared into the flames as if they could give him a vision of what would be coming their way. Vorgon didn't need to touch him to know the tumult of feelings inside the other man. He might be a good hunter, but right now he wasn't doing a very good job of hiding the fears and doubts that plagued him. Or maybe he no longer cared to hide it. Did he trust Vorgon enough now to let his emotions show?

He pulled his attention back to the glowing coals, not wanting the hunter to know he was thinking of him. The steady heat from the fire sank into his clothes—a purple doublet slashed with black, a gold necklace with an amethyst from the mines of Vaemor, breeches in black with matching purple running up the sides. It was fancy compared to Rycard's hard-worn clothing of browns, grays, and greens, suited for the hunt. Perhaps he shouldn't have selected something so elegant. Perhaps Rycard thought him a dandy.

Or perhaps he was simply grateful Vorgon had finally covered up. Nudity didn't bother him, but neither did he wish to make the man uncomfortable, which Vorgon could tell he had done by the way Rycard had been trying not to look at him. Dragons usually wore clothes in Vaemor when in human form, but because one was naked after a dragonshift, there wasn't any shame in being bare either.

Vorgon put another log on the fire and glanced at Rycard again, his mind turning to the difficult task that still stood before them. The man's rugged features were bathed in the firelight, the glow and the shadows making him quite striking. "Do you have a plan to save the men trapped in the town?"

Rycard took a sip of his ale. "Wait until dark. Sneak into Shademere. Get them out."

Vorgon breathed out a half laugh. "Of course. How silly of me."

The hunter sighed out a long breath. His expression

was bleak. "I don't know where they are. Not now. We left them at the inn the morning we set out on Timval's trail. For all I know, they could be thrown in a pit in the camp...or that crazy blood priest could've already fed them to his monster." He rubbed a hand over his eyes. "But I won't leave without the truth. If they live, I'll do everything I can to save them."

"I will help you."

Rycard looked over at him. "You'll help me, but only if I help *you* drive off the Boa Visk, is that it? Those were your terms before. That's why my hunters left me."

Vorgon sighed. "If it's easier to blame me, you may."

Rycard turned to give him a sharp look. "You offered to help, then put impossible conditions on it. We're not soldiers, and we're not dragons. There's no way six people and one dragon can subdue five hundred kerrsgard. I don't blame my people for refusing."

Vorgon heard the truth in Rycard's words. "You're right. I did say that. But I never would have made it a condition for helping get your men out of Shademere."

"Thanks for telling me that now."

Anger flared in him before he could contain it. "Humans," he snarled. He met and held Rycard's gaze, and his words were ice. "They did not leave you because of me. They left because of you. Even without the idea of fighting the Boa Visk, they were still disillusioned. I did not bring them here. You did. You came hunting me, to trade my life for gold. One of your men forces me to defend myself, then you hate me for it. You endanger a child and use him against me. But still I heal you, twice, because you love your hunters and your animals, so I choose to believe there's good in you. Then I free you, free your hunters and your animals. I save your lives. I save your *dog*. And still, your hunters refuse to stand with me. They won't even fight for their friends. But I will. And yet you lay the blame on me? I believed you better than that, hunter."

Rycard couldn't hold his gaze for long. He turned back to the flickering flames and didn't immediately respond. When he did, his voice was subdued. "You're right. You have done nothing but help me, and I've done nothing to deserve it." He finally forced himself to meet Vorgon's eyes again. "Will you accept my apology?"

"I will." With Rycard's apology, the weight of obligation transferred to Vorgon. Now, to keep his own honor and pride, he must forgive and move on. They had blood between them still—Timval's blood—and that was no small thing. But this would be a start, a foundation to build upon.

Rycard nodded and reached down to pet his dog. At his touch, Charza turned over on his back, showing his belly, and made an odd snorting sound.

"I owe you," the hunter said. "I will help you fight the Boa Visk in any way I can. Gansen was right—I'm a hunter, not a soldier, so I'm not sure what good I'll be." He gave a bleak laugh. "But there's nothing left for me anyway. The Splitchain Hunters are finished. I might as well be a rendlich snack as freeze to death in an ice storm."

Vorgon reached out and put a hand on his shoulder, giving him a reassuring squeeze. He could sense the man's inner turmoil, regrets, and worry. "There is always something new. One tale ends, another begins. Don't worry yourself about the distant future when we have tasks enough at present. First let us concentrate on what we must do: find your men and free them."

"Thank you." Simple gratitude resonated in Rycard's voice, and that did much to mollify the last of Vorgon's anger. He had always been a fool for those who needed help. The hunter leaned forward in his chair, clasping his hands together.

Vorgon pondered for a moment. "You're worried about having the skills to save your men. A hunter must be stealthy to stalk his prey. Rely on those skills when you search for them. The curfew in Shademere means there will be few out after dark and most of them will be kerrsgard. The town will provide you with plenty of cover and shadows, but stay away from the kerrsgard camp. Trust your instincts. Do not take unnecessary risks. If you can't find your men, withdraw—we can try again. If you're discovered, run."

"I will." New determination showed in the set of his jaw, the glint in his eyes.

"Don't misunderstand me, this will still be incredibly dangerous." He couldn't help his grin. "Some might even call it stark-raving mad. But it isn't hopeless. I will be there. A dragon tilts the scales in your favor."

"I..." Rycard hesitated, then shook his head slowly, staring up at the ceiling where the firelight danced and flickered along the stone. "You're a good person. Better than I am."

"Peace, my friend," Vorgon said, smiling gently. "After we save your men, we can get drunk and maudlin. Right now, we need rest. You may put your bedroll out here near the fire." He stopped and waited until Rycard looked his way. "Tomorrow will be a long day. Get as much sleep as you can. And welcome to the war, Rycard Serod."

CHAPTER EIGHT

As Vorgon flew him through the moonless night sky, the cold air blew into Rycard's face so hard it made his eyes water and forced him to squint. Beneath him, the dragon's scales felt warm. The heat trapped between their two bodies offset the constant rush of frigid air.

Neither of them spoke much, either aloud or using the kahnsay magic. Vorgon's thoughts were closed off to him anyway, though Rycard could sense the dragon's unease and determination. Rycard was more than a little uneasy himself.

But for his part, Rycard kept his thoughts guarded. Mostly he tried to focus on what was about to come, although his thoughts often veered wildly through his head. One moment he would be thinking about his hunters, where they were now, whether they were safe, why they had left him... The next moment old memories would surface like bubbles slowly rising in a tar pit. Memories of past lovers or challenging hunts he'd endured, even a spring equinox feast years and years ago—his first time with another man. Other memories of men he'd loved. Swimming naked in a river as moonlight played over the water. Thomas telling him he was going to marry a merchant's daughter to save the family fortune. Thomas telling him good-bye with tears in his eyes, but telling him good-bye all the same. And when Rycard hadn't left, Thomas staring right through him and admitting he could never tell his noble family he loved a hunter.

The dragon had stirred these memories, no doubt. In some ways, he understood his attraction to Vorgon. He made a stunning human. His voice, his golden eyes. His power...and his kindness. But on the other hand, it was just like it had been with Thomas. What made him think a noble, wise dragon with hundreds of years of life on him wouldn't say the exact same thing eventually? Look right past him and say, kindly, that he could never be with a mere human hunter. Had Rycard learned nothing in all these years? Never love your betters. It brought only pain.

He gritted his teeth and tried to shake the past and its melancholy away from him. He didn't have the time or the patience to wallow in his own pain. Tonight would be dangerous enough as it was. He had to focus. He would be alone inside enemy territory. Vorgon would be waiting in the fields outside Shademere, close to the river for better cover, staying in dragon form in case trouble came their way. But while he slipped alone through the darkness in Shademere, there would be no one to help him if things went wrong.

Soon he spotted the distant lights of the town—torches, candles, and lanterns—and outside the city, the dozens of campfires of the kerrsgard reinforcements. From this far away in the dark, it was hard to see all the damage Vorgon had caused. The scene even had a quiet beauty to it. The stars. The town lights. The darker ribbon of the river and the trees and bushes around it set against the lighter colors of the crops in the fields. Snow dusting the tops of the mountains around the valley.

The scene was like nothing he'd ever experienced. Flying was thrilling beyond words, sending his heart racing and his blood pumping in his veins. Part of him never wanted it to end. The rest of him wished the whole dangerous night were already over, wished he were curled up in his bedroll by a crackling fire, ready for the peace of sleep.

Vorgon descended through the air as they approached the town. Soon he was flying just a handful of meters above the fields. They landed well outside of town as far from the kerrsgard camp as possible, coming down near the river where the cover was greater and the flowing water helped cover the sound of their landing. The camp was heavily defended, but the town much less so, and that was where he intended to search for his men first.

"If they find me, fly off," Rycard whispered to the dragon. "No sense in two of us getting killed over my problems."

"I will not leave you here alone."

There was such finality in the dragon's words that Rycard could only feel a surge of deep gratitude toward him. He laid a hand on the dragon's side, feeling the heat coming off his blue and white scales, wanting to share his gratitude without relying on his fumbling words. All he said to the dragon, mind-to-mind, was a simple *"Thank you."*

Rycard turned and set off through the fields toward the town, careful to hide from any patrols he spotted. He wished he had Charza at his side. He could use a tail-wag and a friendly lick on the face right about now. But he'd left the dog back at the cave.

Boa Visk sentries guarded the border of Shademere, but the palisade wall had been effectively destroyed. First by Vorgon in his attack on the stronghold, and then by slaves who'd taken much of the remaining wood to fortify the kerrsgard camp. Rycard stayed in the shadows, keeping wide of any torch or lantern. Without any moons in the sky, the darkness was particularly deep. After deliberating, he'd decided to leave his armor behind as well, choosing stealth over protection, to allow him to move quickly and quietly through the darkness.

Sneaking in was the easy part. Finding his men would not be the same.

He slipped along the road to the inn where his men had been stationed, keeping to the trees along the roadside to avoid being seen by the Boa Visk patrols. But he could see long before he reached the inn that the two wagons weren't where they'd left them.

Damn. As he'd feared. When he rounded the corner and got closer to the inn, he saw that the building was empty, quiet and dark.

Bobbing lights came around the corner from his right. A Boa Visk patrol with lanterns. Rycard pressed back against the trees, slipping between the trunks to the left.

More lanterns from the left. A second patrol. Rycard pressed against a tree trunk as the two patrols met at the intersection of their two roads, not two meters from where he stood. He held his breath and tried not to move, not to make a sound as the two patrols spoke together, traded notes about the night's weather, the lack of humans on the streets that night, their disappointment at having found no one to drag back to the kerrsgard and feed to the rendlich.

Rycard's heart lurched as he caught sight of motion near the side of a building. Only a rat. He let his breath out slowly, willing his heartbeat not to thunder in his ears. The rat bumbled back into the deeper shadows, carelessly brushing through a bush and snapping twigs as it went.

The two patrols swung their lanterns in his direction. Rycard froze and hoped the tree trunk was wider than his shoulders. His heart raced and he felt almost lightheaded with the adrenaline rushing through his veins.

"What was that?" one of the Boa Visk said.

"Sounds like vermin," another of them replied.

"Check it out."

"Let the next shift check it out and have it for dinner. It's past time we returned to the barracks."

Rycard couldn't put his head out to see what they were doing. But it sounded as if they'd decided to listen to the last one's advice as footsteps and more of their banter headed away down the road to his right.

He waited a few moments and then risked peering out. The intersection was empty. He let himself heave a deep breath of relief and tried to think about his next move.

The burned out fortress. Perhaps they were being held prisoner there.

He moved through the town's market square,

approaching the burned-out stronghold, when he spotted the crude wooden stage. Above it, a row of bodies were hung upside down, dangling from the top of the thick pole by a rope around their ankles cinched so tight it dug into the swollen flesh. Their throats had been cut.

His heart seemed to stop for a moment and then start again, pounding twice as hard. His chest felt as if a horse had stepped on him, crushing the air out of his lungs. He recognized the two men on the end. Urson and Salcan. They'd been bled dry like butchered pigs.

His head was pounding, a steady throbbing thud like a hammer hitting a shield. There were too many emotions swirling around his mind, none of them good. He couldn't express the sorrow or rage roaring like a tornado inside him. Instead, he fled into the shadows of an alley as another patrol approached from the opposite side of the market square. The sentries didn't bother to look at the half dozen bodies dangling by their ankles. They were clearly used to the sight.

The desire to fall on them with his sword out, cursing and slashing, was nearly too strong to deny. With surprise on his side, he might even kill them all. Had he believed he'd been killing monsters all his life? What a fool he was. The monsters were the Boa Visk. His hand moved for his sword hilt.

But slaying these guards wouldn't bring his men back.

And it wouldn't save the town. It would only result in his pointless death. If he wanted vengeance, if he wanted to stop things like this from happening again, he needed to destroy the real power behind this. The guiding hand and the grinning mask. Hadrak Carn. He needed to rip off his grotesque mask and expose him, before ending him forever.

With his men either dead or gone, he had nothing else to live for.

He headed back to the rendezvous point to tell Vorgon their rescue would not be needed. He stepped out from behind a building near the edge of Shademere, right into the lighted path of a four-sentry patrol.

"Halt!" one of the Boa Visk shouted as the four Boa Visk charged toward him with spears raised.

He stood there, torn between choices. Draw his blade and spill as much Boa Visk blood as he could before they finally brought him down. Or live to pet Charza again, to keep chasing that dream of the little plot by the river, to see Vorgon again. Hear his deep laughter. Feel the warmth spreading inside him whenever they shared a smile...

He turned on his heel and ran like hell for the river.

Wheat stalks whipped and hissed as he sprinted through them. Behind him, horns sounded and drums began to beat. More torches flared to life in the darkness as the encampment stirred to the sound of the alarm. The Boa Visk shouted to each other in their harsh tongue. Torches appeared ahead of him, a unit of kerrsgard angling to cut him off from the river where Vorgon waited. He cut to his left, desperately trying to outrun them.

Wildly shot arrows hissed overhead, missing but coming closer than he liked. Then he heard the snarls and howls of the rendlich. The sound of their pounding feet seemed as loud as the frantic drumbeat.

He was panting hard and beginning to flag. They'd cut him off from the river entirely. Gods, there were so many of them too, all of them eager for his blood. The arrows fell closer. One missed his head by inches, humming like a massive dragonfly as it blew past his ear.

He was a fool. Vorgon deserved better.

Now dozens of torches were closing in on him from all sides. Another arrow barely missed burying itself in his thigh. Rendlich riders were circling him, cutting him off and spiraling in on him now that they had him surrounded.

He drew his sword. No choice now but to stand his ground and try to die well. And take as many of them with him as he could.

Before he knew what was happening, dragon claws settled around him and lifted him from the ground in one smooth motion. The next moment, he was soaring through the air at high speed. When he looked up, all he could see was Vorgon's massive wingspan and his underbelly.

Arrows arced through the air but none came close. Vorgon's speed was breathtaking, his wings pumping hard. He was already past the river, flying low and fast toward the mountains.

The dragon's deep voice entered his mind, filled with concern. *"Did you find your men?"*

"Dead," was the one word he sent back to the dragon. Anything else might have him weeping or see a return of the reckless madness that had seized him earlier.

"Rycard, I am so sorry."

With the words, Rycard sensed the sadness and loss that Vorgon felt for him, a sorrow and regret that they'd been too late to stop this from happening. A sorrow and regret that nearly rivaled his own. Vorgon had never even seen the two wagon drivers—they'd been in town the entire time. But the very fact that a majestic creature such as Vorgon would feel that way at all, especially for humans who had come here to hunt him, had Rycard's throat tightening, had emotion squeezing his chest with the sharp pang of grief he could not hold back any longer. He let out one harsh sob as the cold air whistling past his face drew the tears from his eyes.

In the distance, back near Shademere, a bone-rending screech pierced the night. The shriek echoed across the hills. The draegkal.

Vorgon's sudden rage flashed through their connection. His desire to turn around and fight the draegkal, to destroy it, burned like a forest fire in his mind. The feelings were so strong that Rycard was afraid the dragon would forget he was carrying a human in his claws and drop him.

"I won't drop you. I will destroy the abomination another day. When I have time to enjoy it."

Those words were a bit disquieting. The dragon wasn't all compassion and empathy after all. *"Is it chasing us?"*

"It's challenging me, but it doesn't know where we've gone. We're too far away for it to see our heat. Without any moon in the sky, we are nearly invisible."

Rycard wasn't as comfortable dangling in the dragon's claws as he'd been riding upon Vorgon's back. For one thing, the tops of the trees on the mountain slopes seemed alarmingly close to his body. For another thing, he felt like prey, like a mouse in the talons of a hawk, and it left him uneasy.

The flight home seemed to take forever, but he allowed himself a sigh of relief when he finally spotted Blackgap Canyon. Vorgon circled down and gently set him on the cave ledge. Then he landed beside Rycard and transformed.

Before Rycard could say a word, Charza plowed into him. He went down on his rear, laughing as Charza frantically licked his face, his tail whipping back and forth with wild joy.

"I missed you, too, boy," he said, hugging the dog to him.

Then Vorgon was standing there, holding out a hand to help him up. Rycard took it, gratefully.

* * *

Vorgon was up before the sun and in the air before the stars began to fade with the coming dawn. He needed to fly. Flying helped him clear his mind. It centered him. Besides, he needed to see what was going on in the valley. And it was too dangerous to fly without the cover of darkness to conceal him from the Boa Visk.

But mostly, he was worried about Rycard. The hunter had told him the tale of finding his wagon drivers executed. Rather sheepishly, he'd admitted losing heart for a while and giving in to a reckless despair that had nearly cost him his life.

That was one of the reasons he'd left Rycard asleep on his bedroll with Charza at his side. He knew both the hunter's body and spirit needed rest. The dog had watched Vorgon leave, but even though he'd thumped his tail a few times in greeting, he hadn't left his master's side. Charza understood the pain his master was in, and so did Vorgon.

Rycard hadn't been able to hide it from him last night. When Vorgon had grasped him and carried him into the sky, just before the rendlich reached him, all of Rycard's uncontrolled emotions had flooded Vorgon's mind. Fear, pain, remorse, sadness, and so much guilt.

He wanted to help Rycard, but he was unsure if it was wise to offer comfort. He wouldn't have been surprised if the man rejected any sympathy he showed. After all, they had started out as enemies. Now they were…something else. Still, the man had lost his comrades. His place as a hunter. His life had been upended. Ruined.

The eastern horizon grew steadily lighter. Fortunately, he'd seen no evidence of the kerrsgard in the valley. For now, they seemed to be staying close to Shademere.

He landed on a wide shelf of rock on a mountain slope high above and far to the east of Blackgap Canyon. He stretched his entire body out on the flat expanse of rock and studied the valley below. He didn't spot anything out of the ordinary, but he was certain that after the incursion last night the kerrsgard would begin sending scouts into the valley.

As he watched the fields being lit by the first rays of dawn, his thoughts turned back to Rycard. The hunter was probably awake by now. His eagerness to see the man again made him curious. Was it because they'd flown together? There had been lovers between the dragonriders of old, the humans and the dragonkin. Yet, there hadn't been contact since the retreat to the Isle of Rasella. He'd heard dragon and human love had always been looked upon with concern by the dragonlords—not because they believed there was anything wrong with the love, but because of the strain it put upon the dragon when the human inevitably aged and died. He understood that intellectually, but he was also wise enough to know the heart didn't always obey the intellect.

He shook his head and sent an annoyed blast of smoke from his nostrils. Why was he thinking of such things? Was it because he was developing feelings for the man? He respected the hunter, true. Rycard was as devoted to his animals as he was loyal to his hunters. He was smart and brave and skilled, yes. But there was more than that. The way his face had looked last night, with the light of the fire on his skin... Not handsome, but unforgettable, each scar and nick and imperfection holding secrets he wished to know.

He enjoyed it when he made the man smile. He wanted to take away that haunted look that had crept into his eyes. He wanted to stay in his man-form, just so he could have the thrill of putting his hands on Rycard's body. So he could enjoy the softness of his skin, his lips. He wanted the man to whisper his name.

Or perhaps he was flying too fast in the dark. Last night, the brutal execution of two of his men had pushed Rycard close to the edge. He couldn't play with the man's heart as if this were only a game. He would never do that.

Perhaps it would be best if Vorgon waited to see what happened going forward. Let the snowflakes drift where they would, the raindrops fall as they may. If there were growing feelings between them, so be it. His focus needed to remain what it had always been. Driving the Boa Visk out. Protecting the valley. And now, killing the draegkal.

He was about to finish heading home to wake Rycard, if he wasn't already up, when he spotted movement near the trees. The motion was perhaps a mile or so distant, on the eastern slope of the mountain, skirting the tree line. He used his dragonsight to focus in on the movement. When he saw who it was clambering over the rocks, he growled a curse. Donnel. That shepherd boy would be the death of him.

Unless something bad had happened to the shepherds...

Donnel kept near the trees. He was clearly searching for Vorgon, because he kept scanning the skies, running for a few meters and then slowing to a walk, only to peer around at the heavens again.

He launched himself into the air and glided down to the boy, coming to rest in front of him in a clearing at the base of the foothills. Donnel ran to meet him and pressed himself up against Vorgon's side in a wide hug, surprising him with the unabashed display of affection.

"Dragon!" the boy said. "You came!"

Vorgon curved his long neck around until he could stare at the boy who was still busy hugging him. "What's wrong, Donnel? Are the shepherds safe?"

Donnel pointed toward the mountains to the south of the valley. "We're there right now with the flocks. Weldros says we're safe for a while."

"Why are you here then? It's not safe in the valley."

"Weldros sent me to find you. I have to tell you something bad. The hunters. They took the south road. The Visk caught them, though. Weldros saw it happen."

His heart sank at the boy's words. This would crush Rycard. Even though his hunters had abandoned him, he knew the man still wished them well and wanted them to escape the danger. "Did they kill the hunters?"

"One. They took the others away hurt and all chained

up. Weldros said you would want to know, but I don't know why you'd want to help them. They chained you."

He nodded. "I did want to know. And I have forgiven them."

"You forgave them?" The boy's eyes were wide with shock.

"I did. It is easy to hate. But hate begets hate until everyone suffers. Forgiveness and mercy are what make a noble dragon...and a noble man."

"You sound like Elder Weldros." The boy didn't sound happy about the fact either.

Vorgon grinned. The boy, for his part, didn't flinch from the show of sharp dragon teeth. "Thank you for coming to tell me. And thank Weldros for me as well. I am honored by his friendship. I would fly you back to your people, but I can't risk being seen crossing the valley toward the southern road. It's too dangerous right now."

The boy stared at him with a look of disappointment drawing his lips into a frown. "You're never going to fly me anywhere, are you, dragon?"

"I shall. That's a promise. Now, make sure you do exactly as I say this time. I want you to keep out of sight. Stay beneath the trees as much as you can, cross the valley quickly and return home. Tell all the herders you see to stay far away from Shademere. Tell them to keep out of the valley if they can, too. The dangers are too great. And if they spot another creature flying through the air that breathes fire, don't mistake it for me. It is not a dragon. It belongs to the Boa Visk."

The boy's eyes were wide and he bit at his lip, but he nodded before he hugged Vorgon again. "I'll tell them. I promise," he said and bounded into the trees running as fast as he could go.

Vorgon watched him disappear into the tree line, leaving Vorgon with another problem in a quickly growing list. If he told Rycard what had happened to his hunters, the man would immediately want to try and rescue them, even if he wound up dead. He had nearly been killed last night, and Vorgon didn't think his mind was in the right place to think and strategize clearly. He was all reckless emotion—pain and anger, sorrow and grief.

Vorgon doubted the Boa Visk would wish to kill the hunters right away. Otherwise they wouldn't have taken them prisoner, but would simply have killed them on the road. No, they'd want information. Knowledge of where the dragon was, how they could find him and kill him. Or perhaps he might be too valuable to kill right away. They'd drain him slowly of his blood. Make him suffer.

But that was neither here nor there. Right now he had to make a decision. Tell Rycard what had happened, or keep this from him. Not telling him felt horribly dishonest. But when he considered all the ways telling Rycard could go wrong, his answer was clear. For now, he had to protect Rycard from having to endure the same thing he'd suffered last night. His love for his people would make him desperate and rash. And if he rushed in without a plan, Vorgon was certain the Boa Visk would be ready for him.

He couldn't leave the hunters to suffer at the hands of the Boa Visk. He would go himself to see if they still lived, but not yet. The Boa Visk would be on guard, and he needed time to take the lie of the land and develop a plan. A real plan. This way, if things went badly, Rycard would not torture himself with self-blame.

And he would not die at the hands of the Boa Visk.

Decision made, Vorgon launched himself into the air and flew fast for home. He told himself he was making the right choice.

But if it was the right choice, why did it leave him so uneasy?

CHAPTER NINE

Rycard was careful to make the wine last. Vorgon had only brought one bottle with them into the canyon after their evening meal, and they'd finished half of it already.

They sat in the middle of the canyon, on the edge of a low, flat rock formation next to the stream. Charza was curled up in a tuft of grass near his boots. Redmane stood a little ways off with his head down, probably asleep. The horse seemed happy to spend his days wandering the canyon, eating the grass growing along the stream. His bridle, saddle, and the rest of his tack were safely stored inside Vorgon's home, and the horse didn't seem to miss them in the least. Two moons were out tonight. The pale moon in the west and the red moon to the north, their light mixing strangely and throwing competing shadows. Here in the middle of the canyon, they were far enough from the cliff sides to be in moonlight, not caught in the shadow of the canyon walls. Above them, the sky was a bed of stars for as far as he could see. The air smelled of damp earth and wet stone. The only sound was the musical trickle of the stream and the sigh of the wind in the trees along the canyon ridge. It was peaceful. With his belly full, the wine warming him, and Vorgon beside him, he felt...good. Truly good.

The wine was unlike any he'd tasted before—spiced and buttery and rich. With every sip, he felt pleasant warmth spread throughout his entire body. The wine wasn't strong so much as deeply flavorful. And soothing. Could a wine be soothing?

"Where is this wine from?" he asked. "The Red Hills? Sunderland?"

"From Coromor, on the Isle of Rasella," Vorgon replied. "It's one of my favorites."

The Isle of Rasella. That impressed him. The dragon was sharing a wine that couldn't be had on Anzin. Such a wine would be priceless. "It's excellent."

"I'm glad you like it."

An easy quiet fell between them again.

He frowned, staring down into his wine, remembering

that he didn't have any right to feel good. How could he be here, enjoying himself, when his men had died? What kind of leader did that?

"What troubles you?" Vorgon asked him gently. He wore a fine tunic of red and gold that matched his eyes, dark leather breeches that showed off his powerful legs, and black boots. His golden eyes gleamed in the light of the moons. His face was stunning, beautiful, masculine, commanding. No one could look at him and believe he was not a warrior...or believe he wasn't kind. Because those eyes of his always made Rycard feel as if the dragon could see right into the heart of him and understood.

"What makes you think I'm troubled? Can you read my mind from there?" They were sitting side by side, close but not touching.

"I can read your face. And the feel of you..." He tilted his head, looking up at the sky as if searching for the right words. "Your kahn. It changed slightly. The energy around you darkened."

Rycard didn't answer right away. He wasn't certain how to express all the things he felt. But he also sensed that Vorgon, for whatever reason, genuinely seemed to care. So he took a deep breath and tried.

"This is beautiful. The night. Being here with you. The wine. But how can I enjoy this when so many of my people—

people I was responsible for—are dead?" He swept a hand at the night sky. "They'll never sit in the moonlight and look up at stars, ever again. Why should I be allowed to enjoy it?" He shook his head and took another sip of his wine. "I don't know why I'm telling you this. These aren't your problems."

Vorgon also took his time answering. When he did, his voice was soft, comforting. "I understand the guilt you feel. Many of the dragonkin felt the same when we burned our homeland and fled Anzin. We abandoned all the people to war and death, even our allies, even humans we had loved. Still, if we had stayed, their outcome would not have changed. You must find balance between your grief and your joy. There you will find wisdom and peace within yourself."

"Have you found that?"

Vorgon chuckled and then sighed. "No, not completely. I am as flawed as anyone else trying to make their way through this life. One of the reasons I returned to Anzin was because of how I felt. Unbalanced. As if I had failed to stand up to evil, that I had let down not only the other peoples of Anzin, but the dragonkin and even myself."

"But that evil…it seems unstoppable."

"I can only tell you what works for me, Rycard. I am not trying to destroy all the Boa Visk and free every kingdom. That is too big, even for a dragon. I can only put every bit of my heart into keeping one small part of the world safe. I will die for that. This is where I make my stand. I am at peace with it. Time will help you heal. Time, and places like this, close to the heart of what is best in life, the beauty and the friends to share it with."

Rycard didn't reply. His thoughts and emotions were all jumbled inside him. Twice the dragon had used the word *friend*. Rycard would never have dared use the word after what he'd done to Vorgon...but gratitude filled him all the same. The dragon's words did not magically make his guilt or his sorrow vanish, but his heart felt lighter at hearing them. Knowing Vorgon had experienced the same thing dulled the edges from his pain and doubt. The words were wise. He was determined to take them to heart.

"You're nothing like I imagined," Rycard said quietly, not daring to look the dragon in his golden eyes. He was afraid of what Vorgon might see in his eyes if he did so. Passion, attraction...perhaps even the first ember of love. Fool. He had not felt this way toward another man in years. He didn't want to destroy a new friendship by being as reckless as he'd been last night in Shademere, rushing in desperately without a plan. So he chose the rest of his words carefully. "If someone had asked me, I would've told them that anyone who lived alone in a cave would not be kind. They wouldn't show such caring or...empathy. Not to..." He gritted his teeth, a flood of regret threatening to choke him, making it difficult to get the words out. He charged ahead anyway. He had to say this. "Not to someone who tried to kill them."

Vorgon took a sip of wine and tipped his head back to look up at the sky. "Tell me truly, Rycard Serod. Is it not one of the most life-affirming things in this world when two enemies can become friends?"

Rycard lowered his head. He fought them, but he was helpless to stop the hot tears that ran down his cheeks. He did not sob aloud, at least. His throat burned and ached as if a burning stake were gouging him there, but he managed to remain silent. Still, the tears seemed to let out some of the pain and guilt festering inside him.

Without a word, Vorgon pulled him into a hug. The dragon held him, his heat so very comforting, his wide, strong arms cradling him as if nothing in the world could pull them away, until he had himself under control again. He felt waves of warmth and comfort that Vorgon was sending him through the kahnsay.

"I'm sorry," he said, blinking and wiping at his eyes. "You must think me a weak fool."

"I think nothing of the sort. That is the truth."

Rycard glanced at him. "You are like no one I've ever met. I don't understand you. How can you not be bitter? You've seen darker times than I have, and I am no sheltered princeling living in a palace."

Vorgon gently released him, his brow furrowing as he framed his reply. Rycard already missed the warmth of his touch, the scent of his skin, so close to him.

"It's a decision I made when I came here," the dragon said. "I would not let bitterness sour me on everyone and everything. I came here alone and I needed the time and the silence to heal myself, body and spirit. It is true that it is oftentimes not easy, but it's not a decision I made only once. Every day I must decide again to keep my thoughts full of hope, to believe in the good within people."

"I'm not sure I can do that," Rycard said honestly. "I think that's one of the reasons I wanted to live alone. I had this place I wanted…an image in my mind. A little cabin in the forest, near a river, a plot of land to farm. It is hard to accept that will never happen now."

"It still may. Or something better will happen for you. But I don't want you to hold me up as some sort of paragon of virtue. I meant to protect this valley, and yet I was keeping apart from it. When the Boa Visk first sent their garrison to enforce their rule, I did not attack them. I was not eager to war again, despite all my bold words and all my bluster. People suffered because I wanted to see the good." He sighed and took another sip of his wine, looking off across the canyon at the stark shadows in the moonlight. "I've stayed apart from the valley for too long. I must do more." He indicated the canyon with a wave of his hand. "Living here was necessary. I suppose you could call it a self-imposed isolation. It helped me clear my thinking and shake loose the things that haunted me. But I realize now that it's also lonely."

Rycard's voice was hoarse. "Are you? Lonely, I mean."

The dragon didn't answer right away. When he finally did, his voice was quiet. "Sometimes. I miss my friends. Laughter. Love."

"Why did you leave your island?" He shook his head, then tried a jest to help untangle the knot of emotions inside him. "How could you leave a place that had wine like this?"

Vorgon grinned. "It was not easy leaving Rasella." His expression darkened. "I was in love with a dragon named Tanrev Arelon, of House Cedron. He was older than I, came from a revered line, had status, held power in the council. He loved me too, in his way. But I'd always yearned to return to Anzin—I believed it was a mistake for the dragonkin to abandon the lands to the Boa Visk. One day I finally I told him I was leaving the island and heading back to the mainland. I begged him to come with me. He would not. Neither did he believe I would go. And so I went." He shrugged. "I have not seen him in long years."

"He should have gone with you. If he truly loved

you."

Vorgon shook his head. "I believed the same at the time. But the passing years have also disabused me of some of the more romantic notions of my youth. He believed I would die out here alone. He begged me not to go. One could as easily say I should have stayed, if I'd truly loved him."

"Will you ever go back to find him? This dragon you once loved?"

"We have both moved on, I think. But I cannot return home. Or, I should say, I don't wish to go back." He took a deep breath and let it out slowly. "Yet I may have to, whether I wish it or not."

For a moment, Rycard wasn't certain what he meant. Then he had it. "The draegkal. The blood priest said it had been newly created. You think it might be a new threat to your island because it can fly."

Vorgon nodded. "The dragonkin convinced themselves the Boa Visk could create no new abominations with our blood once we left Anzin. The rendlich, the valgrim, other twisted monsters had all been made during the war, and once created, it's just a matter of breeding them. This draegkal, if it matches the power of the dragons and dragonriders of ancient Vaemor, could mean our undoing. I *must* destroy it, and the dragonkin must be warned what the Boa Visk intend."

"How can all this fall on your shoulders? You can't save the world. Even a dragon can't save the world."

"Wise words, but I can do my best to save these people. And so far, I have not done a good job."

"Can this draegkal kill you?" Rycard demanded.

"I believe it can. It is dangerous. Especially if the blood priest rides it. That means I will face two opponents instead of one." He looked Rycard straight in the eye, although something flickered in his gaze. A momentary doubt? "But you know better than anyone that some things must be done, regardless of the cost."

"I will fight alongside you," Rycard said. "Whatever it takes. Wherever we have to go. You can count on me."

Vorgon reached out and stroked a hand along Rycard's cheek, brushing away the last of the tear tracks there. He leaned forward slowly, his gaze never leaving Rycard's eyes. He drew Rycard toward him.

Emotions roiled inside him like boiling water. Desire, need, yearning, a hint of fear. He wanted this. His heart was pounding hard and fast. He closed his eyes as Vorgon's lips met his.

The kiss was soft at first. The dragon's lips were shockingly warm. That heat sent a thrill racing through him from his brain to his cock, which was already stirring in his breeches.

Vorgon deepened the kiss, pulling Rycard closer to him. He groaned at the feel of the dragon's human body pressed tightly against him. The sensation of their kahn intermixing, their spirit-auras joined at the powerful connection of their lips, had his head swimming. The kiss left him dizzy and aching for more. He could sense Vorgon's lust, his desire, burning like a furnace inside him. That feeling made his heart soar, thrilled him, because he knew he was responsible for making the dragon feel that way. Him. A scarred-up hunter with nothing to his name but a sword, a horse, and a dog.

He wanted more. He yearned for it. He wanted the simple and powerful comfort of Vorgon's hands on his body. He needed the dragon's heat to warm him, to drive off the chill of fear or doubt or sorrow. Above it all, he wanted to give back to this incredible creature, to somehow show his gratitude, his caring, for how the dragon lifted his heart and made him feel like a hero. Made him feel worthy and good. Not a hunter chasing gold, but a man with good in his heart.

Vorgon finally ended the kiss, drawing away far enough to look into his eyes. "I've wanted to do that for a long time," he said softly, but his golden eyes blazed with barely restrained passion.

Rycard's lips were swollen and tingling from the amazing kiss. He gave the dragon a smile. "You should not have waited so long."

He saw a flicker of doubt appear in the dragon's eyes, but Rycard refused to let it last. He settled his hands in Vorgon's doublet and pulled him into another kiss, a kiss he put every bit of his heart into. He threw every doubt away and decided to trust.

Vorgon kissed him back with just as much passion. They broke apart only long enough for the dragon to pull him to his feet before Vorgon was embracing him again, kissing him again.

Rycard groaned into the kiss as he slid his hands down Vorgon's chest, reveling in the firmness of the muscles his fingers trailed across. His cock strained at his breeches, throbbing with need. He didn't want to think about the future. He only wanted the now. He wanted to touch Vorgon's body all over. He wanted the man inside him, driving hard, trembling with pleasure—pleasure that a man had given him. That *Rycard* had given him.

He kissed Vorgon hard as he traced his hands lower, still lower, beneath his belt to the front of his breeches, where he was delighted to find the hard length of his cock pressing against the constraining fabric.

He undid the laces of those breeches as Vorgon drew back enough to watch him. Carefully, he freed Vorgon's cock, and the hard shaft jutted out, thrusting from his body, begging to be touched.

"Beautiful," Rycard whispered. In the moonlight, the long shaft seemed the focus of some kind of erotic dream. Yet when he reached out a trembling hand to touch it, the skin was silken soft and oh so warm.

Pressure seemed to build around his heart as he looked into Vorgon's golden eyes. They were half-lidded with pleasure as Rycard gently stroked his hand up and down his shaft. The lust inside him was coiled like a whip, making it hard to breathe. He began to get down on his knees, wanting to take Vorgon's cock into his mouth, but the dragon stopped him.

A grin was on Vorgon's face, and a wicked glint was in his eyes as he gently but firmly turned Rycard so that the flat rocks they'd been sitting on were behind him. Vorgon's hands skimmed along the bulge in Rycard's breeches, making him catch his breath at the waves of pleasure his touch stirred. Then Vorgon was undoing Rycard's laces and skinning down his breeches to expose the hard length of his cock. Vorgon nudged him, and Rycard sat back on the cool surface of the rock, spreading his legs. The rock was rough against his ass, but Vorgon's hand was like satin as he trailed his fingers up and down Rycard's hardness.

He watched, his eyes widening, as Vorgon went to his knees and took Rycard's cock into his mouth. The sight of the powerful creature on his knees before him, seeing Vorgon staring back into his eyes with that intense, burning gaze, watching Rycard's pleasure as he worked his head up and down, his lips tight around his shaft, was heady, had his thoughts reeling with desire and uncontrollable lust.

He let his head loll back, his eyes fluttering closed, as Vorgon licked along the head of his cock, flicking his tongue against him, teasing him, then encircling his girth with thumb and forefinger and plunging his mouth down again while working him with his hand.

Under that intense assault, Rycard knew he wouldn't last. The orgasm built inside him with frightening intensity. Breathing hard, he reached out and set his hand in Vorgon's hair to warn him he was about to come, but Vorgon didn't relent. If anything, he worked him faster, driving him toward ultimate bliss. He moaned the dragon's name as he came hard, shooting his hot seed down his throat. Vorgon drank him in greedily until he was dry and the intensity of his pleasure slowly started to fade.

He opened his eyes when Vorgon's mouth left him. The air felt cool against his skin, wet from Vorgon's mouth. He reached out for Vorgon's cock, wanting to give him the same pleasure, to drive him to the same heights the dragon had driven him.

Instead, Vorgon caught his hand and pulled him to his

feet. Then Vorgon gently turned Rycard around until he stood there naked and bent forward, his elbows locked, his hands braced against the rocks. Above him, the stars spread in a glittering expanse. The breeze was cool on his skin, making his nipples tighten to hard points. His cock was still semi-erect, and the afterglow of his orgasm still had his body flushed with pleasure. He groaned when Vorgon's hot hands began to stroke their way down the muscles of his back, then cupped his ass, massaging the muscle there, then spreading him wider.

Lips pressed at his hairline, just behind his ear, sending a delightful shiver through his body. Then kisses made their way down his neck, the curve of his spine, to his lower back.

"These dimples," Vorgon's said in a rough voice as he worked his hands on Rycard's ass cheeks, massaging them. "I adore them."

Rycard opened his mouth to reply, then closed it again. He felt too good right now to waste his mind coming up with a response. He only wanted to experience. To *feel*.

Vorgon was unendingly patient, even though Rycard had never minded a flash of pain when pleasure was the reward. But Vorgon used water from the stream to prepare him, slowly, gently teasing his way past that tight muscle until it relaxed enough for him to slip a finger inside, then another, scissoring, teasing him wider. Rycard waited, his head down, his cock stiffening again as the man's gentle touch turned him on once more. His lover's care warmed his heart even more than the heat from his hands warmed Rycard's skin.

He moaned as Vorgon's cock pressed against his hole. He tilted his hips to accommodate the steady push until Vorgon was fully sheathed in him. He closed his eyes and lost himself in the sensations as Vorgon began to make love to him. He was so very hot, the heat seeming to radiate from the silken skin of his manhood out through Rycard's body. His thrusts were slow at first, making sure Rycard had adjusted to him, but quickened as his pleasure grew. Soon Rycard was fully hard again as Vorgon thrust into him from behind. He had his hands on Rycard's hips as he pumped into him. But just when he thought Vorgon was approaching his peak, he surprised him by slowing his pace and leaning forward. He reached around and his hand skimmed the length of Rycard's cock before gripping him. He began to work his hand in time with his thrusts, once again building toward a climax.

Rycard could only stand there lost in the sensations sweeping through his body, the incredible pleasure, the pressure rising in him as the ecstasy built again, the ache inside him deepening. Vorgon thrust harder, reaching his peak and spurting hot seed into him with a groan of purest pleasure that was music to Rycard's ears. Three more quick strokes of Vorgon's hand down the length of his shaft and another orgasm caught Rycard by surprise with its intensity. His seed spilled onto the rocks as Vorgon gradually slowed his strokes. He slowly withdrew from Rycard's channel, and Rycard had a fleeting moment of regret that their connection had ended. He'd loved the feeling of Vorgon inside him, taking him, filling him.

His thoughts were hazy with pleasure as they fell into each other's arms, panting hard. The only sound was the sound of their breathing, the sound of the water, and the sigh of the wind as it brushed its way through the tops of the evergreens.

The two of them lay there together side by side, embracing. The breeze was cool on his skin and his wet cock. Together they looked up at the stars and watched the moons until they set. Neither of them said a word, but that didn't matter. Nothing needed to be said.

It was only as he drifted into a doze that he realized he hadn't once felt any of Vorgon's thoughts.

* * *

Love.

Vorgon was no youngling dragon. He knew what love felt like. He was feeling it now, even as he flew high in the late morning sky, alone with his thoughts and the steady roar of wind against him. He was feeling it for Rycard. In a way, it made little sense that something so intense had any hope of springing up between two enemies. But every moment they'd spent together had been intense. They had shared losses. They had struggled together. Fought alongside one another. Failed each other...

Because he had failed Rycard by not telling him the news of the Boa Visk taking his comrades prisoner. He believed he'd been protecting the man, but perhaps he should've shown more faith. At one point last night, he had meant to tell him everything...but seeing Rycard's tears had broken his heart. And then he had kissed him. It had been all he could do to slam down the shields in his mind to prevent Rycard from knowing his thoughts, knowing the secret he was keeping from him and the festering pain that was growing darker in his heart by not telling Rycard about his men. After that, all his feelings, desires, his need to fill the empty, lonely hole inside himself had taken over. The love they'd made had been beautiful. The connection they shared had been perfect and unforgettable. He couldn't bring himself to kill what had just been born by telling Rycard the fate of his hunters…and how Vorgon had kept it from him.

The truth of the matter had not changed. Rycard would rush off to save his comrades if he knew. Vorgon would not be able to dissuade him. He was a true leader and a brave man. But while the heroes of fairytales never died, true-life heroes died often and bloody, especially against the Boa Visk. A touching song of Rycard's bravery wouldn't bring him back. A poem of his heroics wouldn't be any comfort to Vorgon if he lost the lover he'd only just found.

This morning they'd woken together in Vorgon's bed. They had made love once more. He'd deliberately taken his time, learning exactly what Rycard loved, the ways in which he ached to be touched. He focused on his lover, pouring all he had into making him feel cherished, bringing him to the heights of pleasure. Making him feel alive. But he remained careful to keep his thoughts shielded. Later he'd left Rycard in the canyon walking his dog and seeing to his horse, telling him only that he had to scout the valley for signs of the Boa Visk.

That wasn't a lie, but neither was it the entire truth. He was going to see if he could discover what had become of the hunters. His excuses from yesterday no longer applied—not if he truly loved the man as he claimed. Rycard had a right to know, even if he rushed in to save them. But first, Vorgon had to have a plan in place. And for that, he had to know as much as possible about the state of Shademere and the disposition of the kerrsgard camp.

He was as careful as he could be not to be seen. The only clouds were thin white wisps very high above him, with no sign of rainclouds. The sky was a bright blue. This high, the air had bite. Soon enough he was closing in on Shademere. He didn't know if he was headed straight into battle or if he would only circle high above the encampment, out of range of their weapons and magic, and rely on his dragonsight to search out the hunters. He was ready for either.

Or so he'd thought. But he was not prepared for what he found when he finally reached the town.

The Boa Visk, curse them, had been busy. The town and camp brimmed with activity, but at the sight of him in the sky, horns sounded and drums began to beat wildly. Slaves and soldiers ran in every direction, hiding or taking up arms. The Boa Visk were raising guard towers around the camp, one of which was already complete and bristling with scorpions and bowmen. Two ballistae guarded both the western and eastern sides of the camp, with several others still unfinished. He spotted at least two catapults being frantically loaded with stones by their crews. Dozens more scorpions sat behind dirt embankments. Slaves were digging out tunnels and trenches to protect the camp from fire, and the kerrsgard who drove them slashed at them with whips to make them work faster.

That was far from the worst. What rocked him was what the mad blood priest had done to some of the townsfolk. Humans had been bound to poles or tied to the earth near each siege weapon or large tent. With his dragonsight, he could see they hadn't been killed. They were terrified, watching him with fear and desperation on their faces, and seeing them like that near shattered his heart. As he watched helplessly, kerrsgard soldiers drove more humans from a large pen near the middle of the camp to line up near the guard tower and some of the trenches where their soldiers took cover.

He roared his rage. He couldn't burn the weapons without killing the humans. The filthy dishonor of the Boa Visk repulsed him. They were using the townspeople against him because they knew he wouldn't kill the innocent.

He circled again, unable to attack but still searching for the hunters with his keen dragonsight. He found them. They were on their knees in the middle of the clearing with the draegkal cage, each of them with hands bound and a rope around the neck. The rope was taut, looped around a stake driven deep into the ground. His shadow passed over them as he flew. Their heads turned to follow his flight. He wanted to land and save them, but he couldn't carry them all at once. But the way they were out in the open, it seemed like a trap to lure him down—

A scorpion bolt shot past him, forcing him to change direction. The Boa Visk began to fire their weapons at him, but he was flying too fast and their first shots missed. He raced upward, weaving, trying to get out of their range. But the Boa Visk had kovohl mages who began to work magic against him. He barely avoided an acid-mist cloud that suddenly burst into existence in front of him. Spell-driven winds hammered at him with hurricane force, nearly taking him down before he could bring his own air currents to bear. Draekspell daggers—arrow-like shards of crystallized energy—ripped toward him, and he had to send himself into several spinning barrel rolls to avoid having his wings shredded.

It was too much. They were too strong, and too many, and he could not counterattack without hurting the humans. He'd been outmaneuvered, all his options checked. He roared his defiance again and banked hard, flying westward.

He had only the barest sliver of time to react when the draegkal dove out of the sun and nearly slammed into him. He juked hard, barely dodging what would've been a crushing blow to the middle of his spine. One of the draegkal's claws caught him as it blurred past, ripping into his scales and spilling his blood.

The blood priest was riding on the draegkal's back, strapped to an armored saddle. His black mask with its blank, golden eyes gleamed as the sunlight caught it. The blood priest held a human woman in front of him in the saddle. Her arms were bound with rope. He had one hand wrapped around her throat, the other on the saddle's pommel.

Vorgon roared his outrage, his dragonkin voice shaking the trees as he called out the blood priest's dishonor and shame. The draegkal shrieked in reply, its mindless fury pouring from it with an echoing screech.

"Your death!" the blood priest screamed at him. "Your death, dragon! Accept your end! Sacrifice yourself to the magic and you will live forever!"

Fire licked from Vorgon's jaws, but he couldn't spit flames at the blood priest no matter how much he might wish to burn him to ash. Not unless he wanted to kill the terrified woman the cowardly priest was using as a shield. He had no choice but to retreat. The Boa Visk held all the advantages. Freeing the hunters now was impossible, and he would never be willing to sacrifice innocent lives to his fires.

He raced for the mountains with the draegkal tight on his tail. He was faster, but only barely. Having to veer away from the draegkal's streams of green fire slowed him. This wasn't the battle he'd imagined. There was no hope of destroying the draegkal if he couldn't fight back.

But neither could he lead the blood priest back to the canyon. If he couldn't fight, he had to somehow escape. That wouldn't happen in the sky, so he pulled his wings back against his body and dove toward the earth, shooting toward it faster than an arrow. The draegkal shrieked and gave chase.

Vorgon pulled up an instant before he flew into the tops of the evergreen trees. His blood poured freely from the wound in his side, the pain bright and hot as if he'd been stabbed with a blade of flames. He had to turn some of his magic to stopping the bleeding, and that slowed him further. He was still flying westward, trying to put distance between himself and the town, but the blood priest did not abandon his pursuit.

Another stream of green fire shot toward him. This time he was slow to dodge, whether because the pain from the wound and the magic he had to divert to heal himself had slowed his reflexes or because he was too close to the ground. The fire seared along his wing.

He screamed in pain and dropped, his magic momentarily failing. He shattered through the treetops, sending boughs and splinters in every direction before hitting the ground hard and sliding. By instinct, he dug his claws in to gain traction, gouging deep trenches in the earth. A tree trunk slammed into him, finally stopping him and knocking the wind from him. He could only lay there stunned, breathing hard, bleeding and burned, while the pain nearly destroyed his ability to think.

The draegkal screeched again somewhere overhead. It was circling back, searching for him. Vorgon gathered his concentration, embraced his magic, and shifted into his human form. After the shift, the pain was staggering. All he wanted to do was curl up in a ball and lie there. But he couldn't; he had to get back to Rycard. If he failed, Rycard would never know what had happened to him. And then the hunter would come looking for him...and the Boa Visk would be waiting.

He staggered to his feet and began a loping, shambling run. The draegkal still circled overhead but would not land in the forest. He didn't know if the beast couldn't navigate the thick branches of the evergreens, or if the blood priest simply feared an ambush. Whichever it was, he was able to put distance between himself and the furious draegkal, which banked in ever-widening loops as the blood priest searched for him. But unless the priest got off that flying abomination and tracked him by his blood, Hadrak was not going to be able to find him in the trees.

Now he only had miles to trek through forest to reach

Rycard again. He prayed the man had the good sense to stay out of sight if he spotted the draegkal in the air over the valley. He prayed Rycard wouldn't—

His bare foot slid on muddy, slick pine needles and he went down, tumbling down a small rise and was finally stopped by a fallen trunk covered in bright orange mushrooms. His strength was giving out. He wouldn't be able to make it back to the canyon if he didn't do something quickly. He had to pause and finish healing himself as best he could with what little strength he had left. He closed his eyes and concentrated, but all he could see in his mind was Rycard's face. His lover's face, shining in the light of two moons, waiting for his kiss...

CHAPTER TEN

It was late. Vorgon still hadn't returned, and Rycard was growing ever more worried. The dragon had made it seem as if he'd wanted to scout the valley quickly for any sign of trouble and then come right back. But that had been this morning. Now it was late afternoon and there had been no sign of him since.

What he *had* seen, three times, was the draegkal soaring high overhead. That sent a chill straight through him. This was the first time he'd seen the beast this far west, and he counted that as an ominous sign.

When he'd first spotted the dark shape of the draegkal, he'd quickly led Redmane beneath an outcropping of rock where part of the canyon split and narrowed into a tight defile. After hobbling the horse, he'd taken Charza and headed out of the canyon, careful to stay beneath the trees on the slopes. As he headed west, he kept scanning the sky for Vorgon, but the hours passed quickly and he saw no sign of him. Even the draegkal had long since vanished from overhead, heading north over the mountains, toward the wildlands beyond the borders of Shomogar.

The shadows had grown long, and he was approaching a state of near-panic about Vorgon, when Charza suddenly broke into a sprint and vanished into the trees ahead. He called after the dog, but when Charza did not turn back, Rycard set off after him with his sword in hand.

He found Vorgon leaning against a tree trunk, naked, bloodied, his left arm a mass of pinkish-black burns. Rycard's heart lurched in his chest, and his stomach felt full of ice. Charza whined and paced around Vorgon before looking back at Rycard and barking as if demanding his master fix his new friend at once.

"Hush, little one," Vorgon said to the dog, smiling tightly. He raised his pain-filled eyes to Rycard. "This time I bit off more than even a dragon can chew."

"Gods save us." Rycard ran to him and helped support him before he fell, careful of his injuries. The moment he touched the dragon, the flash of agony he experienced staggered him. He was sharing Vorgon's pain, and that pain was immense. He spoke through gritted teeth. "What happened?"

"I'm afraid I haven't been entirely honorable," the dragon replied, his voice weak, his eyes glazed. "It shames me to admit it. I was thinking of you and what they did…"

"What are you talking about?" He glanced at Vorgon's burned arm. The charred and split flesh made him wince and his stomach turn. But the wound he was most concerned about was the gash in Vorgon's side. It was deep and tacky with his blood, but it looked as if he'd done some minimal amount of healing to it, thank the gods. "Was this the draegkal? Did you fight it?"

"Couldn't fight it," Vorgon gasped. His face was very pale, and he was trembling. His skin felt cold. That had Rycard more afraid than even the blood. The dragon had never felt cold to him before. "The blood priest bastard had a human hostage with him in the saddle. I couldn't attack without hurting her."

Rycard helped him across the uneven ground. He needed to get Vorgon inside right away. "How badly are you hurt?"

"Bastard burned me. Caught me with his claws too." His grin was nearly feral. "I can feel how worried you are. Thank you. I'm sorry about hurting you. Sharing my pain. My control has slipped. Tired and hurt…"

"Pain is nothing new to a hunter," he said. "Now let's get you home."

The trip back to the cave was harrowing and exhausting, but they made it, mostly because the dragon was tougher and stronger than anything Rycard had ever seen before. Once inside the cave, he started a fire and fed Vorgon. He cleaned the dragon's wounds and held his hand as he healed himself a little at a time using his magic. Except to tend to the dog and see to his horse, Rycard never left the dragon's side as night turned to day and day to night once more. Vorgon's heat slowly returned. Rycard began to feel some hope after Vorgon handed back his empty bowl and said in a hoarse voice, "You cook like a newborn dragon, my friend."

He brushed a strand of Vorgon's hair out of his face. "Is that good?"

"No." He coughed laughter. "It means everything is burned."

"I'm glad you're feeling well enough to make jests."

But that night he relapsed, and Rycard spent a sleepless night at his side, tending him, wiping his brow with a damp cloth, trying to keep him comfortable. Charza slept on the bed beside Vorgon. His dog would only eat after the dragon had finished his own food.

But on the third morning, Vorgon had finally

recovered enough strength to climb out of bed. Rycard hovered at his side the entire time, ready to come to his aid if he grew weak.

"Peace, Rycard," Vorgon said, amused. "I haven't been this mothered since I was a youngling."

"If you would stop taking wounds, I could stop mothering you. You bleed more often than any creature I've ever seen."

Vorgon smirked. "I thought you liked your lovers with lots of scars."

Rycard drew him into a deep kiss. He strove to put all his feelings into that kiss, his relief that the dragon was okay, the depth of his passion and tenderness, his desire, how he meant to stay by the dragon's side as long as he would have him. When he finally ended the kiss, they were both breathing heavily.

"If that is the kind of greeting I can expect, I'll have to nearly die more often." Vorgon reached out and gently touched Rycard's face, gratitude shining in his eyes. "Thank you. I caught those feelings. I don't deserve them—"

"Quiet. Now, we've been in this cave for days, and I could use some sunlight. Why don't we head outside for a while, get some fresh air. A walk will do you some good. You can finish telling me the whole story of what happened when you fought the draegkal."

Vorgon sighed. "I suppose it is long past time to tell you everything."

Rycard glanced at him, but the dragon said nothing more. Vorgon had been uncharacteristically taciturn about what had happened. Rycard could sense his deep disquiet and knew something more than a battle had happened. Something had changed. So he'd been patient, knowing the dragon would tell him in good time. He was afraid it was something to do with Shademere, perhaps the people there, and that it would be yet more bad news.

Once outside, they took a seat on the flat rocks where they had spent their incredible night under the stars, when they had made love for the first time. The moment when they'd finally allowed their passion for each other into the open. They sat next to each other, the morning sunlight shining on their faces. The sunlight felt warm on his skin, and the canyon was peaceful. He wished things could stay like this forever. There was no river here as in his dream, only a thin and winding stream, but he had his dog and his horse, and Vorgon. Perhaps that was all he ever needed.

"I love you, Rycard Serod," the dragon said suddenly.

Rycard turned to look into those golden eyes, his heart suddenly pounding as hard as if he'd fought a battle. At first he didn't know what to say, how to respond to the words that had caught him by surprise and warmed him to his core.

Then he simply decided to go with the truth. "You have owned my heart since that moment in the muddy pit when I opened my eyes to find you'd lifted my head to rest in your lap."

Vorgon settled his hands on Rycard's tunic, fisted his hands in the cloth, then drew him into a kiss. A possessive kiss. A claiming of his lips. But also to share the reality of Vorgon's feelings for him. The love. The desire. The friendship.

When he finally ended the kiss, Rycard started to smile, feeling his body already responding to the dragon's touch, but as soon as he looked into Vorgon's eyes, his smile faded. Vorgon wasn't smiling back.

"What's wrong?"

Vorgon took a deep breath. "I have something I must tell you, Rycard. I should never have waited this long. I have brought shame upon myself."

Rycard didn't reply, waiting for the dragon to go on. He assumed this had something to do with not being able to save Shademere, or perhaps with the wagon drivers the Boa Visk had executed.

"Your hunters were captured. They're being held by the blood priest in the kerrsgard camp."

Rycard staggered to his feet. "What? How did this happen?"

"The Boa Visk captured them as they tried to flee the valley. I'm not certain how it happened, but one of the hunters was killed in the fighting. I don't know who. The others are being held prisoner in the camp. I saw them when I flew to Shademere searching for them. But the Boa Visk were waiting for me. The draegkal was waiting."

Blood was pounding in his temples, roaring in his ears. "What do you mean, when you went searching for them? How long have you known this?"

"Days ago. The morning I went flying. Donnel was searching for me. He told me the shepherds saw the hunters taken."

"That night. That's when we..." His throat clamped shut, and he had to stop and force himself to take a breath. "When we made love out here. You knew my people were in danger. And you said nothing. You shielded your thoughts from me."

"They abandoned you, Rycard." His golden eyes were filled with pain and grief. He reached out a hand toward him, but Rycard moved out of the way. He didn't want to be touched right now. The dragon might be able to shield his thoughts, but Rycard could not. The dragon would be able to sense his hurt, his confusion, his utter dismay. How could Vorgon have kept this from him? How could he betray him like this and still claim to love him?

"I told you, they were scared," Rycard replied, his voice unsteady and cold. "You wanted them to fight a war at your side, but they're only hunters. Fighting the Boa Visk is utter madness."

"They left the wagon drivers to their fate," Vorgon countered, his tone hardening. "They forced you to try and save those men alone. And when you found out what happened to your men, it nearly broke you. I couldn't let that happen again."

"The blame for that is on me! I was the one who brought them all here. *I* was the one desperate for gold to keep the Splitchain Hunters going. To escape from Shomogar. To keep them fed until I could hand over the reins and retire from a life constantly on the hunt. This was to be my escape, but I failed them. So I would never blame them for leaving me to deal with my own mess. It will always be my duty to try and save them, even now."

"I blame them!" Vorgon roared. "You had the honor to do the impossible, no matter the cost. But they were cowards! They took the freedom I gave them and they *ran*. You at least stayed behind to save your two men."

"You don't have the right to judge them." He took another step backward. His thoughts spun in his mind as if caught in a whirlpool. His hands were shaking. "You and your talk of mercy and forgiveness. I thought you were better than me. You said you loved me."

"Rycard, I'm so very, very sorry. I know I was wrong to keep it from you. I went to free them, but the Boa Visk were only using them as bait. They will use you as bait against me if they can." He shook his head, anguish on his face. "I could not risk you again. We both know how close you came to death when you tried to save the wagon drivers. The more you mean to me, the more I fear that next time you will fall."

"It's not your choice to make. I have obligations. I can never turn my back on my people. They could turn their backs on me a thousand times, but the moment they need me, I must be there for them. They've earned that much and more. That's what it means to lead. To always be there for those who count on you, no matter what."

A silence spread between them when he finished speaking. He could hear the same wind in the trees, the same trickle of water on stones, and yet it was completely different, because in an instant, everything had changed.

"What will you do?" Vorgon's voice was so quiet that he barely caught it.

"I must save them. However I can."

"I feared this, Rycard. I knew—"

"I have no choice. I can't leave them. Will you come with me? Maybe together…"

"I can't fight them. They're using the townsfolk as shields to protect themselves and all their weapons from my fire. And they have the draegkal. They are waiting for us, Rycard. That's why they're keeping your friends alive. You go, and perhaps they'll kill you, but more likely they'll only torture you to get to me. I'm the one they want. The dragon. You forced me to surrender to save a shepherd boy. Don't you think for an instant I wouldn't do the same to save you."

Rycard stepped past him, careful not to touch him. He didn't want to feel the torment clearly written on Vorgon's face. He didn't want to endure the dark pain in his golden eyes.

He had more than enough of each on his own.

"I need my sword," he said.

He walked away with Charza silent at his side. He thought Vorgon might call him back, but he did not.

As he left, he sent a thought to the dragon, even though they were not touching, and the dragon could not hear him. The anger and hurt had burned away, leaving only a horrible feeling of emptiness and sorrow. *Thank you for showing me the joy of soaring high. I loved you, my friend.*

He couldn't say it aloud, but he said it in his heart.

* * *

Vorgon knew he had failed.

He had believed he was doing the right thing when he'd kept the fate of Rycard's comrades from him. He'd believed he was doing the right thing by trying to free them on his own. Last of all, he'd believed he was doing the right thing when he'd finally told Rycard the truth.

It had all been wrong.

The hurt in his lover's eyes had gutted him. The anguish on Rycard's face at his betrayal had nearly driven Vorgon to his knees. He'd been afraid of exactly this, of losing something so precious to him, all because Rycard's need to protect his people would force him to do something utterly mad. He knew the man. Understood him. He was as predictable as the monsoons.

Under no moon or sun would he allow Rycard to face the Boa Visk alone. Even if the man never spoke to him again, Vorgon would fight by his side—and die by his side. Because that's where this was going to end.

Rycard had stayed by his side throughout the long and difficult healing process when Vorgon's magic seemed to constantly fail him. The wounds inflicted by the draegkal had been different somehow...poisoned or tainted in a way that worked against his powers to heal. The corruption had drained him, turning something that should have been simple into a grueling ordeal. It seemed as though the draegkal and its twisted, foul magic had been designed to do just that—inflict wounds that were almost impossible to heal. Yet even though it had taken him days of exhausting struggle to recover, Rycard had been there for him in every way.

And this was how Vorgon repaid him.

Whatever else might come, he had to make this right. He would not allow Rycard to sacrifice himself. He would save the hunters. And he would kill that filthy, damned draegkal right before he destroyed the demented blood priest who'd created it.

Rycard had set off on his horse, riding eastward toward Shademere with Charza at his side. It would take him the better part of a day to reach the town. Time was short, but he prayed Rycard would not ride through the forest. That would make it harder for Vorgon to spot him from the sky. And Vorgon needed to be able to find him in order to pull off his mad, desperate plan. The plan he had no choice but to set in motion.

He took to the air. Soon he was up high enough to see a wide swath of the meadows and fields of the valley. Rycard's horse had left a trail through the tall grass. He followed the path of bent grass stalks and finally spotted Rycard riding near the foothills of the Eddrassa Mountains.

Vorgon had been raised during the wars with the Boa Visk, so it was nothing at all for him to dive with the sun at his back and pluck Rycard out of the saddle.

As Vorgon's claws settled around him, Rycard's shock and fear flashed into his mind, making him feel as if he'd plunged into a frozen river. The hunter thought he was being grabbed by the draegkal until Vorgon sent him a flood of calming thoughts so he'd know who held him.

Rycard's sharp thought cut across their link, his anger glowing like coals. *"Don't try and soothe me, dragon. How dare you—"*

"Sometimes it is good to know a dragon. Sometimes it is not so good. Now don't wriggle around. I don't want to drop you."

"Put me down!"

"No."

"But Charza and Redmane! I can't leave them alone."

Vorgon felt a wave of pure and simple love for the man. Carried off by a dragon and he was worried about his animals. *"You're a good man, Rycard Serod. I should have told you that before. Your dog is upset, but they will both be fine."*

He could sense the confused swirl of the other man's emotions. Pleasure at the compliment. Consternation that he was being carried through the air, up the slopes of the mountain, like a stolen sheep.

"Where are you taking me?"

"Somewhere we can talk and you can't walk away."

He flew Rycard all the way up to the top of Iolan Peak and set the man down on a snow-covered rock. Then he settled in beside him. The snow started to melt beneath him, gradually turning to slush, but he didn't intend to stay here for long. He had a few things to say, and the stubborn man was going to damn well listen.

Rycard crossed his arms, his breath coming out in white clouds. "What do you want, Vorgon? I won't be dissuaded."

"No. You won't. And that's why I'm here to help you."

"This isn't your fight. They aren't your people."

"It *is* my fight. It was my fight long before you came here. It's also true they aren't my people. But they are important to you, so they are important to me."

He changed back into his human form. He wanted to face his lover man to man. The internal furnace of his magic would keep him warm even without clothes. It spoke of how angry the man sitting beside him was that he didn't even bother to admire Vorgon's naked body as he approached him and took his hand, gripped it hard.

"You are brave, Rycard. And I want nothing more

than to destroy these Boa Visk forever. But I've come to realize that we cannot do this on our own. We need the help of the people we're trying to protect. And they want to help us, if we will lead."

Rycard narrowed his eyes but didn't draw his hand away. That was a good sign. "What do you mean?"

"You'll see. If you will delay only a little while, I have a plan. It will be very dangerous, but perhaps we can restore some pride to the people here."

"I don't relish the idea of waiting. It has been days since they were captured." He clenched his jaw. "They could all be dead by now."

"They were alive when I saw them last. The blood priest wants me. That's all he cares about. A dragon he can use in his dark transformations, creating new abominations with my blood. Making more draegkal. Or something even worse."

Rycard held his gaze for a long moment. Then he snorted in disgust before his mouth curved in the slightest of smiles. "I'm going to trust you, Vorgon." He shook his head and blew on his hands to warm them. "You picked a bloody cold place to discuss it though."

Vorgon pulled him into a fierce kiss. He loved the feel of the other man in his arms. The hunter's lips were soft and cool, and when he deepened the kiss, Rycard responded in kind. This time he didn't shield his thoughts. He let Rycard feel every single one of them, hoping it would be one step toward rebuilding their broken trust.

When Vorgon finally ended the kiss, he didn't draw away. Instead he kept his forehead pressed against Rycard's so he could look him straight in the eye. He didn't want his lover to have any doubts whatsoever.

"I'm sorry I kept something so important from you. Will you forgive me?"

"As you said, you did it to protect me. I believe that in my heart. Besides, how could I not forgive you? You forgave me for hunting you down, taking you prisoner to sell to the Boa Visk, and nearly getting you killed. And how can I not love you back with all my heart? I am yours."

Vorgon's heart soared. "I meant it when I said I loved you, Rycard Serod. You are unlike any man I've ever known. I am proud to stand by your side."

They kissed again, slower this time. A tender kiss, one that spoke of their deepening feelings in a perfect ardent touch. Rycard raised a hand and laid it on his cheek, his fingers roughened with calluses from his lifetime of work. Vorgon never wanted it to end.

But after a moment, Rycard finally pulled away. "So tell me of your plan."

CHAPTER ELEVEN

"Hadrak Carn!" the dragon beneath Rycard bellowed toward the Boa Visk camp. He and Vorgon stood together in a burning field in the midst of smoke and fire, Rycard mounted upon the dragon's back. The vibrations of Vorgon's roar shook through his body. "Face me, blood priest! Face me, *coward*!"

Vorgon spit another stream of flame. Rycard had to turn his face away from the backwash of incredible heat. In the distance, he could barely see Shademere and the kerrsgard encampment through the heat shimmer and billowing smoke. The kerrsgard soldiers were frantically taking positions around the encampment and dragging their siege weapons into position. Their archers loosed a slew of arrows at them, all of which fell short. The remaining rendlich riders were forming up for a charge, but were holding back for now. The wind blew the smoke from the fires Vorgon had started toward the camp, right into the faces of the Boa Visk.

Two long and difficult days had passed since he'd learned the Boa Visk had captured his hunters. Despite the fear constantly eating at him, he'd honored his promise and helped Vorgon set this desperate plan in motion. Now, finally taking action had driven off the last of his fear. All that was left was the clarity of a hunter lining up the perfect strike to bring down the monster.

He tightened his grip on his bow, a war gift from the shepherds. He was tied onto Vorgon's back with a cartload of makeshift straps and rope. Ugly but effective. He needed both hands free to serve as Vorgon's dragonrider, and they had no saddle for a dragon and no time to construct one.

"Are you ready, hunter?" Vorgon's thought burst into his mind, warm and resonant with the comforting familiarity of the dragon, but spiked with undercurrents of battle fury and dark excitement. Hatred of the Boa Visk. Rage. It was so at odds with the kind, noble Vorgon, who'd made such sweet, tender love to him the night before. The power of him, the controlled fury, made Rycard shiver with awe.

He pulled the signal arrow from his quiver. *"I am*

ready."

Vorgon curved his long neck enough to look at Rycard with one beautiful golden eye. *"I love you, my dragonrider."*

He grasped the signal arrow in his bow hand and placed the other against the smooth blue and white scales of Vorgon's neck, so warm and thrumming with powerful magic against his palm. He concentrated, willing the dragon to know the depth of his feelings and the warmth of his love. Then he finished the flood of emotions with a simple and true thought. *"I don't have the words, my friend."*

"I don't need words to know your heart."

A rending screech split the air, pulling Rycard's gaze to the center of the camp and sending a surge of adrenaline through his veins. The draegkal rose through the clouds of drifting smoke, its wings furiously beating the air. On its back rode the blood priest, his hideous mask glinting in the sun.

Rycard glanced at the full quiver mounted at his thigh, then steadied the signal arrow and nocked it against the string. He wasn't as good a shot as either Deacon or Brockon, but he'd been using a bow since he was a lad. Firing from the back of a flying dragon, though, would be a new challenge. Luckily, this first arrow didn't have to hit anything. It only had to fly high and far.

Vorgon let out another vicious dragon roar, his body

vibrating beneath Rycard's legs, and launched himself into the air, his powerful wings driving him upward. Once they were airborne, Vorgon banked and turned them toward the town center. He lifted his head and breathed a stream of fire into the air. Rycard drew back the arrow and shot it high in an arc, sending the shaft, wrapped in oil-soaked cloth, through the edge of the flames. As the shaft skimmed past the dragonfire, the cloth burst into flame and arced through the sky, trailing a tail of black smoke. That was the signal to set their plan in action.

Almost immediately, a commotion broke out inside the kerrsgard camp. Arrows and stones began flying from all directions, piercing kovohl mages in the back, striking down Boa Visk commanders before they could issue orders, raining down upon foot soldiers who broke ranks in confusion, searching for the source of the attack.

The kerrsgard had assembled with all their forces deployed to face Vorgon in the field outside the camp, but this attack came from within their lines. As they dragged slaves and townsfolk into their ranks for protection, the humans began fighting back with hidden weapons. The sheep suddenly changed into wolves and turned against their startled captors. Confusion spread as fires set by the townsfolk flared to life inside the encampment. Arrows falling among the rendlich startled them into breaking formation and stampeding out of control.

"They're doing it," he thought to the dragon, watching as the shepherds who'd infiltrated the town took full advantage of the confusion, attacking from all sides with bows and slings and freeing the human slaves that the Boa Visk had bound to the weapons and tents as shields.

"Now let's help them!" came Vorgon's return thought on a wave of battle euphoria.

Vorgon's plan had been to take the herders up on their promise of assistance and ask for help freeing Shademere from the Boa Visk. It was not something the dragon had done lightly, for they all knew the cost would be high. Yet, the shepherds had agreed to his plan. All yesterday they had infiltrated Shademere, bringing in wool in wagons as if to sell at market, all the while hiding weapons in the sacks. They gathered the remaining townsfolk who were willing to fight, no matter the sacrifice, and awaited their signal.

Vorgon flew toward the camp at such speed that Rycard's stomach felt as though he'd left it a hundred meters behind him. The dragon shot straight for the draegkal, churning the smoke that rose over the crackling fires.

The draegkal spread its wings, checking its forward flight and lifting its claws to face Vorgon. The blood priest clung to the saddle with one arm, his other arm wrapped around the slave woman seated before him as a shield. The draegkal shot a blast of green fire that Vorgon dodged, juking so hard to the right that Rycard had to grit his teeth against the force that yanked him in the other direction.

Vorgon's return stream of fire forced the draegkal to dive to avoid having its head scorched. Vorgon immediately dove after him. They flew low over the lines of kerrsgard who were beginning to recover from the surprise attack by the humans.

As he pursued the draegkal, Vorgon breathed a long stream of fire along the ranks of kerrsgard, scattering soldiers and burning the rendlich riders who had managed to form up again. His flames sent the beasts charging wildly through the ranks once again, some of them like moving bonfires that spread chaos and flames in their wake. The sharpened stakes driven into the ground around the perimeter caught fire, and smoke billowed into the air in great black clouds.

Rycard nocked another arrow and shot at the draegkal's wing as they pursued it. He missed. He drew again and fired, but Vorgon was veering hard to stay on the tail of the draegkal, and he missed again. He cursed and reached for yet another shaft.

The blood priest turned in the saddle and looked at them from behind that grotesque mask. He moved his hands in an elaborate gesture, and a black, swirling mist gathered around him, coalescing around the hand he raised toward them. With one smooth motion, Rycard drew and released an arrow. Its shaft ripped through the thin black miasma. The monster let out an ear-piercing shriek and banked hard. The sudden, jarring movement from his mount threw off the blood priest's concentration. He lost control of his spell and the black mist trailed away with the spell uncast.

Vorgon flew faster, his big wings pumping, driving them through the air at breath-taking speeds until he was right on top of the draegkal. Before the monster had a chance to veer away, Rycard sighted in with his bow. Right at the center of the blood priest's back.

The blood priest yelled some command to the draegkal, which spun in a tight circle and hovered in the air, facing them with is wide distorted jaws open and seeping small tongues of flame. The blood priest's grotesque, black lacquer mask grinned insanely, the golden mesh of the eye sockets gleaming in the sunlight as he began motioning his hands for another spell. Rycard suddenly found his sight aimed directly at the face of the terrified slave woman the priest was using as a shield.

He drew away. The woman met his gaze with wide, pleading eyes as she clutched desperately at the saddle in front of her, having no bindings holding her in like the blood priest. She was young, just a girl barely into her teens. Just a child. Rycard let out a frustrated curse. He wasn't a good enough shot to hit the blood priest over the girl's shoulder, if he could hit him at all.

Then she made a gesture of blessing, her hands circling her head, her lips, her heart, and then, absurdly, mimed the shooting of an arrow.

It took Rycard a moment to process. Then she threw herself forward over the draegkal's neck.

Rycard didn't hesitate, didn't think, he just sighted the blood priest and drew as another black miasma of magic circled the blood priest's hand. He let the arrow fly. As soon as the shaft left the bowstring humming before him, he knew he had shot true.

Just as the blood priest thrust his hand forward to release his spell, the arrow punched directly through the mask's gold-mesh eye-socket. The blood priest fell backward over the draegkal's hindquarters, kept in the saddle only by the straps around his legs.

"Got him!" he thought to Vorgon in purest glee.

Vorgon's surge of triumph was his only reply. The dragon immediately tucked his wings and plunged after the draegkal as it dove to evade them. Vorgon slammed into the back of the monster, digging his claws into its wing and its saddle and drawing out a terrified screech from the creature. Vorgon thrummed his wings heavily for balance as he drew the monster in close with his powerful claws. Rycard slipped the bow over his shoulders and lunged forward, grabbing for the frightened girl still in the saddle. He strained against the straps holding him and wrapped his hands around each of her arms. She launched herself at him and threw her arms around his neck so tightly he could barely breathe, let alone see where they were going.

"Got her!" he thought to the dragon the instant he felt her legs leave the saddle.

Vorgon roared and shoved away from the screeching draegkal. Rycard tried to pull the woman onto Vorgon's back in front of him, but she was clutching him so tightly he couldn't quite move her. She seemed to realize what he wanted, and a moment later, she swung her leg over Vorgon's neck and sat facing him in an awkward embrace. Rycard gave a bark of relieved laughter at her bravery, and wrapped his arms around her more tightly as she took a cautious glance over his shoulder to gaze down at the view below. He drew her close against him as Vorgon twisted in midair and dropped to the ground like a diving bird of prey, pulling a scream that was part terror, part delight, from the girl.

Rycard looked down at the direction of Vorgon's dive. Below them, the ground was coming up to meet them fast. Smoke rose around them everywhere, choking him. The noise of battle was loud and constant, screams and clashing weapons, curses and shouts, crackling fire, the terrified roaring of the rendlich, and off in the distance, the horrible screech of the draegkal.

"Free your friends!" Vorgon's thought roared in his mind.

It took Rycard a moment to spot his hunters through the smoke and confusion. They were bound to poles in the clearing where he'd first seen the draegkal what seemed like ages ago.

Vorgon spread his wings wide at the last moment, slowing and turning upward, then slamming down on his rear legs in the middle of the encampment. The shock rattled Rycard's teeth and sent the girl's head slamming up into his chin.

Rycard didn't need to be told twice. He put his hands on the girl's waist and lifted her off Vorgon's back, but she tightened her hold on his neck and squeezed.

"Thank you, dragonrider," she said in a soft soprano. Then she looked up at him with a doe-eyed smile and planted a kiss on his cheek. She swung her leg over Vorgon's neck like some kind of backward dismount from a horse and leaped down, landing nimbly on her feet with one hand to the ground to steady herself. Then she glanced up at him once more and ran off, disappearing into the smoky battlefield.

Rycard felt his heart swell with the satisfaction of a life saved. But he couldn't let himself dwell on it. He drew his knife to slash at the ropes and straps holding him atop Vorgon. Finally free, he vaulted off the dragon's back, hit the ground, and came up with his knife ready.

Wordlessly, Vorgon took off again after the draegkal who was fleeing in panic with the dead blood priest still dangling in the saddle on its back. Rycard tore his gaze from the sky and ran.

He sprinted across the smoky field toward the spot where his hunters stood bound to their posts. He dodged the bodies of dead shepherds and townsfolk and more than a few fallen Boa Visk. The sight of the dead shepherds grieved him, but he didn't have time to indulge in those emotions now. Dezarie, Gansen, Brockon, and Deacon were there, bloodied and beaten but alive. Yero was not. Rycard felt his heart break for the small, dark spearman. He reached his hunters, who all began crying out to him at once.

"Rycard! You're alive!" Dezarie shouted.

He felt a wave of relief, joy, amazement at seeing his company, hearing their familiar voices over the din of the battle around them. He reached Deacon and cut the archer loose first, pulling his bow and quiver off and tossing them into the archer's outstretched grip. Deacon had the first arrow nocked and loosed and planted in the chest of a Boa

Visk spearman before Rycard had Dezarie freed.

She threw her arms around him and hugged him. "I'm so glad to see you," she said, not wasting any more time before turning to search the fallen around her for weapons. She came up with a dagger and began to cut Gansen loose, just as Rycard was slipping the ropes from Brockon.

He drew his sword. "Find weapons!" he yelled. "We're fighting until this town is free!"

Gansen rubbed at the rope burns on his wrists and gave Rycard a look that was half shame, half relief. "Rycard, I—"

Rycard cut him off. "Go find a weapon. Move."

Gansen trotted off to retrieve one of the dead Boa Visk of his long black carska spear. Brockon had picked up a bow and an ugly black Boa Visk quiver and was standing beside Deacon, firing toward a ragtag line of Boa Visk spearmen. Two humans, a townsman and a shepherd, stepped up beside them to join their rank, the townsman with a bow of his own, the shepherd with a sling and a sack of rocks around his shoulder. One of the Boa Visk took an arrow to the gut, the other half dozen turned and ran.

"Dezarie, Gansen, with me." Rycard led them toward a charred but still functional ballista whose crew was struggling to load a deadly looking bolt to shoot at Vorgon.

Rycard fell on them with his sword slashing, striking

cobra fast, and taking down three of the ballista crew in the time that Dezarie and Gansen got the other two. He felt the familiar rush of excitement, standing there side by side with his hunters, killing things that should never walk the earth.

The Boa Visk had hired him for a monster hunt, and he was going to give them one. Even if he did it for free.

* * *

Vorgon circled around hard, breathing fire at one of the guard towers and engulfing it as he chased the draegkal. The blood priest was still strapped to the saddle, flopping this way and that as the draegkal dodged and wheeled and dove to avoid Vorgon's fire. The draegkal was hurt too, but it was far from beaten. Twice it had nearly seared Vorgon with its fiery breath.

Whenever his pursuit of the draegkal took him close to the ground, Vorgon attacked the Boa Visk with flame. Most of the humans they were using as shields had been freed, and the slaves had fled in all directions. The death of the blood priest seemed to have left the kerrsgard in temporary confusion. But there were still far, far more kerrsgard than humans down below.

The draegkal sensed his pursuit. It veered around and came at him again, shattering the air with its discordant shriek and spitting fire. Vorgon twisted into a spiral, avoiding the stream of green flames. The draegkal overextended itself and was too slow recovering from its attack. Vorgon saw his opening. He drew all his power, all the energy of his magic, and opened up with a torrent of flames. The stream of brilliant fire struck the draegkal in the head. Vorgon's fire was so intense it incinerated the draegkal's black scales, burning deep into its flesh. He summoned currents of air to fan the flames to temperatures that had Vorgon wheeling quickly away to avoid being scorched. The draegkal's head went from fire to glowing coals to ash in moments, then the creature's headless body plummeted to the ground and smashed onto an earthen embankment bristling with sharpened wooden spikes that punched through its dark corpse.

A wave of elation drove Vorgon to roar so loud that the troops on the ground all stopped and looked upward in dread. He shot a column of fire straight into the air. The abomination was dead, and with it the hideous blood priest, and with them both the threat to the dragonkin on the Isle of Rasella was ended. At least for now. Vorgon had no idea if they'd created any more of the hideous creatures elsewhere, but he prayed to the gods they had not.

He wheeled back, stoking his inner fires once more. He could not revel in his victory yet. The kerrsgard had regrouped and were driving back the lightly armed humans.

Not for long.

He roared again as he flew low, appearing through the smoke, scorching the kerrsgard and bathing their battle lines in fire. They screamed as his flames consumed them. Their lines broke. Those few who had survived the fighting and the fires turned and fled their encampment, running into the fields, leaping into the trenches, fleeing his shadow. He let them go, for now, because he needed to find Rycard. He needed to know he was safe.

He circled the encampment, desperately searching for the man he loved. He took out a half-charred ballista, surrounded by a group of dead Boa Visk. No sense leaving that in one piece. His heart ached at the sight of so many fallen humans. At all the fire and smoke, collapsed and burning tents, the widespread destruction.

But the bodies that littered the ground were not all human. The dead Boa Visk, and their kerrsgard, outnumbered the humans ten to one, twenty to one.

Vorgon soared over the camp and then over the center of the town where the burned-out stronghold was smoldering once more. The sight below made his heart sing again. The humans held the camp and the town. The fighting seemed to be over. Below him, people where scurrying about, but not fighting, not scared. They were leaping about, shaking their weapons in the air in victory. He swooped lower. Their faces were those of the vanquishing army, not the vanquished.

They'd routed the Boa Visk. Gods above him, they'd done it. They'd all done it.

He roared again in triumph. But it didn't feel complete. He still could not find Rycard.

The men and women were already starting a human chain to haul water from the river to help quench the fires. A sense of dread began to creep up on him again, forming in the pit of his being. He soared closer to the ground, scanning each face that stopped to look up at him. He found two more Boa Visk hiding outside the town who had somehow avoided the flames. He incinerated them, even as his sense of panic grew. No Rycard.

He spotted two of Rycard's archers in the line of people collecting weapons from the dead Boa Visk on the battlefield and loading them into a cart. He landed gently beside them.

The humans turned to him, pausing in their work to begin a litany of thanks for his efforts in securing their town.

He bowed his head briefly to them, but he couldn't appreciate their thanks or their sense of victory while terrified that Rycard's body could be lying on the battlefield somewhere, dead.

"Have you seen Rycard?" he asked the archers.

They gave him the same looks of relief and excitement that the townspeople had.

"I think he, Dezarie, and Gansen were off by the kerrsgard camp," the quiet one with the shaved head said to him.

"Last I saw, they were hacking up a bunch of Boa Visk," the other, Brockon, said.

Vorgon nodded his thanks and opened his wings to take off.

"Wait," Brockon said.

Vorgon folded his wings and turned to him.

The man was looking at him with an expression of remorse almost as tight and dark as the feeling in Vorgon's heart. "I owe you an apology. Rycard too. We never should have left."

"This isn't the time," Vorgon said. He knew in his higher nature that he should forgive this man. Hadn't he given Rycard a lecture on the merits of forgiveness, and Donnel too? But after seeing Rycard so distraught, and after all the chain of events that led them to this moment, it was hard to take his own advice. Especially now, when the only thing he wanted to feel was the relief of seeing Rycard alive and well. "There will be time for righting wrongs after I find Rycard."

Footsteps approached him from behind. "What wrongs are you looking to right?"

Vorgon turned. Rycard, Dezarie, and Gansen were trudging up the field, battered, bloody, and edged with soot from the smoky field.

Pure relief swept through him at the sight of his lover. Rycard smiled at him, and the look of joy on the man's face lifted Vorgon's soul higher than he could ever hope to fly. Rycard tossed aside his weapons and ran to him, his harsh, hardened warrior grinning and laughing like a lunatic.

He shifted back into human form. He needed to hold the man he loved. Hold him, and maybe never let him go again. Vorgon threw himself into Rycard's arms, covering his face with eager kisses.

The smoke did not matter to him. The victory was forgotten. The only thing that mattered was that the man in his arms was safe and this was finally over.

"Dragon! Dragon!"

Vorgon looked down at the blur of motion racing toward him. Before he could react, a set of small arms in shepherd's robes threw themselves around his and Rycard's bodies.

"You saved us! I knew you would! And the hunters too!"

Vorgon looked down at the shaggy head that tipped back and smiled up at him.

"Donnel!" Vorgon felt his temper soar. "What in the name of the gods are you doing out here? Weldon clearly told you to stay back at your camp with the other children!"

"And miss the war? It was amazing! You burned all those Boa Visk bastards to charcoal!"

"Donnel!"

"What? You did! And that flying monster, too. You're heroes!"

Rycard snorted with laughter. Vorgon turned to glare at him, and Rycard cleared his throat and forced his face to resume its harsh countenance. "Right. You should always obey your elders."

Donnel smiled up at him. "I will, I promise." He turned his face back to Vorgon and nearly danced with excitement. "Can you take me flying now? *Pleeeeease*?"

Vorgon gave him a stern look. "Are you kidding? After you disobeyed us all? *Again*?"

Rycard gave him a nudge in the side. "Come on, what was he supposed to do, miss the war?"

"Yay!" Donnel cheered.

Vorgon turned to Rycard and glared at him. "You will pay for this. Later." And he stole one more lingering kiss from the human he loved before stepping out of the way of the crowd and shifting.

* * *

Rycard sat in the tavern below the inn where they'd first set up their wagons after arriving in Shademere. He had a tankard of ale in one hand. His other hand rested lightly on Vorgon's legs, which were crossed at the ankles and in Rycard's lap. Charza sat beside his chair, his muzzle resting on his foot. They sat at the fireside, the tavern bursting at the seams around them, filled with the noisy laughter of townspeople and shepherds getting drunk on Boa Visk ale and taking second and third helpings of the kerrsgard's supply of sidon, which the shepherds were roasting over spits outside. The part of town where the inn stood had managed to avoid the greater part of the fighting. So once the fires were out, the inn became the center of the victory feast and celebration.

"I was thinking about your cabin by the river," Vorgon thought to him.

"And?"

"I know of a pretty little clearing, near a stream. Not quite a river, but the water's clear. Good grazing for Redmane, and Charza likes chasing the little ground mice. And I hear the neighbor is nice."

"Neighbor? I was hoping to find a place with some solitude."

"Oh, there's solitude, all right."

"This sounds familiar," he thought to his dragon, unable to hide his smile. *"If I remember correctly, it's a little isolated. There aren't any stairs, just a rope ladder. Cozy though."*

"So you are interested?"

"I wouldn't be anywhere else in the world, my friend."

"What's the matter with you two?" Dezarie asked. "You look like you're hearing voices or something."

"It is noisy enough in here without voices inside my head," Rycard said, ducking the question as he glanced at the four hunters seated with them near the fireplace.

Dezarie and Deacon, Brockon and Gansen. They'd all had their fill of roasted sidon, and Brockon was already starting yawn where he sat with the comforting heat of the fire washing against them. Rycard felt a bittersweet happiness that they'd rescued his last four hunters, but a sadness at the loss of the rest. So much sacrifice. From his people, from the shepherds and townsfolk. He wished the price had not been so high.

"We honor their sacrifices by living and loving." Vorgon's thought was warm but tinged with sorrow for the fallen. *"We remember them and hold them in our hearts. That is all we can do."*

He cocked an eyebrow at the other man. *"Do you ever grow weary of being right?"*

Vorgon only laughed.

Charza lifted his head and licked at his hand. Rycard set his tankard down and rewarded his loyal dog with all the petting he deserved. His spirits lifted, thanks to Vorgon and Charza. He was so lucky to have them in his life.

Dezarie glanced between them again suspiciously. Her puzzled from told him she definitely suspected something was going on. "Did I tell you we found the wagons?"

Rycard stole a sip of ale before answering. The firelight painted Dezarie's face with its orange, flickering glow. A fat pink line ran down the side of her cheek where she'd taken a cut from a Boa Visk spear. Vorgon had healed the cut and cleansed the poison. The scar didn't mar her beauty at all. "You didn't. Where were they?"

"In the old mine shafts in the foothills that the Boa Visk garrison used for storage."

"That's wonderful. Were all the supplies intact?"

"No. They'd looted everything. But it doesn't matter. I don't think we'll need them."

Her words caught him off guard. "What do you mean?"

Before she replied, Gansen interrupted with a heavy sigh. "Rycard, I'm sorry."

Rycard turned to the burly man seated across from him. He'd said hardly anything all evening, which was nothing at all like him. His face was drawn, his eyes held a haunted look.

"I shouldn't have left you back at the gorge," Gansen said, leaning forward. "It was foolish. I was a coward. A stupid, arrogant coward, thinking I had all the answers. I was more wrong than I can ever say."

Rycard glanced at the faces around him. They all seemed to echo the sentiment, with furrowed brows and downward glances.

Vorgon broke the silence first. "I think we all did things over the last few days that we regret. But when the hour came, we stood together."

Rycard gave him a wry smile. "I believe that's an understatement."

"But not like me," Gansen said. "The Boa Visk captured us because of me. Yero's dead because of me."

Dezarie put a consoling hand on his arm. "The Boa

Visk would have caught us regardless."

Gansen shook his head and turned to Rycard. "We were headed down the road and Yero decided he didn't want to come with us. He tried to talk me into going back. To going into Shademere to find Urson and Salcan with you. We argued. Instead of keeping quiet and trying to evade the Boa Visk, I shouted at him. I led them right to us. Yero took the first arrow."

"Dezarie's right," Deacon said. "They would have caught us anyway. Shouting or no, they had found us."

"But maybe they wouldn't have!"

"Gansen," Rycard said. He understood exactly what the man was feeling. "Peace. We all made mistakes these last days. The gods know I made more than my share. Yero was our friend. His brave spirit forgives you, if there's anything to forgive."

Gansen closed his eyes and rubbed at the bridge of his nose. His voice was choked with emotion. "Yero's blood is on my hands."

Rycard reached out and grabbed the man's other hand, squeezing it reassuringly. "Enough, my friend. It's on the Boa Visk. They were the ones doing the killing."

Vorgon took another sip of his ale. His voice held both wisdom and empathy. "This is the burden of leadership. Those in your charge don't always live. Remember him always, but allow yourself to be forgiven."

"Well, I've had enough of leadership," Gansen said. "I ask *you* to forgive me, Rycard. And I want you to know that I'll move on and be on my way in the morning."

"You're not going anywhere, Gansen," Dezarie said. "We talked about this. We're staying. And you're staying with us."

Rycard wasn't sure he'd heard her correctly. "You're staying?"

She favored him with a wistful smile. "We all know it's too late in the season to try to ride for the winter camp. So, given the state of things in Shademere, Deacon came up with the idea that we could spend the winter here. The people are going to have a lot of work to do rebuilding the place, repairing the damage. The last crops are in the fields and they weren't all destroyed. They can't bring them in all by themselves and build new homes as well. So we figured we'd help out. There will be plenty of work to be done."

"And we can train the people how to use the weapons the Boa Visk left all over the place," Brockon added. "Once we clean them, that is."

Vorgon sat forward in his chair, his golden eyes narrowing. "You mean to train the people to be an army."

Brockon snorted with derision. "We don't have the first idea how to be an army. We kill monsters. But we sure as hell know how to use swords and spears and bows." He shrugged. "It wouldn't be enough on its own, but with a dragon around..."

Vorgon turned to Rycard. "It might be necessary. The passes will be blocked in winter, but come spring..."

Gansen was about to speak again when Dezarie wheeled on him with an expression so fierce that Rycard sat back in his chair. "If say so much as one word, you big oaf, I'll cut you."

Gansen gave her a reluctant smile. "Jeez, woman. All right. Calm yourself."

"Don't tell me to calm myself."

Gansen rolled his eyes. "Damn shrewish woman." Then to the rest of the party, "I'm going to get another ale." But Rycard didn't miss the hand he trailed over Dezarie's shoulder as he rose and headed for the bar.

Rycard looked around at his hunters. It was selfish, but he wanted them to stay. And the idea of training the townsfolk in how to use the huge cache of weapons might go a long way to ensure that they could hold their own against attacks by the Boa Visk. Well, with a dragon on their side at least.

Vorgon took his legs from Rycard's lap and moved his chair closer. He took Rycard's face in his hands and looked at him gravely. "You realize this means it's over. We've won.

All of us. Your hunters. The people of the valley. Us. With weapons and warriors and help rebuilding the houses and bringing in the crops, and all this damned sidon, the people here are safe. I believe with winter coming and snows sealing the mountain passes, the Boa Visk won't be able to get another foothold in this valley."

"Certainly not with a dragon around."

Vorgon placed a soft kiss on his lips. "Maybe more than that."

Rycard pulled back to stare into Vorgon's beautiful golden eyes, as enigmatic as ever, this time clearly holding secrets. "What is it?"

"I've decided to take your advice."

Rycard looked up at him suspiciously. "What advice was that?"

"I'm going to return to Rasella."

Rycard's heart leaped into his throat and he suddenly felt cold, despite the fire in the hearth. "No, you can't. Not when everything's going so well here. I... I don't want to be without you."

Vorgon looked at him strangely. "Well, I'm not planning to go without you. You were right. We need to convince dragonkin to fight for their home. The time for hiding is over. Anzin needs us. And even if they don't agree, we need to at least warn them of the draegkal."

Rycard smiled at him, his heart still pounding hard. "You'll take me with you to the floating citadel?"

"You don't think I'd leave you here, do you? We'll even bring Charza."

Rycard planted a kiss on Vorgon's lips. *"You wouldn't get three feet in the air before I dragged you back."*

"Think we can get three feet toward the door before your hunters realize we're gone?"

"If we're quiet."

Rycard stood and took a soft step toward the door. Charza scrambled to his feet, tongue out, his tail wagging happily and thumping against the side of the chair, attracting everyone's attention. So much for a quiet getaway.

Dezarie glanced at them both, her mouth curved in a knowing smile. "Headed out?"

Vorgon slipped an arm around Rycard's shoulders. "Yes. I wish to say one final prayer at Timval's grave." He looked into Rycard's eyes, the kindness and love there warming him from the heart outward. "And then we'll go home."

Rycard caught her eye, then looked at Brockon and Deacon. "Will you be okay?"

Deacon only raised his tankard in a silent salute. Brockon took Rycard's place closer to the fire and stretched. Dezarie leaned back in her seat, glanced at Gansen, then met his gaze once again. "I think we will be."

Charza led the way to the door, tail still wagging. Rycard and Vorgon followed, murmuring good-byes to the shepherds and townsfolk as they left. A moment later they were through the doors and into the brisk night air. A chill was definitely coming down from the mountaintops, threatening winter.

"We'll be back before the spring?" Rycard asked, slipping his arm around Vorgon, reveling in the warmth coming off his body.

"We will. I promise."

"Good. Because I don't think Donnel could stand not having his dragon around." The boy had been ecstatic about his flight on Vorgon, even though the dragon had kept to the fields to the west where there hadn't been fighting and had kept his maneuvers safe and tame. He wasn't sure the shepherd boy's parents had been thrilled about it, though.

Although as Vorgon often said, it was good to know a dragon.

Vorgon took his hand and guided him toward the tree line, their dog trotting alongside, the sounds of the townspeople laughing and celebrating growing fainter and fainter behind them, the wind blowing cool through his hair, and Vorgon's warm hand reminding him he was finally home.

Home was with the dragon he loved. And always would be.

~ ABOUT THE AUTHOR ~

A. C. Fox writes m/m fiction and has fallen in love with creating stories of fantasy romance, a longtime pleasure. A. C. works an office job in a tall building with terrible parking and keeps meaning to take the stairs instead of the elevator. Meanwhile, there are plenty of new stories to dream up.

A.C.'s M/M fantasy romances are *The General's Hostage, The Captive Prince, The Dragon Hunter, The Warrior's Mage, The Gladiator's Slave, Marked,* and *Chains. Hold the Sky* is an M/M contemporary romance.

Discover more about AC Fox here

http://acfoxbooks.wordpress.com/

The Captive Prince

A. C. Fox

Save the land, or follow his heart?

Time has run out for Lord Domlen. The Fortress of Rain has been cursed by the enemy Boa Visk, his people trapped as phantoms within its walls, and the rain ever falling across his lands. If he does not break the curse soon, the trapped spirits will become revenir, ghosts that feed upon the life force of the living. He needs a miracle. And he gets one. He learns of a ritual that can break the curse and free his people. But nothing comes without a price, and the price is one Lord Domlen cannot bring himself to pay: the ritual demands blood—royal blood. Desperate, he abducts Prince

Falken of Teirlan to be his blood sacrifice on the night of the red moon and forces all gentle emotion far, far away. He must save his people, even at the cost of an innocent life. But as the time of the ritual draws near, how will he find the strength to kill an innocent man? Especially one who reignites all the emotions he believed he'd buried so deeply away?

Prince Falken, sorcerer from Teirlan, needs his magic to escape the Fortress of Rain, but the shackles on his wrists have cut him off from his power. When he discovers the servants around him are actually spirits, he understands the stronghold is bound by dark forces—a curse that somehow revolves around his grim, noble captor. There is dark magic here, but how can he help the strong, enigmatic Domlen while he's trapped, his powers bound? There is greater magic than that of the curse, and Falken has resources beyond Domlen's ken. But when the ritual goes horribly wrong, how will Falken make his enemy trust him? And how will he save the man he's coming to love?

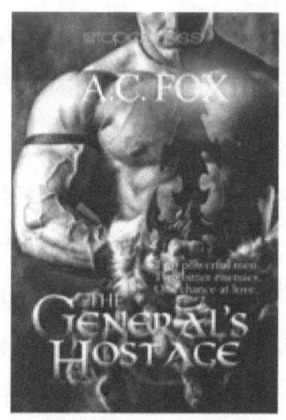

The General's Hostage

A. C. Fox

Two powerful men. Two bitter enemies. One chance at love.

Tav Cyrdath, a powerful wind adept and a brilliant general, leads the last free humans in a war against the Boa Visk, monsters who have enslaved most of humanity. But when the man who rules Illunvia refuses to surrender, Tav is forced to take the city by sword and magic. Victorious, he intends to execute the human traitor who has done so much harm by defying him. But when the defeated ruler, Duric Darmain, begs him to spare the citizens of Illunvia, Tav finds himself overcome by sudden mercy. He takes the man as a hostage instead, intending to use him in a trap against the monsters who have set this war in motion. Duric is defeated, broken...and yet Tav can't get his enemy out of his mind. But how could he ever feel this way about a man who has betrayed all Tav stands for?

Duric knows he was only a puppet ruler for the Boa Visk, yet he has done all he can to shield his people from the cruel overlords. Now he is a prisoner, fallen from power, hated and scorned as a traitor. And yet the enemy general begins to treat him with a curious respect and eventually even kindness. He dares not trust again, but this one-time enemy makes him want to yield his heart as hostage, even as he struggles to conquer the fears he can't escape...

Magic can heal wounds, but hearts must be mended with love. Both men have deep scars. Both have seen dark times. But the chance at love exists...if only they can embrace it before the Boa Visk return.

Hold the Sky
AC Fox

When love competes, will anyone win?

Harry has just begun his career as an architect with a well-known Chicago firm, but when he runs up against the talented, successful, not to mention stunningly handsome Garrett Reed, he quickly loses both his cool and his first big contract to the other man. Now a second job has just come up for bid, a huge project that can make Harry's career. And Garrett is after the same prize.

Garrett is fascinated with Harry. He admires the man's drive and talent, not to mention his incredible good looks. But as the wild attraction between them burns hotter, the cool, aloof Garrett finds himself in an uncomfortable position. Can the two of them find a way to temper the passion that flares between them, or will their competitive natures tear their tentative love to pieces?